Hawke's Tor

By the same author

THE MUSIC MAKERS
CRY ONCE ALONE
BECKY
GOD'S HIGHLANDER
CASSIE
WYCHWOOD
BLUE DRESS GIRL
TOLPUDDLE WOMAN
LEWIN'S MEAD
MOONTIDE
CAST NO SHADOWS
SOMEWHERE A BIRD IS SINGING
WINDS OF FORTUNE
SEEK A NEW DAWN
THE LOST YEARS
PATHS OF DESTINY
TOMORROW IS FOR EVER
THE VAGRANT KING
THOUGH THE HEAVENS MAY FALL
NO LESS THAN THE JOURNEY
CHURCHYARD AND HAWKE
THE DREAM TRADERS
BEYOND THE STORM

The Retallick Saga

BEN RETALLICK
CHASE THE WIND
HARVEST OF THE SUN
SINGING SPEARS
THE STRICKEN LAND
LOTTIE TRAGO
RUDDLEMOOR
FIRES OF EVENING
BROTHERS IN WAR

The Jagos of Cornwall

THE RESTLESS SEA
POLRUDDEN
MISTRESS OF POLRUDDEN

As James Munro

HOMELAND

Hawke's Tor

E.V. THOMPSON

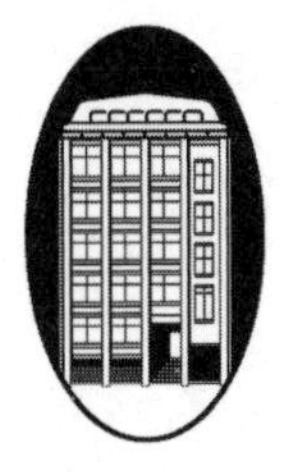

ROBERT HALE · LONDON

First published in Great Britain 2011

Hardback ISBN 978-0-7090-9279-7
Paperback C Format ISBN 978-0-7090-9373-2

Robert Hale Limited
Clerkenwell House
Clerkenwell Green
London EC1R 0HT

www.halebooks.com

2 4 6 8 10 9 7 5 3 1

Typeset in 11/16.8pt Palatino
Printed in Great Britain by the MPG Books Group,
Bodmin and King's Lynn

Prologue

'HUSH NOW. THAT'S quite enough of your noise. I swear I've never known such a teasy child! We're going out to meet your father but if you keep up that noise he'll be in an even worse mood than the one he's had these last few weeks.'

Completing the task of wrapping a woollen shawl about her baby, Kerensa Morgan picked him up so roughly that, taken by surprise, he ceased his grizzling immediately.

'That's better. You stay quiet like that and I won't feel so inclined to throw you in the river when we cross over the bridge.'

Despite her stern warning and rough handling of him, Kerensa hugged the two-month-old baby to her and kissed his smooth-skinned forehead. When he responded with a lop-sided smile, she said happily, 'That's *much* better. You keep that smile when you grow-up and you'll capture the heart of every young maid you meet up with, Albert Morgan.'

Unimpressed by his mother's forecast of what life might have in store for him in the future, baby Albert began to protest once again about the restrictions placed upon the movement of his limbs by the tightly bound shawl. However, moments later he was carried from the house and, captivated by the sounds and movement of rooks that had their nests in a tall elm tree that towered above the lane outside the cottage occupied by the Morgan family, immediately became quiet.

The lane led to the wooded slopes of Bodmin Moor from the tiny, scattered hamlet of Trelyn, which was at the heart of the vast country estate from which it drew its name.

There were only two isolated cottages between the Morgans' home and the River Lynher. Beyond the river a belt of thick woodland covered the north eastern slope of the moor for as far as could be seen.

Kerensa walked past the second of the cottages with the baby, keeping her glance firmly fixed ahead of her, aware that the occupier, the elderly spinster Jemima Rowe, would be watching from behind the lace curtain of the sitting-room window. If she thought Kerensa had seen her Jemima would beckon for her to come inside with the baby and keep her talking for far longer than she could afford to be held up.

Jemima was a tall, autocratic woman who until her retirement had been housekeeper at Trelyn Hall. An inveterate gossip, she missed nothing that happened around her and no one who passed by her isolated retirement cottage. Kerensa tried to tell herself the retired housekeeper meant well, but there always seemed to be a thinly disguised malicious element in whatever she said about anyone. It was a trait with which Kerensa felt uncomfortable.

At the lowest point of the lane, Kerensa stopped to look over the bridge which crossed the river there. Only a short distance upstream from where she was standing, the waters of the Lynher were augmented by the Witheybrook which tumbled from the moor in a series of chuckling cataracts, adding an urgency to the river's progress which had hitherto been lacking.

For a minute or two she watched a dipper, bobbing obeisance

to the river before deserting its precarious perch on a water-polished rock to plunge into the fast moving waters and walk against the current on the shallow river-bed, searching for sustenance.

Moving off, Kerensa continued along the lane for only a short distance before turning onto a path that climbed between the trees, heading up a steep slope towards an impressive outcrop comprised of giant slabs of weathered granite piled one upon another and known as Hawk's Tor, which dominated the outline of the moor above her.

Dusk was not very far away but the path here was easy to follow, its centuries-old course having been further defined by horses owned by the Trelyn estate, as they dragged off huge tree trunks, felled by woodsmen in a tree-felling operation on the upper fringes of the wood.

Kerensa had no fear of losing her way, she knew this path well and had walked it on very many occasions before today.

Emerging on to the high moor from the shadow of the trees, she paused for a few moments to regain her breath and look about her. It had been a steep climb, especially with a baby in her arms. The path continued across the moor, but when Kerensa regained her breath she turned off it, to wander in a seemingly aimless manner across the carpet of coarse grass that lay between her and the tor that soon towered like a non-accessible fortress high above her.

The warm rays of the sun had not yet abandoned the upland and she enjoyed its warmth until she detected a movement in the shadows immediately below the tor. Increasing her pace, she hurried towards the spot.

Entering the ribbon of shadow she paused for a moment having lost the movement among the scattering of free-standing granite boulders, some of which were twice the height of a man.

When she arrived at the place where she thought she had seen the movement, she paused, puzzled, and called out, startling the baby she carried in her arms.

Albert, frightened, began to cry and for a few moments Kerensa turned her attention to the baby, anxious to pacify him.

He stopped momentarily and, suddenly, she heard a sound behind her.

Turning abruptly, a greeting on her lips, she stopped before it was uttered and her eyes opened wide in an expression of disbelief … which quickly turned to horror.

She opened her mouth again, this time to scream, but it was already too late. A fiercely wielded rock struck her a bone-shattering blow on the forehead … and Kerensa knew no more.

Twenty minutes later Hawk's Tor and the surrounding moor was silent and deserted, as though nothing untoward had ever occurred there. But hidden among the boulders beneath the tor and cloaked by the deepening shadow of darkness, the body of Kerensa Morgan lay still, her life's blood soaking into the earth that lay beneath the coarse grass of Bodmin Moor.

Chapter 1

THE WEEKLY REPORTS from Cornwall's police districts to the Bodmin headquarters rarely contained anything of great interest and Superintendent Amos Hawke found the task of sifting through them one of his more boring tasks. The vast majority of arrests listed were for vagrancy offences, committed by penniless and homeless veterans of the Crimean War, drawn to Cornwall in increasing numbers recently, the county's perceived warmer climate attracting those who were forced by circumstances to live at the mercy of the elements.

Other offences involved drunkenness among the hard-working, hard-living miners who were also responsible for fifteen cases of assaulting constables, this being one of their most popular diversions, especially on pay days when much of their money changed hands in the many grog-shops, beerhouses and kiddleywinks which had sprung up like weeds around the often remote mines. There were also many petty thefts – usually blamed on the vagrants – and reports of absconding apprentices.

Amos also noted three reports of missing persons. One was an old man with failing mental faculties, who he remembered as having gone missing on a number of previous occasions. Another was a young woman believed to have eloped with a gypsy lover.

But it was the third missing person's report which claimed his attention. A young married woman had gone missing with her two-month-old baby and this report was only a few hours old, having been hastily added to the Launceston police district's return that very morning, just before it was despatched by mounted messenger to the Bodmin headquarters.

It was possible Amos took particular interest in this item in the first instance because there was so little of note in any of the other reports, but the scanty details of the report informed him that the twenty-four year-old missing woman was the wife of the estate steward responsible for Trelyn, an estate owned by one of Cornwall's most influential landowners and who was also a county magistrate.

Amos had just finished reading the sketchy details and was giving it some thought when there came a knock upon the open door of his office and Sergeant Tom Churchyard, the headquarters superintendent's clerk who was also Amos's right-hand man, entered the office with a batch of papers in his hand.

'Ah! You are just the man I was thinking about, Tom,' Amos said, by way of a greeting, 'Are you particularly busy at the moment?'

Tom Churchyard shrugged, 'Not really, I have been dealing with two sheep-stealers from up on the moor, but now they've been committed to the Assizes and remanded in custody I can forget them for a few weeks. There is a complaint from a mine manager up at Caradon Consuls about someone deliberately damaging mine machinery and tampering with the man-engine, which he says could endanger the lives of his miners. I was thinking of going up there tomorrow but I believe the sergeant at Rilla Mill is already dealing with it.'

'Caradon, you say? That's not very far from Trelyn, the private estate owned by Magistrate Trethewy. A woman went missing from there last night, taking a baby with her. I have an uneasy feeling about it.'

Tom looked at him in surprise, 'Any particular reason why?'

Amos shook his head, 'Nothing that makes any sense. Call it an ex-detective's intuition if you like. Of course, I could be wrong. She might just have gone off to visit her mother, or something similar, thinking she'd told her husband about it, but as her husband's employer is a magistrate it won't do any harm to show we're taking the report seriously.'

Looking at the clock on the wall of his office, Amos said, 'Let's go out there together right now, Tom. I haven't had the horse out for almost a week and a gallop across the moor is just what it needs. You can take the new pony that was bought last week for the chief constable – but don't get too reckless on it. Hurt yourself or the pony and we'll both have some awkward questions to answer.'

The Cornwall Constabulary was a force formed only four years before, in 1857, and all members below the rank of superintendent were expected to go about their duties on foot. Indeed, one constable had actually been dismissed for accepting a lift on a farm cart when on his way to investigate an incident.

Nevertheless, Tom Churchyard held a unique position in the force. Officially Amos's sergeant clerk, he was *unofficially* a detective, carrying out investigations on his superior's behalf. It was work not approved of by the county's police authority, being considered an unethical intrusion into the lives of the residents of the county, many of whom were still resentful of a constabulary forced upon them by a government in London.

Although after four years it was now grudgingly recognized by some as serving a useful purpose, when Amos had raised the question of having a small detective force, the police authority had declared firmly that 'policemen were there to be recognized, wearing an official uniform in order to *prevent* crime, not skulking about spying upon innocent people'.

Nevertheless, the Metropolitan Police's Scotland Yard had already proven the value of such a unit within a police force; Amos had himself been working for them when called to Cornwall to help solve a series of brutal murders before the Cornwall Constabulary's formation. It was his success in this investigation that had led to his appointment as the new Cornwall Constabulary's senior superintendent.

He had later recruited Tom Churchyard from London to help him with another difficult case, making use of Tom's extensive knowledge of the criminal world.

Now, putting the remaining police district reports to one side, Amos was confident that if there was anything suspicious about the disappearance of the wife and child of the Trelyn estate steward, Tom Churchyard was the best man to help him investigate the matter.

It was mid-afternoon when the two policemen arrived at the small hamlet and Tom declared it to be the prettiest place he had seen since coming to Cornwall from London, two years before. Comprised of no more than ten tidily thatched cottages, some hidden among the trees but each with a neat and well-tended garden, Trelyn possessed an air of settled tranquillity.

Making their way to Trelyn Hall, a very imposing house built in the river valley immediately below the hamlet, they slowed their horses as they rode up the driveway to the house and, inconsequentially, Amos counted the windows on the front of the house. There were thirty-nine and thinking about the number there must be on the other three sides of the house, he decided a full-time window cleaner must be employed to work on them.

When the two policemen reached the building Amos hesitated for only a moment before choosing to ride up to the front entrance and not to the kitchen door. He wanted Magistrate Trethewy to see them and know they were taking the report of his estate steward's missing wife seriously. The influential landowner would also no doubt wish to know what action they intended taking in order to find her and the steward's baby son.

The door was opened by the family's butler who made it clear by his frosty manner when Amos and Tom identified themselves that he felt it beneath his dignity to open the door to *policemen*. However, when Mrs Trethewy put in an appearance, she immediately invited them inside the house, informing Amos that Colonel Trethewy was absent on magisterial duties but before leaving had expressed serious misgivings about the missing woman and child. Despite her own evident concern, Amos gained the impression she did not entirely approve of the estate steward's wife.

During conversation with Mrs Trethewy the two policemen were surprised to learn that a police sergeant had recently been stationed in the village by the inspector in charge of the district and after assuring Mrs Trethewy the police would do everything in their power to find the missing woman and child, Amos and Tom made their way to the sergeant's home.

Sergeant Dreadon lived close to the village farm with his wife and two sons, in a house that had a separate lock-up cell built at the rear of the building. Amos quickly learned the policeman had been one of the first to join the Cornwall Constabulary when it was formed, four years earlier, and had been quickly promoted to his present rank.

When Tom expressed his surprise that at a time when the force was experiencing problems in recruiting enough constables to bring it up to strength, a sergeant should have been detached to serve in such a tiny, out of the way hamlet, Francis Dreadon smiled. 'Out of the way Trelyn certainly is, but Colonel Trethewy lives here and he is not only an important landowner but also a magistrate; Deputy Lieutenant; former High Sheriff of Cornwall – and a member of the police authority. Need I say more? The chief constable makes certain he is well looked after.'

'Of course!' Amos was fully aware just how important the goodwill of Colonel Trethewy was to the Cornwall Constabulary, 'but what do you know of the missing woman, Kerensa Morgan, is she a local girl?'

'Very much so, she was born less than a mile from here, at North Hill, and has lived in the area all her life.'

'What about her husband, the estate steward? Is he local too?'

'Horace Morgan? No, he was brought in from Wales by Colonel Trethewy, a couple of years back. He was working as a land steward there, although I believe he spent some years in India before that. It didn't go down very well with the men around here when he was appointed. As far as I can gather the estate steward at Trelyn has always been a Cornishman, so Morgan has never really been accepted by the locals.'

'But that didn't stop Kerensa from marrying him?'

Giving a short laugh, Sergeant Dreadon replied, 'I never knew her before she was married, but from all I've learned while I've been stationed here she would never have caught one of the local men ... not to marry, anyway, she'd built up too much of a reputation for herself ... but you'll need to speak to some of the local men or women to find out about her. By all accounts she has had a fling with most of the single men in this corner of Cornwall, and one or two of the married ones as well, or so I've heard. Of course, it's all hearsay, she was already married to Horace Morgan by the time I was posted here.'

'Do you think her husband knew of the reputation she had when he married her?'

'I doubt it. Nobody spends very much time talking to him and apparently he has never gone out of his way to get to know any local folk. But he was so besotted with his wife it would probably have made no difference anyway.'

'What if he found out later ... very recently, perhaps?'

Giving Amos a searching look, Sergeant Dreadon said, 'I can see where your questions are leading, and Horace Morgan is not a man to be trifled with, but as far as I know he has never laid a hand on Kerensa – and he thinks the world of that baby of theirs.'

Putting aside that line of questioning for the moment, Amos asked, 'Is there anyone she and the baby might be staying with? A relative, or a close friend?'

'She has no close family – no family at all, so I'm told – and no close friends either. There's always the chance there's a man involved somehow, in view of her past record, but I can't think of any man in Trelyn who would care to cuckold Horace Morgan, he carries too much power on the estate. Besides, this is a small community, if she'd been seeing someone from outside it would be common knowledge ... and no one would keep a secret in order to protect Kerensa Morgan!'

'Well, she has posed us quite a problem and at the moment I can't see there being a happy ending to it, but Sergeant Churchyard and I had better speak to Horace Morgan before returning to Bodmin. As you've said, his employer is a very important man in the county, the chief constable will want it to be seen that everything possible is being done to find Mrs Morgan and her baby.'

'You'll find Morgan in the woods on the other side of the bridge across the Lynher, down by the old mill. It seems Kerensa liked taking the baby there sometimes to hear the birds, or so she said. He believes it's possible she went there yesterday and met with an accident. He's taken some of the estate workers up there to carry out a search.'

'You didn't consider going with them?' Amos's question implied criticism of Sergeant Dreadon.

'He has plenty of men with him who know the woods better than I do and before you arrived I sent someone to Launceston to ask the inspector in charge if he could spare a few men to help with a search up on the moor. I don't think it a good idea to concentrate on a single area unless there is something to go on, and at the moment her disappearance remains a complete mystery. I decided I should stay here in case someone comes in with information about Kerensa and the baby, otherwise there would be no one around to do anything about it.'

Nodding acceptance of the other man's reasoning, Amos said, 'If you can point Sergeant Churchyard and me in the right direction we'll go off and find Horace Morgan and see whether he and his men have had any success.'

Chapter 2

RIDING THEIR HORSES carefully along the narrow and steep lane which led down to the equally narrow bridge spanning the Lynher river, the two policemen were passing a small cottage built inside a niche cut into the rocky hillside when they saw a tall elderly woman on her knees in the garden, weeding a colourful flowerbed. She looked up at the sound of the horses and, rising to her feet, watched the riders approaching, at the same time kneading her aching back with the knuckles of one hand.

Smiling in her direction, Amos said, 'Good afternoon, ma'am, gardening on such a steep slope must be hard work, but you have a wonderful display of flowers to show for it.'

'There have been better years,' came the reply, 'but then, I've also had worse. Who are you?'

Both men brought their horses to a halt and Amos said, 'I'm Police Superintendent Amos Hawke from Bodmin and this is Sergeant Tom Churchyard, ma'am.'

'What have you come all this way from Bodmin for? We already have a policeman in Trelyn ... he's a sergeant too.'

'We're here because Mrs Morgan and her baby have gone missing and everyone's worried about them.'

'Mrs Morgan ... are you talking of Kerensa Tonks, as was? I saw her only last evening taking that baby of hers up towards the place that has a name the same as yours, *Hawk's* Tor and although the baby was wrapped in a shawl it was far too late to have it out. I'm not surprised she got herself lost; it would have been nigh on dark by the time she got to wherever it was she was going. Not that it would have stopped her from doing what it was she wanted, Kerensa Tonks got up to more than most in the dark and having a baby hasn't put a stop to her ways, nor has having a husband, much as he might have hoped it would. It's in the blood, her mother was no better ... and they used to say *her* mother looked more like the master up at the hall than any of his own children.'

The two policemen exchanged glances, aware that the woman to whom they were talking probably knew more about Kerensa Morgan and everything that went on in the hamlet than anyone else they were likely to meet up with.

Dismounting from his horse, and signalling for Tom to do the same, Amos said, 'I'd like Sergeant Churchyard to make a few notes about what you've just told me, ma'am. It's quite likely you're the last person to have seen Mrs Morgan and it could prove a great help in finding her.'

'You'll only find Kerensa Tonks – or Morgan, as she's called now – if she wants to be found, though you're both presentable young men, so you might stand more chance than most.'

Choosing for the moment to ignore the woman's implication, Amos said, 'Do you mind if I ask your name, and whether you know more or less what time it was when you saw Mrs Morgan and the baby?'

'I'm Jemima Rowe, *Miss* Rowe, although everybody calls me Jemima. Until I retired nigh on twenty years ago I was housekeeper up at the Hall, though it was a different place in my young days. The master up there then was a colonel too, same as the one who's there now, but he'd no more think of taking on a "foreigner" as his estate steward than he would of allowing any of his servants to marry one.'

'Can you give me an idea of what time it was when you saw Mrs Morgan?' Amos persisted.

'I wasn't watching the clock, but it must have been half an hour or so before dark. Immediately after she passed by I went out to fetch in my washing and saw her take the track that leads up to the moor.'

'Are you quite certain of that? She wouldn't have been going into the woods? That's where her husband seems to think she might have gone, to meet him.'

'She was heading up towards the moor, whatever her husband thought. He'd be the last one to know where she was going off to, whatever time of day or night it was.'

'What makes you say that?' Tom stopped writing and looked searchingly at her.

'Because I've seen him coming past here looking for her more than once,' Jemima said, scornfully, '*and* heard them arguing about it when he found her and they were on their way home together. Him demanding to know where she'd been when she should have been at home preparing a meal for him when he finished work, and Kerensa telling him she was fed up with being tied to the house all day and had gone out for a walk and forgotten what time it was.'

'When was the last time you heard such an argument?'

'Some time last week, Thursday, I think. It was getting dark then too. But if she's gone missing she'll come back in her own time, baby or no baby, but she'll do it once too often, you mark my words. She has that man of hers under her thumb now because she's young and pretty, but she'll get old like the rest of us and find she has nothing else to keep him.'

'You didn't see her husband going up that way looking for her?'

'No one else came past the cottage before dark, although I have no idea what might have happened after that, I had my curtains drawn and the bolt on the door.'

Tom had been taking notes in his pocket-book while she was talking, now, at a signal from Amos, he closed the book and slipped it into an inside pocket of his frock coat, as Amos said, 'Thank you very much, Jemima. The next time I'm around this way I'll call in to say "Hello" and admire this lovely garden of yours once more.'

Secretly pleased with his praise for her garden, Jemima said, 'I don't doubt you have better things to do than waste time on an old lady, but if you need to know anything about Trelyn, or the folk who live here then you're very welcome to call in and ask me about them. I've lived hereabouts for close to ninety years and I know more than anyone else you're likely to talk to about what goes on, or *has* gone on here.'

Leaving the old woman lowering herself gingerly to her knees, Amos said to Tom, 'In view of what Miss Rowe said, you'd better go up on the moor and have a look around, Tom. I'll join you when I've spoken to Morgan … but be careful, I've heard a lot about the marshland up there. If Kerensa Morgan wandered into it in the dark she and her baby may never be found.'

Once over the narrow, single arch bridge spanning the river the two policemen parted company and Amos found Horace Morgan about half a mile along the side of the wooded slope of the moor. He had formed the estate workers into a spaced-out line, and they were making their way through the woods as though beating for a shooting party. It was easy to locate them because of the noise they were making, calling out either 'Kerensa', or 'Mrs Morgan' as they went.

Horace Morgan was a big, heavily-built man and Amos was surprised to find he was in his forties, or perhaps even early fifties. Knowing him to be the father of a young baby Amos had imagined he would be a younger man.

Restlessly distraught at the disappearance of his wife and baby, the estate steward seemed convinced his wife would be found somewhere in the woods, even when he was informed that Jemima Rowe claimed to have seen her taking the path to the moor.

'Jemima Rowe is getting old,' he said, 'These days she is seeing less and imagining more. She probably *thought* that was where Kerensa was going with the baby because just recently she's sometimes met me when I was on my way home from checking on work at Trewortha, a farm way out on the moor. But I told Kerensa I wouldn't be out there yesterday because I was supervising replanting at the far edge of this strip of woodland. If she had decided to meet me she'd have expected me to come back through the woods. That's why I'm concentrating my search here, although I sent someone out to Trewortha earlier this morning, because she doesn't always remember what I tell her. The moor isn't a good place to be at night, especially with a baby and *had* she gone there she'd have no doubt stayed the night and not tried to get home.'

'That would have been the sensible thing to do,' Amos agreed, 'I've heard there are some particularly deep bogs to be found up there.'

Horace Morgan shook his head, 'That's true enough, but Kerensa knows where they all are. She wouldn't be likely to wander into any of them, not even in the dark – but if you listened to the tales the older folk hereabouts tell about the moor you'd think there was far more to worry about than the odd marsh, or two. If you believed some of them you'd find more dragons up there than we've ever had in Wales … or something every bit as fierce. They are convinced there's a mysterious animal that roams the moor at night killing sheep and foals – and humans too, if they're foolish enough to be up there after dark!'

After maintaining a thoughtful silence for some moments, Amos asked, 'When did the stories begin about this mysterious beast? Was there something particular that happened to give credence to such a belief?'

'As far as I can tell there have always been such stories around the moor. Every so often we come across a half-eaten sheep, or the bones of a foal might be found picked clean, but it's only to be expected. Animals die of natural causes, same as humans and you've always got foxes, buzzards, ravens – and even dogs – scavenging around up there. The moorland bogs are far more dangerous. I wouldn't fancy the chances of anyone, or anything, wandering into one of them, day or night but, as I said, Kerensa knows the moor as well as anyone and she wouldn't put Albert's life at risk.… No, if she's hurt herself somewhere it'll be here, in the woods.'

'When was it you first became anxious about her, Mr Morgan?

'When I got home after dark and found she wasn't home. She often goes wandering around, even though she has a baby now, but she would rarely keep him out after dark.'

'You said you thought she might have come to meet you from work. If she *had* remembered where you were working and come to find you wouldn't you have been likely to run into each other somewhere along the way?' Amos posed the question mindful that the ex-Trelyn Hall housekeeper had seen Kerensa heading for the high moor and not taking the path through the woods.

'Yes – had I been coming back the usual way, but I wanted to check that the tenant in Treveniel Farm had repaired a fence his cattle had knocked down, so I took a short cut there instead of coming back through the woods.'

'What time would that have been?'

'I don't know, about four o'clock, I suppose. Then I went back to my office in the Hall and caught up with some paperwork.'

'And you stayed working in the office until dark?'

'Yes, I'm used to doing that, although not so often since I've been married. It wasn't until the butler came to the office and asked when I'd be leaving because he wanted to lock up the Hall that I realized how late it was!'

'How late was it?'

'Gone ten o'clock. I knew Kerensa would be worrying – and getting cross too if she'd cooked something for me.'

'What did you do when you found she wasn't at home?'

'To be honest with you I didn't know *what* to do. I left the house and went down past the mill towards the path that goes through the woods. I would have called in to ask Jemima if she'd seen anything of her, but just before I reached the woods I met up with Ivan Bartlett, the estate's head gamekeeper. He'd just come along the path through the woods and said he'd neither seen nor heard anyone. I knew that if he'd seen no sign of her I would have no chance, so believing she must have gone to Trewortha and decided to stay there, I walked home and went to bed, 'though I didn't sleep much, I can tell you. But I'm not going to find her while I'm standing here talking to you. If you really want to help you can join the line of beaters – although you'll need to leave your horse behind, there are places along here where it wouldn't get through.'

'I think we need to follow up every possible lead,' Amos replied, 'Even one given by an old lady who might or might not have seen her. I've sent my sergeant up to the moor and I'll go up there to join him … but I'd appreciate having someone with us who knows the moor really well. Is there anyone here you can spare?'

'I could do with *more* men to help me search the wood, not send them off with you on a wild goose chase….'

Even as he was speaking, Horace Morgan caught sight of two young boys at the end of his line of estate employees. The line had stopped, waiting for the search to recommence and the boys, aged about ten and eight had become bored and were having a battle, throwing acorns and oak apples at each other.

'You can take the Coumbe boys. They're young but since they lost their father some years ago they've been allowed to run wild on the moor and know it as well as any man on the estate.'

The two boys accompanied Amos back through the woods and, after he had refused requests from them to ride on his horse, they began finding small items to throw at each other again. He urged his horse to a faster pace, forcing them to cease their sibling battle in order to keep up and when they reached the steep track that needed to be negotiated in order to reach the moor they ceased their game altogether.

Once on the moor the path narrowed to pass by the granite height that was Hawk's Tor. From here Amos could see Tom leading his horse and picking his way around a patch of marshland that was easily discernible now but would have been far less visible in bad light.

Waving to Tom, Amos set the two boys searching among the scattering of large boulders around the tor. He intended riding out on the other side of the path, beyond Tom, in order to cover as much ground as was possible.

Before he could set off, Jenken Coumbe, the older of the two brothers, asked, 'What exactly are we looking for? Mrs Morgan will hardly have been hiding all night and most of today among the rocks up here.'

'We're looking for anything that might tell us she has been here,' Amos replied.

'Do you want me to climb up the tor itself?' Jenken queried.

Amos hesitated for a moment then, looking up at the fortress-like granite height, he said, 'She'd have been hardly likely to take a baby up there … and neither would anyone else. If we don't find anything down here it might be necessary to search up there, but, if we do, either the sergeant or myself will go, it's far too dangerous for you boys….'

At that moment a stoat broke cover from a clump of stunted gorse and with outstretched tail ran towards the tor.

With a shout of glee, Billy, the younger of the two brothers ran after it, ignoring Amos's call for him to come back. Darting in and out among the rocks scattered about the tor, the small boy kept appearing then disappearing, shouting all the while that he could still see the stoat.

Suddenly, when he reached the base of the towering tor he disappeared from view and his shouting ceased abruptly. Moments later he came into view once more … but all his excitement had gone and there was a look of wide-eyed horror on his face.

'What is it?' Amos demanded. 'What have you seen?'

'I … It's … I think it's her … Mrs Morgan!'

'You *think*?' Amos swung down from his horse. 'Is it a woman … is she all right?'

Gulping in air, Billy shook his head. 'It's a woman, but I can't tell anything about her properly.... Her face ...!' He suddenly burst into tears and ran to his brother and clung to him, sobbing uncontrollably.

'Stay with him,' Amos said to Jenken, '... and keep an eye on my horse.'

Running to the spot from where Billy had appeared, he saw why the young boy had been so shocked. The body lying on the ground immediately beneath an almost sheer cliff face *was* that of a woman – or so it would appear from her clothing, but the face had been so disfigured it was virtually impossible to distinguish any features.

After confirming the woman was dead, something that was never really in doubt, Amos returned to where Billy still clung to his older brother. Attracting the attention of Tom, and waving for him to come to him Amos spoke to the older of the two boys.

'Jenken, take Billy home to your mother. When things have settled down go along and see Sergeant Dreadon, he'll have a little reward for you both.'

Chapter 3

DURING HIS POLICE service in London's East End, before coming to Cornwall, Tom Churchyard had witnessed violence and its consequences on numerous occasions and been forced to deal with death in many forms but, called to the tor by Amos, he winced when he saw the disfigured face of the woman lying at the foot of the steep rock face.

Looking up towards the summit of the tor he said to Amos, 'It looks as though she must fallen from the top, poor woman.'

'If that's the case, then where's her baby?' Amos countered.

Looking up at the tor once more, Tom said, 'It could still be up there … but if it is I doubt whether it would have survived the night, it isn't very old.'

'You'd better find a way up there and go and check,' Amos said, 'Although I doubt if it's there – or that Kerensa Morgan was ever there either, if this is her. But whoever she is, she certainly didn't fall to her death. Someone killed her.'

Startled, Tom said, 'What makes you think that?'

'I don't *think* it, Tom … I know!' Amos replied grimly. Pointing to an irregularly shaped chunk of granite, about half the size of a man's head, which was balancing on a flat rock several paces from where they stood, he added, 'There's blood on that rock, lots of it. There's no doubting it's what was used to batter her to death.'

'But *why*?' Tom queried. 'Who'd want to kill a young woman who has just had a baby?'

'Perhaps we'll learn more when we find the baby. You'd better climb to the top of the tor and make quite certain the baby isn't there, then ride down to Trelyn and tell Sergeant Dreadon to arrange to have the body carried down to his house and put in the cell. It can stay there until we can have it taken into Launceston for an autopsy. When that's done we'll see if Horace Morgan can identify her from the clothes she's wearing. Dreadon's already sent to Launceston asking for help in searching the moor but see if he can hurry things up. I'd like to cover as much ground as possible before dark if you don't find the baby on the tor – and I doubt very much if you will.'

Baby Albert Morgan was not on the tor and when Tom had ridden off to Trelyn, Amos made a detailed search of the area surrounding Hawk's Tor. Any doubts he might have entertained about the cause of the woman's death were quickly dispelled. There was what appeared to be a large bloodstain on hard ground close to one of the huge granite boulders some distance from the tor. By walking in a direct line between this spot and the body Amos found a number of bloodstains on the rocky ground.

Whoever had attacked the as yet unidentified woman had killed her a little distance away then dragged her body to a spot where it was less likely to be seen by anyone passing along the nearby path. It was a feat requiring considerable strength, but his discoveries brought him no closer to solving the mystery of what had happened to the baby, or finding *why* the woman had been killed.

Had it been a random killing, or one with a sexual motive, the murderer would hardly have taken the baby off with him, unless perhaps it was felt its crying would attract someone to the scene. But would not a vicious murderer have killed the baby and left its body with that of its mother?

Of course, there was a remote possibility that the body was *not* that of Kerensa, or that the baby had been carried away by some unknown creature....

Amos rejected both these ideas. What was more certain was that this was not going to be an easy crime to solve. However, he was determined it *would* be solved, and the first step was to have the body identified.

Horace Morgan did not wait for the body to be brought down to Trelyn for identification. The two Coumbe boys had met a gardener from Trelyn Hall when they reached the hamlet on their way home and told him what they had found on the moor. The gardener immediately hurried away to the wooded slopes to pass on the news to the estate steward.

Tom was returning to Amos after speaking to Sergeant Dreadon when he saw Horace Morgan toiling up the slope to Hawk's Tor. Urging his reluctant pony to a faster pace up the steep slope, Tom caught up with him and found him fighting for breath but still doggedly pursuing a course towards the tor.

Guessing the Coumbe brothers had been unable to keep silent about Billy's gruesome discovery, Tom slowed his horse to match Morgan's pace when he drew alongside him.

'You've heard a body's been found up by Hawk's Tor, Mr Morgan?'

Morgan nodded without slowing his pace, not replying until the path levelled out slightly, enabling speech to come easier.

'Is it ... Kerensa?'

'We can't be certain. I am afraid she's suffered very severe injuries, Mr Morgan. It will be necessary to identify her by her clothes, or any jewellery she might be wearing.'

'Albert … the baby … what of him?'

'He hadn't been found when I left Superintendent Hawke but I'll go ahead to find out what's been happening while I've been away. I'd like to offer to take you behind me, but it's as much as the pony can manage to carry me up this slope. I suggest you take it a little more slowly too. Sadly there's nothing you can do for Mrs Morgan – if it is her – and when we find the baby he'll need his father.'

Kneeing his pony forward, Tom went on ahead to tell Amos that Morgan was on his way and in his understandably distraught state might prove difficult to reason with.

Amos and Tom left the shadow of the tor together to meet Morgan before he reached them and his first words were, 'Where is she? Where's Kerensa? Have you found Albert?'

'It's not absolutely certain yet that it is Mrs Morgan,' Amos replied, blocking the path of the desperate man, 'and there is no sign of a baby … but please wait a moment and listen to me, Mr Morgan. I want to warn you that, whoever the woman is, she has suffered severe facial injuries. I would much rather you did not see her at all just yet, but she needs to be identified, even if only by her clothing.'

'What sort of injuries – and how did she come by them? Has she had a fall … and why isn't Albert with her?'

'I can't answer the last question and the cause of her death will not be fully known until an autopsy has been carried out, but it would be better if you stayed here while I find something with which to cover her face.'

'You'll do no such thing. I want to see what's happened to her and if it is Kerensa I'll get every man from the Trelyn Estate up here to search for Albert.'

'That would be a great help. I have already sent to Launceston for all available constables to help in the search for him. We will be able to make use of anyone else who can join them but, with all due respect, I feel it would be far better if you did not see her face until the doctor who will carry out an autopsy has been able to examine her and perhaps clean her up....'

'Why does there have to be an autopsy? Isn't it enough that she should have fallen and disfigured herself, if that's what has happened to her? Does her body have to be mutilated as well?'

'I am afraid it is necessary, Mr Morgan, because I do not believe her injuries to have been caused by an accident.'

Startled, it was some moments before Morgan seemed able to take in what Amos had said, then, in a strangled voice he queried, 'Not an accident ... what do you mean?'

'I mean that she appears to have been murdered. Now, I regret the need for this, but do you mind coming up to the tor with us and checking whether the body is that of your wife but, if it is, please don't touch her?'

Horace Morgan was able to confirm that the body lying on the moor at the base of Hawk's Tor was that of his wife, Kerensa. He not only recognized the clothes she was wearing, but also identified the wedding ring which, when removed from the stiff third finger of her left hand revealed the inscription, '*K & H*' engraved inside the gold band.

Trying hard not to look at her disfigured face, he demanded tearfully, 'Who would do such a thing to her, and why ... and where can Albert be? What would they have done with him?'

The Trelyn estate steward glanced up at the tor towering above them and, correctly reading his thoughts, Amos said, 'Sergeant Churchyard has been up there and found nothing, but as soon as policemen from Launceston arrive here we will organize a thorough search of the rest of the moor.'

Seemingly grateful for an opportunity to do something positive, Morgan said, 'There's no need to wait for them, I'll bring every man from the estate up here and begin the search right away. If Albert is on the moor he'll have been out in the open all night, that's already far too long for a helpless baby.'

'That's a splendid idea,' Amos agreed. 'Take Sergeant Churchyard's pony and gather all the men you can. We will wait here until Sergeant Dreadon comes to take your wife's body down to Trelyn.'

'What do you intend doing about finding Kerensa's killer?' Some of Horace Morgan's natural aggression returned when he posed the question to Amos.

'While you're away we will see if we can find anything up here that might help us, but our main investigation will begin when we have the results of the autopsy and know exactly how and when she died. We will also have to obtain a statement from you, Mr Morgan, distressing though it might be for you. We *will* find your wife's killer, and your son too, but I am afraid nothing we are able to do is going to bring your wife back to you.'

Chapter 4

NEWS OF KERENSA'S murder and the disappearance of baby Albert spread quickly and soon the party searching the moor was augmented by miners from many of the nearby copper mines. They scoured a vast area until poor light brought the search to an end, but nothing was found of the child.

When darkness fell not a single searcher remained on the moor. Rumours of a 'beast' or some supernatural creature roaming the high ground at night was not wholly believed by everyone but with the unexplained death of Kerensa Morgan no one was willing to put it to the test and in the inns and drinking dens that night even the most sceptical of disbelievers were unusually subdued.

Kerensa's body was conveyed to Launceston and, at Amos's request an autopsy carried out immediately. The results confirmed his belief that she had been killed with the bloody rock found close to Hawk's Tor. Tiny fragments of granite were found embedded in her skull and the doctor conducting the autopsy reported that her death had been the result of a 'frenzied attack'.

Late that night, back at the superintendent's office in the police headquarters in Bodmin, Amos and Tom, both weary after the day's exertions, were discussing the events of the day. They had been friends for a long while and when none of their colleagues was present there was a relaxed informality between them.

'This is going to be a very difficult case to solve,' Tom declared. 'At the moment we have no apparent motive and the disappearance of the baby is a complete mystery.'

'It's certainly baffling to say the least,' Amos agreed, 'but the answer is out there somewhere and we have to find it. What do you make of Horace Morgan?'

Tom looked at Amos sharply. 'I was going to ask you the same question. He certainly *appears* to be absolutely devastated by all that has happened, but I had a feeling everything is not quite what it appears to be. He is no fool or he wouldn't be the estate steward for Trelyn, so I doubt whether he was as ignorant of her past behaviour as he would have us believe, and if Jemima Rowe is to be believed about the arguments he and Kerensa had then she hasn't changed too much since they were married.'

'I agree and, as we both know, infidelity is probably behind more murders than anything else, but it doesn't explain the disappearance of the baby. According to all we've heard Morgan was besotted with him.'

'What if he discovered the baby wasn't his?'

'Now *that* would provide an answer,' Amos mused, 'and although it would be difficult to dispose of a woman's body up there on the moor, a baby could be carried down and thrown in the river and would be miles away in a matter of hours. We'll go back to Trelyn tomorrow and while I follow up on some of the stories we've heard about Kerensa I would like you to interview Morgan. See what you can learn about his background, there might be something there to help us....'

Pushing himself up from his chair with a show of weariness, Amos said, 'I don't know about you, but I think it's time we went home. We'll make an early start in the morning and take the horse and pony again.'

As the two men walked down the stairs of the police station, Amos asked, 'Have you heard from Flora recently?'

Flora was a young housekeeper whom Tom had met when he and Amos were investigating another murder at one of Cornwall's great houses, some two years before. Romance had blossomed between them and it had been assumed by everyone who knew them that they would marry. However, after moving on as housekeeper to the tragically widowed Dowager Lady Hogg whom she had known for many years, Flora had accompanied her elderly employer to Canada, where three of the dowager's sons by an earlier marriage were living together with a number of her grandchildren. Lady Hogg had felt a need to be with them.

Flora had accompanied her on the voyage intending to return again when she had seen her employer settled in her new home, but her letters made it clear she had fallen in love with the country and was also reluctant to leave the frail, yet indomitable peeress.

Tom grimaced. 'When Flora left for Canada nobody expected Lady Hogg to live for very long, but the country seems to agree with her health and it's beginning to look as though she might live forever – except when Flora mentions coming home to marry me. Then she suddenly becomes all ill and helpless. Flora's letters have been few and far between just lately and when they do come they are all about Canada and not about us. I was very upset at first, but I'm beginning to accept the inevitable.'

'You've never thought of going to Canada yourself?'

Tom gave Amos a lop-sided, mirthless smile. 'I don't think I would be welcomed there by Lady Hogg and her family, do you? Besides, I enjoy what I'm doing here.'

Tom had been instrumental in arresting Lady Hogg's youngest son on criminal charges and, although they were eventually dropped due to the family's influence in the county, the incident created such a scandal that the son involved was forced to leave the country and go to Canada where the family owned a great deal of land. Tom knew he could never go there – not even for Flora.

'Well, you must come to the house and discuss it with Talwyn. She said I was to invite you to dinner tomorrow anyway. You can speak to her then.'

Amos's wife, Talwyn, taught school but she was very supportive of her husband and his work and he would often discuss particularly difficult cases with her. Amos wished Tom had someone like her with whom to discuss his problems. He felt the sergeant was becoming an increasingly lonely man.

'I would like that,' Tom replied. 'Flora was very fond of Talwyn, but I believe it's too late for any suggestions about our future.' Suddenly despondent, he changed the subject abruptly. 'Anyway, I have an idea we are going to be working on this case for longer than any of us would like. We'll see what Morgan has to say tomorrow.'

On the way to the two-bedroom annexe of a house close to the Launceston police station which he shared with Horace Halloran, the Cornwall Constabulary's sergeant major, and a fellow ex-Royal Marine, Tom thought of his conversation with Amos.

When Flora had left Cornwall for Canada, he had been very unhappy and after she had informed him she could not foresee a return in the immediate future, he *had* considered going to Canada, despite the problems he would face there. However, Flora's letters became fewer and when they did arrive were full, not of a life together, but of the vibrancy and excitement of being in a new, young country and he gradually realized he was probably never going to see her again.

Once he accepted this he felt less guilty about allowing his work to dominate his own life and in consequence was now able to go for many days at a time without thinking about her.

When the two policemen reached Trelyn the following morning Tom went on to the Hall to speak to Horace Morgan, while Amos decided that before he interviewed anyone else he would pay another call on Jemima Rowe. He found the ex-Trelyn Hall housekeeper making bread in the kitchen of her cottage and was not surprised to learn she had heard of the discovery of Kerensa's body and the disappearance of baby Albert.

Digging her knuckles into a mound of dough being kneaded on a dusting of flour scattered upon the scrubbed table-top, she commented, 'I'm not one to speak evil of the dead, but if ever a girl brought about such a violent end to her own life, it was Kerensa Tonks.'

'That may be so,' Amos agreed, 'but she did not deserve such a death – and the baby certainly never harmed anyone.'

'Then he's assured of a place with the Lord … although he might not be dead. It could be that he has found a good life right here on earth – and that's more than he could look forward to with his mother.'

'What exactly do you mean by that?'

The ex-housekeeper's thin-lipped mouth clamped shut as though to indicate she had said enough, but Amos persisted. 'Do I need to remind you this is a murder case, Jemima?'

From the cross positioned above the fireplace and the framed religious tapestries adorning the walls of the cottage, Amos had assumed the ex-housekeeper was a practising Christian and he added, 'I think I'm right in saying that the sixth commandment declares, "Thou shalt not commit murder".'

'The seventh says "Thou shalt not commit adultery",' Jemima retorted, 'but she paid no heed to that one, so don't quote commandments to me when you're talking about Kerensa Tonks, young man. I've spent my whole life living by them, but I doubt whether *she* had even heard of them.'

'Then we should feel sorry for her, Jemima, but my job is to uphold the law here in Cornwall and the most serious crime that can be committed against that law coincides with one of the Commandments. Whatever Kerensa Morgan had done, she is the victim of a very serious and particularly violent murder and it's my duty to bring whoever did it to justice. It is your duty, both as a law-abiding citizen and a Christian, to give me all the help you can, so I'll ask you once more. What did you mean when you said baby Albert Morgan might be able to live a better life than the one he had with his rightful parents?'

For some moments Jemima Rowe remained silent and Amos thought his pleas had fallen upon deaf ears, but suddenly her shoulders sagged and she said resignedly, 'You're right, of course, I'm being unchristian. I've never liked the girl, but no one deserves to die the way she did and the baby might have brought some real happiness into her life – there was little enough of it there before he was born.'

'Wasn't she happy with her husband?'

'Him? Horace Morgan gave her his name and a respectability she hadn't known before, but little more than that. He wasn't a generous man in any way. He was as tight with his money as he is with praise for anyone who does anything for him.'

'Yet he gave her baby Albert.'

It was a policeman's baited statement, and Jemima responded as Amos had hoped.

'As long as Horace Morgan believes that it's not for anyone else to say otherwise, whatever they may think.'

'Is there any other man you can think of who *might* have been the father?'

Jemima gave an unladylike snort of derision. 'I'm trying to be charitable towards the girl's memory but there are limits! Had Horace Morgan not come along when he did a great many men would have been quaking in their boots for fear she'd name them as the baby's father.'

It hardly narrowed down the list of possible suspects for Kerensa Morgan's murder and Amos returned to his earlier line of questioning. 'Explain what you meant when you spoke about the possibility of the baby being better off now ... if he's still alive.'

Jemima looked uncomfortable, 'I was referring to something that happened years ago ... just gossip, no more.'

'I'd still like you to tell me about it.'

'All right, but it happened some years ago and couldn't possibly have anything to do with the disappearance of Albert Morgan.'

'Let me be the judge of that,' Amos persisted.

'Well, as I said, it was no more than a rumour concerning simple Annie Dawe, daughter of Harold Dawe who farms at Bowland, out on the moor. She wasn't seen for a long time and word went around she'd got herself in trouble – by her own father some said. Then the Dawes were snowed in for weeks during the bad winter we had some years ago and when folks were able to get about again Annie told old Bessie Harris, the midwife at North Hill, that she'd had the baby and her father had paid one of the gypsies camped out at Sharptor to take it away and give it to someone he knew who desperately wanted a child.'

Amos frowned, 'You're not suggesting this gypsy might have murdered Kerensa Morgan just to get hold of a baby for someone?'

'I'm not suggesting anything, I'm just telling you what I heard happened to the Dawe girl's baby, as you asked me. It was rumoured at the time that it wasn't the first unwanted baby this particular gypsy had got rid of for someone in trouble – and I believe he's still around.'

Amos thought about what Jemima had told him. If Kerensa had been killed by a man with a good reason to murder her, but who could not bring himself to murder a baby – possibly even *his* baby – it could have been a way to dispose of Albert Morgan.

'I don't know, Jemima, it's one thing to take a baby from a girl who's got herself in trouble, but something quite different when it means getting involved with murder. Every gypsy I've ever known would be far too astute for that.'

'I suppose it would depend how much money he was offered,' Jemima retorted. 'Anyway, as I said, it was probably just gossip.'

'Nevertheless, it might be worthwhile having a chat with this gypsy, do you know his name?'

'I can't say I ever heard it mentioned – and you won't be able to get it from poor, simple Annie. She hanged herself in her father's barn only months after all this was supposed to have happened. Bessie Harris is the one to speak to. She still lives at North Hill and delivers most of the babies hereabouts ... both those that are wanted and those that are not.'

Chapter 5

WHILST AMOS WAS interviewing Jemima, Tom was having a frustrating time at Trelyn Hall, where Horace Morgan had an office at the rear of the great house.

After dismissing Tom's words of sympathy with an impatient gesture, Morgan demanded, 'Have you got anywhere yet with your search for Albert?'

'We have a great many men working on it and are pursuing a number of lines of enquiry, Mr Morgan, but I'm here to fill in some of the background of both you and the late Mrs Morgan, to see if we can find any possible connection with the tragedy you've suffered.'

'I suppose that's a long-winded way of saying "no",' Morgan commented, curtly. 'Well, you're not going to find him here so you'd be better out there with the others.'

The estate steward showed evidence of having had very little sleep since the murder of his wife and the inexplicable disappearance of his baby son. Tom would normally have shown great sympathy towards the man, but he found it difficult, and Morgan *was* a suspect and, so far, the only one they had.

'I'll try not to take up any more of your time than is absolutely necessary, Mr Morgan, but we all want to discover what happened up there on the moor, and why. Can you think of anyone who might have had any serious grudge against either you or your wife? Is there anything you can think of that might have happened before you came to Cornwall, perhaps, that might throw any light on what has happened here?'

For just a moment Tom thought Morgan hesitated, as though he might have thought of something, then the estate steward shook his head vigorously. 'Nothing at all. Besides, as far as I know nobody I've ever known is even aware I am working in Cornwall. I have no relatives and there was no reason for me to tell anybody else.'

'How about before then ... when you were in India?'

Morgan was startled now. 'How did you know I had been in India – and how can that possibly have anything to do with what has happened here? Anyway, it was so long ago everyone I knew there will have forgotten me.'

At that moment the door to the steward's office opened and a short, dapper man with a ruddy face and a bristling moustache entered the room. He was dressed for riding and Tom immediately recognized him as Colonel Trethewy, magistrate and owner of the Trelyn Estate. He and Tom were acquainted with each other by sight, the latter having given evidence against defendants in the magistrate's courtroom.

Colonel Trethewy had come to visit his steward, but it was Tom to whom he spoke. 'What are you doing here, have you found Morgan's missing child yet?'

'No, sir, but we have every available man out on the moor searching – as we had yesterday.'

'I trust you also have men searching vehicles leaving the county – especially the caravans of those damned gypsies who've been making such a nuisance of themselves in these parts lately. My head gamekeeper tells me they have been setting so many snares around the estate it's a wonder I have any game left.'

'There are constables on every bridge across the Tamar, sir, and we are searching all gypsy camps around the moor.'

'You are unlikely to find anything now, it's probably far too late. They will have spirited the boy away long before the body of his mother was found, but what *are* you doing here?'

Aware that Colonel Trethewy was one of the men of influence who had been bitterly opposed to the formation of a police force in Cornwall, and who stood with those who refused to allow a detective branch to be set up, Tom realized he needed to be careful how he replied.

'Superintendent Hawke is personally looking into the murder of Mrs Morgan, sir, he's sent me here to ask Mr Morgan a few questions.'

'What sort of questions?' Colonel Trethewy demanded.

'Whether there is anyone who might nurse a grudge against him, or who might hate him sufficiently to want to attack his wife. After all, he has an important post here with you, and important men make enemies.'

'So they might, but very few enemies resort to murder. Besides, I told Morgan when I took him on that I did not want him becoming too friendly with any of the local people, or taking on employees he might have worked with in the past. Morgan has orders to neither ask nor offer favours because of the post he holds at Trelyn. I am satisfied he has heeded my words by breaking all links with his past and taking a local wife with no family to come begging for favours. In other words, he has proven himself to be an ideal man for the post he holds at Trelyn. In view of this you need trouble him no more, Sergeant, he has more than enough to distract him from his duties right now, although had he not been adamant that he needs something to take his mind off the tragic happenings of the last couple of days, I would have insisted he take time off. The last thing he wants right now is to have you here asking questions of no consequence to distress him. I suggest you return to Superintendent Hawke and tell him he is to concentrate on gypsies and vagabonds in his search for whoever killed Mrs Morgan and abducted the child.'

'We were lucky to escape with only a "suggestion" from Colonel Trethewy,' Amos commented to Tom, when the two men met later that morning at the police house home of Sergeant Dreadon. 'Vagabonds and gypsies are his pet hates – although policemen are not far behind them. Anyway, we now know we can eliminate anyone in Morgan's background from the inquiry.'

'I don't think we can,' Tom replied. 'As a matter of fact I believe we should look into his background very thoroughly.'

Surprised by Tom's positive response, Amos asked, 'Why? If he broke all links with his past when he came here it's hardly likely anyone with a grudge will have found him. Trelyn is about as far as you can get from anywhere.'

'I might have agreed with you half an hour ago,' Tom explained, 'but I've just had a cup of tea with Sergeant Dreadon and he happened to mention that when he was speaking to the letter carrier the other day, the man was impressed to have just delivered a letter from the Honourable East India Company addressed to Morgan, at Trelyn Hall. It means Morgan was not telling the truth when he said nobody was aware of his whereabouts.'

'It could be he didn't feel the East India Company counted as "a person",' Amos commented.

'Perhaps ... but I'm not convinced. I felt all the time we were talking that there's something in Morgan's background he'd rather we knew nothing about.'

Amos had known the sergeant for too long to dismiss his hunches out of hand. 'Well, we need to follow up every possible lead, Tom. Write a letter to the East India Company and see if they can tell you anything about Morgan. If there's anything worth looking into further I'll ask the chief constable to authorize you to go up to London and dig a little deeper. We'll go to North Hill now and have a chat with a certain Bessie Harris. Jemima tells me she's the one who is sent for when a baby is being born. It also seems she knows of a gypsy who takes babies from unmarried mothers – for a sum of money, of course – and sells them on to women who are desperate for a baby but unable to have one themselves.'

'Now *that* could explain baby Albert's mysterious disappearance,' Tom declared. 'Although I would never have thought of such a thing as a possible explanation!'

'Don't get too excited about it, Tom, Jemima's information is a few years old, but it's worth checking out. When we've done that we'll see if the landlord of the Ring o' Bells at North Hill has a private room where we can get something to eat. It might also be a useful opportunity to learn something more about Kerensa Morgan. She worked there before she was married and – again according to Jemima – it seems she did a lot more there than satisfy the customers' thirst. We might learn something of significance.'

Chapter 6

BESSIE HARRIS'S HOME was a tiny thatched cottage at the edge of North Hill village. The front garden was occupied by a grey-muzzled dog of uncertain breeding, which looked through clouded eyes in the general direction of the two policemen and, as they opened the gate, barked ferociously, at the same time wagging its tail in greeting.

The sound brought two cats to the window-sill inside the house and Amos and Tom would learn they were only one-fifth of the number kept by the woman who during a long lifetime had brought most of the residents of the surrounding villages into the world.

Bessie was a short, grossly overweight, grey-haired woman who waddled rather than walked when she led the two men across the single downstairs room, shooing cats off the two chairs on which she invited her visitors to sit after she had somewhat reluctantly allowed them inside her home.

The room was cluttered with knick-knacks gathered from a lifetime and smelled uncomfortably strongly of the animals which shared the cottage with her. Tom wrinkled his nose in distaste and it did not pass unnoticed by Bessie.

Addressing Amos, she said sharply, 'I don't suppose you came here just to clutter up my cottage, so what is it you're wanting?'

'Information, Bessie. We've been told you might be able to give us the name of a gypsy who's been known to find homes for unwanted babies.'

'Me? How am I supposed to know something like that? I just help mothers best I can to bring their babies into this world. What they do with them afterwards is their business, not mine – nor anybody else's as far as I'm concerned.'

'I wouldn't argue with that, Bessie,' Amos replied, adding soothingly, 'From all I've heard you're probably the best midwife in the whole of Cornwall and I am not here to make any accusations against you. The women around here are very lucky to have you, but Sergeant Churchyard and I are investigating a murder, a particularly brutal murder, as well as the disappearance of a baby you will have helped to bring into the world – Albert Morgan.'

'I did, and a right screamer his mother turned out to be … but I mustn't speak ill of the dead, not even if it is Kerensa Morgan, but what's this gypsy you're talking about got to do with her, or with me?'

'I want to speak to him to see if he knows anything about Mrs Morgan's death, or can give me any clues as to the whereabouts of her baby….'

Bessie's mouth immediately became a tight-lipped thin line and Amos added, hurriedly, '… I am not interested in the babies he's found homes for, especially if they've gone to homes where they're wanted. They'll no doubt live better lives than they might otherwise have had, but I am seeking a murderer and this gypsy has to be a suspect, even though he is not the only one right now.'

'*That* doesn't surprise me. I could name you half-a dozen *women* who have wished Kerensa Morgan in her grave … not that they'd actually be ready to put her there,' she added hastily, '... and as for Jed Smith, he wouldn't hurt a soul.'

Amos now had the gypsy's name and, nodding at Tom to make a note of it, he asked, 'Where can I find this Jed Smith?'

Aware she had given away the gypsy's name, Bessie made no further effort to keep anything about him secret. 'He has a caravan over at Slippery Hill, a couple of miles up the road towards Launceston. He married a non-gypsy woman from out Temple way and his people wouldn't have much to do with him after that, not even after she died, a year or so back. He used to have his caravan up at Sharptor, but as his daughter grew older and prettier she began attracting too many of the miners who work up that way, so he moved off. Like I say, he's not the sort to murder anyone – or steal any babies, either. You hit the nail on the head when you said the babies he's passed on go to better homes than they would have had with their natural mothers.'

Bessie had said far more than she deemed was wise and now she added hurriedly, 'Not that *I've* ever had anything to do with that sort of thing myself, but I know the man. I think I can promise you he doesn't have a violent bone in his body. If he can possibly help you find Albert Morgan, he will.'

'Thank you, Bessie, you have been very helpful – but you mentioned half-a-dozen women who would have wished Mrs Morgan in her grave ... can you give me names?'

'That was just my foolish way of saying Kerensa was disliked by a great many women; I wasn't saying any of them would have actually killed her!'

'Of course not, but *someone* did and one of those women might well be able to point us in the direction of the murderer. Name them for me, Bessie, and tell me why it is they dislike her so much.'

'It's the same reason with every one of them – Kerensa played fast and loose with their husbands. Mind you, they're only the ones folk knew about – not that Kerensa ever cared overmuch about keeping her goings on secret, not even from her own husband, so perhaps you ought to be speaking to him instead of raking up old scandals that are best forgotten.'

'They probably would have been forgotten had someone not murdered her and stolen her baby, so if you tell me the names of these women, Sergeant Churchyard and I will be on our way. Horace Morgan has more than enough to cope with at the moment and we have spoken to him on a number of occasions, the last only this morning. I would like to leave him in peace until we have some information for him. As for raking up old scandals … We are not out to break up anyone's marriage, Bessie, we'll be as discreet as is possible given the circumstances, but we do need to talk to them.'

For some moments Bessie thought over what Amos had said. Arriving at a decision, she nodded her head vigorously. 'It might not hurt to have some husbands reminded of their shortcomings. I'll tell you of a couple of Kerensa's affairs that everyone knew of. One was with George Kendall who lives down by the bridge at Berriow, just below the village here. He's a nasty piece of work who used to be a gamekeeper up at Trelyn until Morgan came along and gave him the sack – possibly because he'd heard about what had gone on between Kendall and his wife. Kendall went to work up at the Notter mine then but he's well known for being handy with his fists, especially where his own wife is concerned. She had two black eyes the day I went to deliver her fifth – another girl – less than a year ago, and she's due her sixth any time now. His affair with Kerensa was the talk of the village for a long time and he wasn't very happy when she upped and married Morgan.

'Then there's Jowan Hodge. He's a miner, a hard worker and one of the few to make and keep his money when he was working up at the Phoenix mine. He bid for a pitch that turned out to contain a very rich lode and used his earnings to buy shares in the mine. They paid off handsomely and he's worth a bob or two now. That's probably the reason Kerensa latched on to him. Gossip had it they were planning to go off together – and this was after she'd married Morgan. Fortunately, Jowan came to his senses and settled down again with his wife who is a good, sound woman. She comes from a Christian family and goes off preaching when the call comes to her.

'That's two of 'em for you to be getting on with … but you should have a word with Alfie Kittow too. He's landlord at the Ring o' Bells, right here in the village. Kerensa worked for him – and again, this is just rumour – it might not have been only Alfie's customers she kept happy. If Florrie, Alfie's wife, was at the pub she'd tell you a different story. She and Alfie have always been a close couple, but Florrie hasn't been there for a while. She's lost a few babies in the past, most being stillborn and she's desperate for a child. She went away a while ago and Alfie spread word she was expecting again and had gone back to her family, somewhere outside Cornwall so they would be around to help when her time came, but his story never convinced me. She never looked very pregnant – and I should know a pregnant woman when I see one! I think she might have another reason for going away, but no doubt you'll be able to get to the bottom of it.

'Anyway, you wanted some names and now you've got 'em, so you can get on your way before I get a bad name for talking too much to policemen.' Tom had been taking notes while Bessie was talking and now he shut his notebook gratefully eager to be first out of the door.

Once outside he took in a deep breath, saying, 'It's good to be out in the fresh air. I don't think I would want Bessie delivering a baby for anyone in my family!'

'I agree, Tom, but she has given us more to go on than anyone else we have spoken to.'

'So, what do we do now?' Tom queried.

'We'll go to the Ring o' Bells and see what the landlord has to offer by way of food. While we're eating we can have a few words and see if there's any truth in the rumours about him and Kerensa, although I have a feeling he'll prefer telling us more about the other men she met while she was working for him. Either way, it will be worthwhile I don't doubt.'

Chapter 7

IN NORTH HILL'S Ring o' Bells public house, an effusive landlord showed the two policemen to a private room away from the public bar where perhaps half-a-dozen men wearing the garb favoured by miners were drinking.

'You'll be here looking into that terrible business up on the moor,' he said, as they seated themselves at one of three tables in the room. 'The whole village is shocked. We've never had anything like it around here before and I still can't believe it! Do you have any suspects yet?'

'One or two,' Amos replied, laconically. 'I believe the victim used to work here for you?'

'Yes, Kerensa was a very cheerful girl, the customers liked her.'

'From what we've been hearing she liked them too … perhaps a little too much?'

'I wouldn't say that, but she was a single girl and fancy free.'

'And so she might have been, but most of your customers aren't!'

'Well … this is a small village. Those who live here thrive on rumours and the like. She did her job well enough and I had no cause for complaint.'

The Ring o' Bells landlord was inclined to be less garrulous now, but Amos persisted.

'From what I have heard very few *men* complained, although it might have been a different story where the women were concerned. Did your wife like her?'

Now Alfie Kittow was clearly uncomfortable, 'They had very little to do with each other. Kerensa's place was down here in the bar and Florrie rarely comes down, she says the atmosphere doesn't agree with her.'

'We would like to speak to her, so perhaps you'll take us up to see her after we've eaten?'

'I'm afraid that won't be possible, she's gone away for a while. She's expecting, you see and ... well, she's had a number of miscarriages and lost babies before. She blames the sort of life we lead here, at the Ring o' Bells, so has gone off to her family. If everything goes well and the baby's all right she'll stay there until it's a bit stronger, then she'll either come back here or I'll sell up and join her there – but I'd rather you kept that bit of information to yourself.'

Perspiration glistened on Alfie's upper lip now but Amos had not finished questioning him. 'When is the baby due?'

'She's probably had it already, but I haven't heard from her for a while. I keep telling myself I must try to find out what's happening, or go up and see her – and the baby. Trouble is, I'm not much of a writer.'

'We'll need to get in touch with her, so we would like her address, please.'

'That's another problem. I haven't got it written down and my memory has never been very good for names at the best of times. I can't remember the *exact* address, although it's in Wiltshire. I could take you there if I had to, but why do you want to speak to Florrie, she wasn't even here when Kerensa was murdered?'

'We need to follow up every possible line of inquiry, speak to anyone who knew Kerensa Morgan.'

'Then you're going to be kept busy enough right here in Cornwall without gallivanting off to Wiltshire. We've had half the miners on Bodmin Moor in the Ring o' Bells at some time or another and they all knew Kerensa. She was a very popular girl.'

Amos thought Alfie was more confident now he believed they had accepted his story about his wife and he said, 'We'll be busy, certainly, but I intend calling in as many of my policemen as necessary to help – and if I think going to Wiltshire to interview your wife will be helpful then either Sergeant Churchyard or myself will go there. Of course, if we can narrow down the list of suspects right here in Cornwall that won't be necessary. That's why we're here talking to you now. We thought there might perhaps be someone in particular who seemed close to Kerensa … or who caused trouble because of her. I've heard the name of Jowan Hodge mentioned, do you know him?'

It was quite apparent Alfie was being deliberately vague about his wife because he did not want her to be interviewed. Amos had no intention of allowing the matter of her whereabouts to remain a mystery, but for now he hoped the Ring o' Bells landlord might be more forthcoming if he believed he could divert their attention away from her by giving them something else to concentrate on. The ploy worked.

'There was talk about her and Jowan Hodge at one time, but I'm sure it was no more than talk. He's happy with his wife, and she's strict chapel so wouldn't put up with him playing around. If Kerensa set her cap at him it was because when he struck it rich up at the Phoenix he came in here buying drinks for everyone. She was never one to pass up an opportunity with someone who was generous with his money.'

He looked at Amos hoping he might have diverted attention from himself and his wife, but he was met with an expression that told him nothing.

For a moment, Alfie faltered before saying, 'There *is* someone else who was smitten with Kerensa and caused trouble in here because of it – even though he's a married man – and that's George Kendall.'

'His name has been mentioned,' Amos said, nodding approval at Tom who had his pocket book out, taking notes. 'Tell me more about him.'

'Well, I don't like talking about my customers, but Kendall isn't one of them anymore and hasn't been since before Kerensa met up with Horace Morgan. He's always been violent, even when he was a boy, and I pity that poor wife of his, she's had more black eyes than any prize-fighter. It's fairly certain there was something going on between him and Kerensa, but she put a stop to it when she and Morgan started going out seriously together. She didn't stay here for long after that, but Kendall wouldn't accept it was over between them and before she left he came into the Ring o' Bells more than once threatening what he'd do to her if she didn't change her mind. The last time he'd already had too much to drink somewhere else and mouthed off at her, as usual. One of the miners who was in here drinking told him to leave her alone and a fight broke out. It took a half-dozen of the miner's friends to better Kendall and throw him out. I warned him then never to come back in the Ring o' Bells again and he never has. I believe he caused more trouble for Kerensa once or twice after that, but it wasn't inside here so it was none of my business. Thinking about it, he's got to be one of your main suspects.'

'Thank you.' Reserving his opinion on why Alfie Kittow might be so keen to throw suspicion on someone else for Kerensa's murder and the abduction of Albert Morgan, Amos asked, 'Where might we find this George Kendall?'

'He lives down at Berriow Bridge, but he won't be home again until tomorrow. A couple of the miners who work with him up at the Notter mine were in here last night. Kendall and the men he works with have struck a profitable lode and are working double shifts to clear as much of it as they can before their pitch comes up for auction again.'

Amos knew little about mining, but he was aware there was a bidding system on a great many mines where at set intervals particular working places would be auctioned off, the bidding miners agreeing the percentage they would retain of the mined ore's value. It seemed that George Kendall had been fortunate enough to come upon a promising lode on his particular pitch.

Satisfied their visit to the Ring o' Bells had not been entirely wasted, Amos and Tom settled down to enjoy the meal that was sent in to them by the landlord of the Ring o' Bells, 'compliments of the house'. While they ate the two men chatted over what they had learned so far from their visit to North Hill.

Tom was still not convinced that Horace Morgan was not implicated in some way in Kerensa's murder and declared he intended finding out more about the estate steward's past. He agreed with Amos that it seemed unlikely he would have done anything to harm his baby son and pointed out they had no evidence that the baby *had* been harmed. At the moment he was merely missing.

The two policemen also decided there were flaws in the story given to them by the landlord of the inn where they were eating that his wife had gone away to have a baby. Both men were sceptical about his claim that he was unable to remember the address where his wife was staying.

'I might be able to find out where she is,' Tom said. 'Alfie Kittow mentioned having received letters from his wife and any letter delivery man worthy of his calling will read the postmark on letters he carries. We know the local man was aware a letter he delivered to Horace Morgan came from the East India Company offices – he will probably remember the postmark on the letters Kittow received from his wife. That should help us.'

'Good thinking,' Amos said. 'If Kittow announces to all and sundry that his wife has had a baby boy and he gives up the Ring o' Bells to go and join her, then no one will query it – but it could possibly explain the mystery of what has happened to baby Albert Morgan! A number of gaps remain to be filled in before we have any chance of making a case against him, but he is certainly very worried about something. We'll go into it further, but not until we have spoken to both the men Alfie has told us about. Even if they have nothing to do with the case they might have their own ideas on why he has been so eager to divert attention from himself. There is also this gypsy, Jed Smith. We need to speak to him. He might be able to throw some light upon the disappearance of baby Albert, but I think we have a long way to go with this case yet, Tom.'

Chapter 8

RIDING BACK TOWARDS Bodmin across the moor later that day, Amos and Tom were talking of all they had learned to date. They were forced to admit they had made little real progress and, as yet, there was no single suspect. The afternoon had proved particularly frustrating as neither of the men mentioned by both Bessie Harris and the landlord of the Ring o' Bells was at home.

As Alfie had informed them, George Kendall was working a double shift on the Notter Mine and Jowan Hodge and his wife had not been at home when they called.

It had become increasingly apparent that Kerensa had been altogether as promiscuous as they had been led to believe and, as a result, the list of possible suspects was growing instead of reducing, as they had hoped it would when they had ridden to North Hill earlier in the day.

'There can't be many homes in the area where the man of the house isn't fearing he'll be next to have us knocking on the door,' Tom commented.

'No, and most will no doubt behave much as Alfie Kittow did and try to divert attention from themselves by giving us even more names of men we will need to question.'

'Do you think Alfie had an affair with Kerensa Morgan?' Tom asked.

'He certainly wasn't happy having us asking him so many questions, especially when we were inquiring about his wife. Bessie Harris believes his wife could have left him as a result of an affair with Kerensa and not because she was having a baby and wanted to be somewhere quieter than a busy and sometimes rowdy public house.'

'If he wanted his wife back do you believe he might have been desperate enough to murder Kerensa to get her out of the way?'

'It's possible and if he did he might – quite literally – have been able to kill two birds with one stone. He hinted he might give up the Ring o' Bells and go off to join his wife if her baby was born safe and well. What if he killed Kerensa, and had baby Albert taken to his wife, perhaps by this gypsy, Jed Smith? If Alfie's wife is seen with a baby at some later date it would arouse no suspicion as long as the baby isn't brought back here – at least, not until it has changed beyond recognition, as babies do. Besides, for all we know Alfie might even be the baby's real father. It's not beyond the realms of possibility.'

'It's an interesting theory,' Tom agreed, 'So what do we do … go off to find Alfie's wife and check on her?'

Amos shook his head. 'It *is* only a theory. I don't think the chief constable would agree to pay for one of us to travel all the way to Wiltshire, where Alfie claims his wife is, unless we have something more to go on. A lot depends on what we get from this gypsy, Jed Smith. He might want to tell us something if he took a baby to Alfie's wife and realizes it's likely to involve him in a murder investigation….'

Looking up at the sky, which had become overcast since they began their journey, Amos said, 'Anyway, let's speed up a bit. I promised Talwyn I would try to get home early for dinner tonight – our visitor was due to arrive today and you're coming to dinner, remember?'

'Who is this visitor, you said it was no one you know?'

'That's right, she's a nurse who will be with us for a night or two. She is in Cornwall trying to recruit new nurses from girls attending schools here. She served with Florence Nightingale in the Crimea before going on to India where she must have been kept busy during the mutiny there. If she's anything like the nurses I met when I was in Miss Nightingale's Scutari hospital, she'll be something of a 'battleaxe'. I think Talwyn suggested I bring you home to dinner for support. We couldn't really refuse to take her in; she is related to the man who funds the school where Talwyn teaches. Unfortunately, he and his family are away from Cornwall during her visit so he asked Talwyn to take care of her while she is here. In view of the money he puts into her school she could hardly say no.'

It had been a hard day and although Tom welcomed the opportunity to enjoy Talwyn's cooking, he would rather have spent the evening talking with just Amos and his wife about the events of the past few days. Talwyn was a very intelligent woman who had been of considerable help to Amos when he first came to Cornwall from Scotland Yard on a murder investigation, and both men were appreciative of her acumen.

Nevertheless, shaking out his reins in order to keep up with Amos's mount, Tom said, 'Oh well, we're neither of us patients now and I think for one night I can put up with a battle-axe. After all, Florence Nightingale and her nurses did a great deal for our wounded men when they had most need of women like her. I'll be on my best behaviour.'

*

A shock awaited the two policemen when they arrived at the Hawkes' house and were introduced to the nursing battle-axe. In her early thirties, Verity Pendleton was a tall and elegant fair-haired woman who would have turned the head of any man at a social gathering.

She was also well-educated and possessed a surprising knowledge of police work and procedures. The reason for this became clear when she explained that she had grown up in a police environment, her stepfather being an ex-Royal Navy captain who, on retirement, had been appointed as Chief Constable of the Wiltshire Constabulary, a force which had been formed almost twenty years before that of Cornwall.

Over dinner the conversation was for a while about the Crimea war and the military hospital at Scutari, in nearby Turkey, where a newly qualified Verity had served as a nurse with Florence Nightingale and where Amos had been a patient as a result of a wound suffered during the war. However, after they ascertained that he had been returned to duty before Verity's arrival at the hospital, their talk turned to India where she had nursed both troops and civilians during the mutiny of East India Company native troops in 1857 and 1858.

She was immediately interested when it was mentioned that the husband of the woman whose murder was being investigated by Amos and Tom had been an employee of the Honourable East India Company and who, according to available information, had been in India during the mutiny.

'Do you have any idea where he was stationed while he was there?' Verity enquired.

'No, but speaking to you has given me an opportunity to find out a little more of exactly what he did there,' Amos replied. 'Magistrate Trethewy is his employer at Trelyn and is also benefactor of the school at nearby North Hill. If you could possibly find time to talk to the girls there I will take you to meet Colonel Trethewy and drop into the conversation that you were in India during the mutiny. With any luck he will suggest you meet Morgan. You might be able to find out a little more than I did about his time in India.'

'Is there any particular reason you wish to know more about him?' Verity asked. 'Surely you do not suspect him of murdering his wife and doing away with his own baby son?'

'He has not been ruled out as a suspect,' Amos admitted, 'and he has been extremely vague about his life before coming to Cornwall. If he has something to hide I would like to know about it. If he hasn't...? Well, then we can concentrate on our other suspects – and unfortunately there are a growing number!'

'As your stepfather is Chief Constable of the Wiltshire force there is another matter on which you might be able to help us,' Tom broke into their conversation. He had taken out his pocket book while Verity and Amos were talking and now, turning to the entries of the day, he said, 'The landlord of the Ring o' Bells at North Hill is also a suspect and claims his wife is in a Wiltshire village where she has gone to have a baby. In fact, he declared she has probably had the baby by now – this despite the fact that the local midwife in North Hill is not at all convinced she *was* pregnant when she left Cornwall. Amos and I think it possible a gypsy we have been told about might have been involved in obtaining a baby for her. That, in turn, could have something to do with the disappearance of baby Albert Morgan, although at the moment it's no more than speculation.'

'How intriguing. Where in Wiltshire is this woman?'

'That is a problem,' Amos admitted. 'Alfie Kittow claims to have forgotten the address ... although he says he could take us there!'

'Do you believe him?'

'Quite frankly, no! But Tom is going to speak to the local mail carrier. We are hoping he might remember the postmarks on the letters from Mrs Kittow that he's delivered to the Ring o' Bells while she's been away. If he has you might know the place from which they were sent and be able to tell us about it.'

'I know many places in Wiltshire, although I certainly haven't been to every one of them,' Verity admitted, 'But even if I don't know a place you are interested in I can ask my stepfather to send someone to make enquiries about this woman if you think it might help.'

'It would be *very* helpful,' Amos said. 'Thank you.'

Chapter 9

LATER THAT EVENING, after dinner had been eaten and enjoyed, Tom and Verity found themselves together in the Hawkes' garden. Amos had pleaded that he needed to complete a report on Kerensa's murder and the apparent abduction of baby Albert for the chief constable, and Talwyn had ushered them outside, claiming she needed to supervise their maid-of-all-work clearing away the dinner things in the kitchen.

Tom was showing Verity the rose bush he had bought for Amos and Talwyn as a wedding anniversary present. The bush was in flower and exuding a wonderful scent. After commenting on the flower's beauty and fragrance, Verity said, 'I have an uncomfortable feeling that Amos and Talwyn are deliberately throwing us together, Tom.'

'Probably,' Tom replied with a smile. 'They are a wonderful couple and very happy together, but Talwyn, in particular, worries about me. She would like to see me safely settled and as contented as they are.'

'Unfortunately, she is wasting her time, Tom. I am settled and contented with my present way of life, but Talwyn *is* a very kind and considerate woman.' After a slight hesitation, Verity added, 'Have you never felt the need to marry?'

It was an honest question with no ulterior motive and Tom replied equally frankly.

'A couple of years ago I thought I *was* heading for marriage.'

'What went wrong?'

'Flora, the girl I was going to marry, was housekeeper to the Dowager Lady Hogg, who went to Canada to be with her sons. She is an elderly lady and Flora felt duty bound to accompany her on the journey. She intended to return to England once Lady Hogg was settled in, but something always seemed to get in the way and it was never the right time to leave.'

'Did you never think of going to Canada to be with her?'

Tom gave a wry smile, 'I wouldn't have been welcome there. Lady Hogg doted on her youngest son and Amos and I were responsible for him being forced to leave this country. We arrested him for being involved in a burglary and a plot to defraud a number of influential people – and for a while he was also a murder suspect. In fact, had he not belonged to such an influential family he would either have spent a great many years in prison, or been transported to Australia. Fortunately for him, an agreement was reached that instead of being taken before a judge, he would be allowed to leave the country and go to Canada where the Hogg family have large estates. Lady Hogg went there to be with him. Actually, it was as a result of that investigation that Flora and I met in the first place.'

'How intriguing! You and Amos must tell me more, while I am here.'

Looking at Verity and seeing a very attractive woman, Tom asked, 'How about you … is there no one in your life?' He realized as soon as the words were out that it was an impertinent question, but Verity did not appear to be offended.

'Miss Nightingale never allowed any of her nurses to become

involved with men. She insisted they be wedded to their vocation – as she herself is – and it *is* a very demanding vocation but one I love very much.'

'Yet you left actual nursing some years ago and are performing a different task now, lecturing and recruiting nurses, surely the same rules no longer apply?'

'To be perfectly honest I have never found time to even think about it, I have been kept far too busy.... But shall we change the subject? Tell me more about the man you wish me to speak to, the husband of this murdered woman.'

'There is very little Amos and I know about him, really. We have been told he worked in Wales before he came to Trelyn and spent time in India before that, but we have no idea why he left either place.'

'I can think of a couple of reasons why he might have left India. One is because the mutiny there shook everyone to the core. Before then they all enjoyed a good life ... well the Europeans did. Most were employees of the East India Company, the *Honourable* East India Company, which controlled the country. They lived well and felt safe, but the mutiny changed everything, it was a terrifying time, especially for the women and children. When it ended the Crown took over the running of the country and many Europeans, frightened of what had occurred and realizing the opportunity to amass huge fortunes had passed, decided to leave India. Not only that, with the British Government now involved in the affairs of the country, certain men were afraid they might be brought to account for their actions during earlier years.'

'I've always thought it must be a fascinating country,' Tom commented, aware that Verity had also been in India during the mutiny and must have been subject to the dangers faced by other

Europeans there. 'With your knowledge of the place it would be interesting to have you meet Horace Morgan and see what you make of him. He doesn't seem to have made any friends since coming to Cornwall and keeps himself very much to himself.'

'I am perfectly willing to speak to him if an opportunity can be arranged by Amos, but do you really think it might help with your inquiries into the murder of his wife?'

'I don't know,' Tom confessed. 'Both Amos and I have the feeling that he is not quite what he seems to be and, as he *is* a suspect, we need to learn all we can about him, to either find a possible motive, or rule him out.'

'Well, I only intended to be in Cornwall for a few days, but if Talwyn doesn't mind if I remain here for a day or two longer I will be happy to talk to the girls at North Hill school … and any other school of her choosing. That *is* why I am in Cornwall, after all, and if it means I can help you in any way – and Amos, of course – I will be thrilled. When I was a young girl in Wiltshire and something exciting occurred I used to wish I had been born a boy so I might join the constabulary and be involved with what was going on. If I were able to help you with your murder inquiry it would be something exciting to tell my stepfather!'

'I think the life you led in both Scutari and India was probably far more exciting than speaking to Horace Morgan, but your help would certainly be appreciated by Amos … by both of us.'

Tom was aware that Verity's background was very different to his own and she was totally dedicated to her work. Furthermore, the social gulf between them was far too deep to be bridged, but she *was* a beautiful woman and he enjoyed speaking to her. He hoped she might remain in Cornwall for a while and give him an opportunity to spend more time in her company.

In the kitchen of the house, Amos was standing behind Talwyn, hands on her shoulders and they were both looking out through the window at the pair walking around the garden together.

'They seem to be getting along very well.' This from Talwyn.

'They do,' Amos agreed, 'but I hope Tom will not become too smitten with her.'

'Why? Verity is a very nice woman.' Talwyn turned her head to look up at her husband.

'I agree, but nothing can come of it, their backgrounds are poles apart. She obviously comes from a very good family, and is a friend of people like Florence Nightingale. Tom comes from a poor part of London and is only a policeman.'

'*Only* a policeman? Is that how you see *yourself*, Amos, as less than others?'

Amused by her sudden eruption of indignation, Amos smiled and tightened the grip he had on her shoulders, 'No, of course not, but then, as you are so fond of telling me, *I* have an arrogant nature.'

'And so you have!' She reached up and touched his hand affectionately. 'But you *are* as good as any man I have ever met – and *better* than most. So too is Tom. As you have said yourself, if he wasn't so loyal to you and left headquarters he could opt for rapid promotion elsewhere in the force and – again quoting you – he would be snapped up for a senior post in any constabulary in the country if he ever decided to leave Cornwall.'

'True,' Amos agreed, 'but you mustn't get your hopes up about Tom's chances with Verity even if the social gap wasn't there. She is a dedicated nurse and committed to what she is doing.'

'Perhaps,' Talwyn replied, enigmatically, 'but I'm not giving up yet. I see a lot of the same strength of character in Tom that I first saw in you … but without the arrogance! Verity is no fool, she will be able to recognize it too.'

Chapter 10

TOM HAD SOME work to carry out in the Bodmin police headquarters before he sought out suspects in the murder of Kerensa Morgan and it was Amos who took Verity to Trelyn in the hope that she might meet Horace Morgan and learn more of his life in India, but it was Tom who was the early subject of conversation when the two first set out.

They were travelling using a pony and trap that Amos had at his disposal and Talwyn gave her husband a brief but smug 'I told you so' look when Verity expressed disappointment that Tom would not be accompanying them.

Verity saw the look too and said, easily, 'Tom has had a very interesting life and I enjoyed talking to him last evening.'

'We're likely to meet up with him later in the day,' Amos explained. 'He has one or two things to do at headquarters, but they shouldn't take him too long. When they are done he will be riding to North Hill to try to interview two possible suspects who were unavailable yesterday.'

Verity quietly accepted this and, although during the drive to Trelyn she put a great many questions about the man they were hoping to meet, she also succeeded in finding out more about Tom.

Amos was aware of this and wondered whether Talwyn's acumen might prove superior to his own where Verity was concerned. He conceded that it would not be for the first time.

Arriving at Trelyn Hall, they were greeted with thinly disguised disapproval by the butler and seated in the entrance hall while Colonel Trethewy was informed of their presence.

The magistrate kept them waiting for some fifteen minutes before putting in an appearance and it was immediately apparent that he was annoyed at being disturbed by Amos. His irritation dissipated somewhat when he saw Verity but, still frowning, he demanded, 'What is it the police want this time, Hawke?'

Gesturing towards Verity, he added, 'and who is this?'

Giving Colonel Trethewy a brief introduction to Verity, Amos explained the purpose of their visit, but it failed to mollify the bad-tempered landowner. 'Talk to schoolgirls about becoming nurses? What sort of a future is that for decent country girls, eh? I'm surprised Chief Constable Gilbert allows his most senior superintendent to waste time aiding a woman who is attempting to lure young girls into almost certain immorality when he should be investigating a murder. I shall most certainly have words with him about it.'

'It is because I was coming here as part of that investigation that I offered to bring Miss Pendleton with me to speak to you, sir. As for the mission that brought her to Cornwall, I have no doubt she will be able to put your mind at rest.'

'Thank you, Amos. Colonel Trethewy is not the first man to have misconceptions about the nursing service. It is something Miss Nightingale has needed to fight against for very many years. Whenever the word nurse is mentioned to senior army officers of the past they immediately think of camp followers, the women who follow soldiers into battle for a wide variety of reasons and who are the only ones to care for soldiers when they are wounded in battle. Many are well intentioned and do their very best for the men – others do not. All lack the skills necessary to help the recovery of the men they tend. Miss Nightingale is aware of this and with the full support of Her Majesty Queen Victoria she has trained and organized a force of women whose skills are often superior to the doctors they support and whose dedication and discipline have transformed the nursing service. In order to expand and improve the reputation of these women, bright, honest and intelligent girls are being recruited to receive training in some of London's top hospitals. It is a scheme that has the backing of the Prime Minister, Lord Palmerston, and its success is very close to Queen Victoria's heart, as Her Majesty told me herself.'

Startled, Colonel Trethewy looked at Verity in disbelief, 'You have met the Queen?'

'On more than one occasion,' Verity replied matter-of-factly. 'She has taken a keen interest in all the many aspects of nursing ever since Miss Nightingale proved its worth during the Crimean War. A school of midwives has recently been opened in London which we hope will revolutionize childbirth and do away with many of the old women who carry out the task – particularly in the countryside – and who are positively dangerous for both mother and child. And, of course, the importance of having a trained nurse assisting at childbirth is a subject with which Her Majesty has personal experience.'

Colonel Trethewy appeared embarrassed by the conversation but Amos thought of the conditions in which Bessie Harris lived and from which she sallied forth to bring babies into the world.

Recovering some of his composure, Colonel Trethewy realized

he was speaking to someone who undoubtedly had considerable influence close to the seat of power in the country's capital and he tempered his tone accordingly.

'I have, of course, heard of Miss Nightingale's sterling efforts on behalf of wounded soldiers during the Crimean War and Her Majesty's concern for those who fight in her name is well known and appreciated. As an ex-soldier myself, anything that makes their lot easier has my fullest support. Now you have explained your purpose in coming to Cornwall more fully I will be delighted to arrange for you to give a talk to the girls of our school. Would you like me to have the girls brought here, to the Hall?'

'No, Colonel, but thank you for suggesting it. I feel the weather is so pleasant that I will take the girls out of school and find a grassy bank on which to sit while I talk to them.'

'As you wish. I believe there are a couple of very bright pupils among them, but I doubt very much whether you will be able to persuade them to leave Cornwall. Most girls have already decided who they will marry, even before they leave school.'

'I think you will find Miss Pendleton is not easily deterred from her purpose, sir. Had she been she would never have survived the Crimean War *and* the Indian Mutiny.'

Amos's words had the effect for which he had been hoping. Eager now to make a favourable impression upon his well-connected visitor, Colonel Trethewy said to Verity, 'You were caught up in the troubles in India as well as the Crimea? I wonder if you ever met Horace Morgan, my estate steward, while you were there?'

'The name sounds familiar, where was he stationed?'

'I really don't know, but he spent many years with the Honourable East India Company. I will have him brought to my study and you two can have a chat together while Superintendent Hawke brings me up to date on his inquiries into the murder of Morgan's wife and the disappearance of his baby son. I have no doubt Hawke has already told you all about it? It is a dreadful business ... dreadful!'

Chapter 11

TOM ACCEPTED THAT as the Cornwall Constabulary's most senior superintendent Amos was the right man to introduce Verity to the Trelyn magistrate and was very much aware of the huge social gulf between himself and the Nightingale nurse. However, there was not too great a difference in their ages and he had found it easy to talk to her. In fact, she was probably the most interesting woman he had ever met.

Not that there had been very many women in Tom's life, the unsociable hours kept by a policeman had seen to that. He would like to have spent a little more time with Verity, preferably just the two of them, but he knew she would be leaving Cornwall in just a few days – and he had a murder to investigate.

When he had completed the paperwork that required his attention in the Bodmin police headquarters, Tom set off on Amos's riding horse for North Hill and Berriow Bridge, his intention being to interview the two possible suspects who had not been available on the previous day.

His first call would be on George Kendall, the man reputed to have a violent temper and who, although married, was said to have had a tempestuous affair with Kerensa and been extremely angry when she had ended it.

He would next visit the home of Jowan Hodge, who he felt must be a very lucky and shrewd man. Few copper miners had made money from their vocation … and kept it. Although rumoured to have had an affair with Kerensa, he was said to be happily married, in sharp contrast to Kendall.

Hodge was said by the landlord of the Ring o' Bells to have had trouble with Kerensa because she did not want the affair to end, even though she was married and had a baby. The inn-keeper had suggested this was because, thanks to his wise investments, Hodge was now a comparatively wealthy man.

Halfway across Bodmin Moor and lost in thought about the questions he was going to put to the two men, Tom looked up and saw a young girl hurrying across the moor ahead of him. As he drew nearer he could see she was dressed in the manner of a gypsy, wearing a brightly coloured blouse and a skirt which was shorter than was customary among countrywomen. She was also barefooted and her long black hair hung loose almost to her waist. When he came close enough for her to hear horse and rider she turned her head but did not slow her pace.

Reaching the gypsy girl, Tom reined in the horse alongside her and said cheerfully, 'Hello, you're a long way from anywhere.'

Giving him only the briefest of glances, she replied, 'I could say the same of you.'

'True,' Tom conceded. 'Where are you going?'

'That's none of your business. Where are *you* going?'

'I'm heading for North Hill. I thought if you were going that way I might offer you a lift, up behind me.' The girl was small and slight and he believed the horse would be hardly aware of the extra weight.

This time the girl's glance was longer and more searching and Tom was aware she was considering the advisability of accepting his offer. He was about to explain he was a policeman when he remembered that gypsies and policemen rarely got along together. He checked himself – and would be glad he did so.

'All right. I've certainly done more than enough walking for one day – and it'll get me home a sight faster.... Give me your hand.'

He reached down and, grasping his extended hand, she leaped up and the next moment was straddling the horse behind him, exposing an expanse of leg which would have shocked women who lived more settled lives. Now, having helped to lift her on to the horse, Tom realized he had been right about her weight, it must have been less than half his own, even though she was probably eighteen or twenty years of age.

They rode in silence for a while, with Tom very conscious of her arms which tightened about his waist whenever the horse made an unexpected movement. He was also aware that she occasionally rested her head against his back, as though tired.

He was first to break the silence between them, saying, 'This must be better than walking. Had you walked far before I met up with you?'

'*Too* far. I left our wagon at dawn this morning to walk to my grandmother's home, about three miles from where you met me, and was on my way back again.'

'That's a long walk in one day, but I've been backwards and forwards across the moor in the last few days and haven't seen any gypsy wagons ... not actually on the moor, anyway.'

'My grandmother doesn't live in a wagon caravan. She's a *gorgio*, like my *dai* – my mother. My Dado was working on their farm when they met and they were married in a proper church. His family never forgave him, but my mother's family welcomed him – well, most of them – and he's very fond of my grandmother. She's not too well right now and I thought he might have gone there to see how she was, but she hasn't seen him.'

'Are you saying he's gone missing?'

'I wish I knew. But he hasn't been home for a couple of days and although he often disappears for a day or two he always tells me when he's going to be away. This time he didn't.'

Something in what the girl had said struck a chord in Tom's mind and, recalling what Bessie Harris had mentioned when he and Amos visited her, he said, 'That must be a worry for you … but we haven't introduced ourselves. I'm Tom … and you?'

'Zillah … Zillah Smith.'

'Zillah is a very unusual name … but a pretty one. Is your wagon actually in North Hill village, Zillah?'

'No, it's actually at Slippery Hill, on the Launceston road.'

Now Tom knew his surmise had been right. He was giving a ride to the daughter of Jed Smith, the gypsy who dealt in unwanted babies. 'That's a couple of miles beyond North Hill, I'll take you there then come back to North Hill.'

He felt her draw back from him and she demanded, 'Why would you do that, what do you expect from me in return?'

'Only your company. Besides, after what happened at Trelyn on Tuesday night I'd like to make certain you get home safely.'

'What happened on Tuesday night?'

The question surprised Tom, then he realized that if Zillah had been alone in her wagon home since the murder she could have spoken to no one who knew what had happened to Kerensa Morgan and her baby. It was also highly unlikely the news would have reached her grandmother at her remote farmhouse on the moor.

'There was a particularly nasty murder up here, at Hawk's Tor. The wife of the estate steward at Trelyn Hall was found battered to death and her baby who was with her at the time is missing.'

Zillah was behind him so Tom was unable to see her face but he sensed she was startled.

'You mean … Kerensa Morgan?'

'Yes, did you know her?'

'I met her once or twice when we had our wagon on Sharptor, but my Dado didn't like me talking to her. She did have me make a shawl for her when she was expecting, but he said she wasn't a nice girl for me to know.'

'From all I've heard about her your father's opinion was probably right.'

'*What* have you heard about her, you're not from these parts or I would have seen you before – and you don't talk like a Cornishman? Where did you hear about Kerensa's murder and how do you know what sort of girl she was?'

Tom hesitated before replying. The chances were that if he told her the truth she would want nothing more to do with him. The duties of a policemen were seen as including moving on gypsies. To the establishment they were perceived as invariably dishonest and classed as vagrants. As a result, a mutual antipathy had developed between gypsies and those whose duty it was to uphold the law.

Nevertheless, Tom knew that if he lied to Zillah now he would never have her trust in the future … and it was something he might need, especially as there now appeared to be a mystery concerning her father's whereabouts. Tom felt strongly that the gypsy's disappearance was somehow connected with Kerensa's death and the missing baby.

'I actually come from London, Zillah. I came to Cornwall a couple of years ago to help with a murder that was committed at

Laneglos House and stayed on. Now I'm investigating the murder of Kerensa.'

'You're a policeman?' The question came out in the form of an accusation, 'but you're not wearing a uniform.'

'It wouldn't be very practical to wear a policeman's top hat when riding a horse, would it?' Then, deciding to tweak the truth just a little, he added, 'Besides, I spend most of my time in the police headquarters in Bodmin and don't carry out normal police duties. I'm only out here now to help with the murder inquiries.'

'And so you might be, but I don't want to be seen with a policeman. I'll get off your horse before we reach North Hill.'

'That will still leave you with a couple of miles to go. Why don't we skirt the village and I'll take you all the way home, to see if your father's back yet. If he's not then we really should make a serious attempt to find him. There is so much going on around here at the moment that anything could have happened to him.'

'Why pretend you're interested in finding him for me? What is it you *really* want? The sergeant at Trelyn would be only too happy if he never saw him again. He'd have had both of us out of Cornwall long ago if Mrs Hocking down at Slippery Hill hadn't let us stay on her farmland.'

'I'm not the Trelyn sergeant. If you and your father are causing nobody any trouble you're entitled to stay wherever you like … and with a murderer on the loose I'd be far happier knowing you weren't staying in a wagon on your own.'

Zillah spent some time thinking about what Tom had said before replying, then she asked, 'Is that *really* what you are thinking? There's no other reason you want to take me all the way home? It's not because I'm only a gypsy woman and you know there'll be no one else around when we get there and so you think you'll be able to do whatever you like with me?'

'Zillah, if your father is there I'll be very glad for you. I'll pass the time of day with him and go off happy in the knowledge that you have someone to look after you.'

Tom knew that if Jed Smith *had* returned he would be having more to say to him than merely passing the time of day, but he *was* concerned about Zillah being in a gypsy wagon on her own in a remote part of the countryside with a killer out there somewhere.

Zillah interrupted his thoughts by saying, 'If you are going to take me all the way to Slippery Hill before you do whatever you've got to do at North Hill, I'll show you a short cut which will take us to the west of both North Hill and Trelyn.'

Delighted, Tom said, 'That's fine. On the way you can tell me when it was you last saw your father and try to think of somewhere he might have gone – and anything else that might help me find him for you.'

Chapter 12

WHEN HORACE MORGAN entered the room where Colonel Trethewy was talking to the two visitors to Trelyn and was introduced, it was immediately apparent that he felt uncomfortable about meeting Verity. Amos was quick to realize the Trelyn land steward was unlikely to reveal anything of importance about his past in the presence of his employer.

Turning to the landowner, he said, 'Shall we leave the two of them to discuss people and places they might both know in India, sir? I would like to know of any problems you might be having here, in Trelyn, and ask you what you think of Sergeant Dreadon, whether in your opinion he should be considered for further promotion....'

When the two men had left the study, Verity tried to put Morgan at his ease. 'I don't think Superintendent Hawke is terribly interested in India, but I know he wants to discuss with Colonel Trethewy his investigation into the dreadful loss you have suffered, Mr Morgan.'

'If there is any progress being made *I* would like to be the first to know about it,' Morgan replied, belligerently.

'I am quite certain you will be the first to know when he has something positive to tell. I believe he and Sergeant

Churchyard are following up a number of lines of inquiry at the moment.'

Her sympathetic tone proved effective and Morgan relaxed. 'It's an absolute nightmare. I thought I had left such happenings behind me when I left India.'

'Were you there during the mutiny?'

'Yes.'

If he thought such a brief reply would satisfy Verity, Horace Morgan was mistaken.

'Where were you during the troubles?'

'I was stationed at Cawnpore, but when the mutiny broke out I had been called away to settle problems on an estate in the Punjab. I tried to get back to Cawnpore but it was already under siege and return was impossible. By the time I was able to return, at the end of July in 'fifty-seven it was too late….'

His voice tapered off and Verity was shocked by the distress she saw written on his face. It was many moments before he regained control of himself and continued, uncertainly, 'You know what Nana Sahib did there … the massacre?'

'Yes, it was absolutely dreadful.'

Verity was aware he was talking of the treachery of the leader of the mutineers who, with his army had invested the garrison at Cawnpore where a great many women and children had taken refuge when fighting began in the area and suffered unbelievable hardships as a result.

The appalling scene of carnage that greeted the British soldiers who captured Cawnpore after a brief but bloody battle so enraged them that their retribution, carried out with primitive ruthlessness, was swift, indiscriminate and almost as brutal as the killings they were avenging.

Showing genuine sympathy now, Verity said, 'I visited

Cawnpore some time after it was taken by our army and it was a horrible experience ... but how fortunate for you that you were not there when it happened.'

'Fortunate? There have been times when I wished I *had* stayed at Cawnpore with the others.'

It was a moment of unguarded emotion and Verity said, 'It could not have been easy returning to the scene having known so many who perished there. Were any particularly close to you?'

Horace Morgan's expression hardened. The moment of exposed raw emotion had passed and he said, 'It's not something I want to even think about ... especially now.'

'Of course not. It was insensitive of me to remind you of it. I apologize, Mr Morgan, let us talk of some of the happier things we both remember about India, no doubt there were many for you.'

Leaving Trelyn in the pony and trap, Amos and Verity headed for North Hill school. Colonel Trethewy had sent one of his footmen ahead of them with instructions that the schoolmistress was to arrange for the most senior of her girl pupils to be gathered together in order that Verity might speak on the prospects open to them in Florence Nightingale's burgeoning nursing service.

On the way, Verity spoke of what little she had been able to glean from the Trelyn land steward in her conversation with him.

'It was difficult to form any firm opinion of him,' she said, choosing her words carefully. 'He was certainly very lucky to have escaped when trouble broke out in Cawnpore. That incident scarred the minds of everyone who was close to it in any way. What has happened to his wife and son here in Cornwall must have stirred many appalling memories that he has been trying hard to forget.'

'So you think I might eliminate Horace Morgan from my list of suspects?'

Verity hesitated before replying. 'No, I don't think you can. I am trying hard not to allow emotion and sympathy to cloud my judgement, but it is not easy. I visited Cawnpore when evidence of what had occurred was still apparent. Anyone as closely involved as Morgan with the people who died there will carry thoughts in their minds for ever of what they experienced and I have deep sympathy with him because of that, but – and I am unable to give you a logical reason for my thinking – I believe Morgan was far more closely connected with all that went on there than he is willing to say. He will certainly be no stranger to death in its most violent forms. I think you must keep him on your list of suspects, at least until you learn a little more about his background. I will try to help you if I can. I made a number of friends among those who worked for the East India Company while I was in India and many are back in this country now. I will make enquiries and try to find out whether any of them know anything about Horace Morgan and his time in India.'

'Thank you ... but here we are at the school and it looks as though the teacher has mustered girls of all ages for you. I'll go off and see whether Tom has arrived to question the two other North Hill suspects. I'll see you back here in a couple of hours' time.'

Chapter 13

THE WAGON OWNED and occupied by Zillah Smith and her father was a well-kept vehicle which had gleaming patterned paintwork on the outside and an interior that reflected the care lavished on the outside. However, Tom was only able to admire the internal fittings of the wagon through an open stable-type doorway at the front of the gypsy home: Zillah did not invite him to enter.

After a quick check inside the wagon she returned to the doorway, her concern heightened. 'He's not here, and hasn't been home. I really am worried about him now.'

'I can see that, Zillah,' Tom spoke with genuine sympathy, 'but you told me that whenever he went away for any length of time he would always let you know when he expected to be back here. What made him behave differently this time?'

'That's what's so worrying. I don't believe he intended being away for very long.'

'Didn't he say *anything* to you before he went?'

Zillah hesitated for a moment before replying with a non-informative, 'No.'

Not prepared to accept such a brief and unsatisfactory reply, Tom said, 'I'm not happy about leaving you here alone with a killer at large and your father away from home, Zillah. I doubt very much if it's what he would want, either. Is there anywhere you could stay until he returns? If there is I am quite willing to take you there.'

Once again voicing the suspicions she had about his motives for being helpful towards her, Zillah said, 'Why should you be so concerned? You'd never even met me before today.'

'I'm concerned because you find yourself in a situation you can do nothing about for yourself. The chances are that *I* won't be able to do very much, either, but I can try and – if necessary – can call on a great many resources to help find your father.'

'All right, so you might be able to be of some help to me – but why should you *want* to be? As far as you and all the other *muskerros* – policemen – are concerned I'm only a Romany *chi*, a no-account gypsy girl, good for only one thing – but you'll not be getting *that* from me, so why bother?'

As amused as he was embarrassed, Tom replied, 'I know policemen are not liked by your people, Zillah, and it's a feeling reciprocated by many constables – perhaps with some justification on both sides – but when I was sworn in as a policeman I took an oath that I'd carry out my duties "without favour or affection, malice or ill-will". I took that oath seriously and it means I behave the same way towards gypsies and non-gypsies, whether they are young women or cantankerous old men.'

Suddenly smiling, he added, 'Mind you, it's an oath that's easier to remember when you're dealing with a pretty girl rather than with a crusty old man – even if there's no reward at the end of it.'

Zillah looked at Tom for a long time without making any comment and he knew she was trying to make up her mind whether or not she could trust him. Then, reaching a decision, she asked, 'Just how do you think you might be able to help when I have no idea where he went when he left our wagon?'

'First, I need you to tell me everything you know about the circumstances in which he left the wagon. Do you have any idea what time it was – and did he say nothing at all about where he was going?'

Zillah suddenly appeared ill-at-ease. Aware she was reluctant to be frank and open with him Tom decided to take a chance and tell her what he already knew about her father.

'If you want me to help you find your father you need to be honest and tell me all you can about the time you last saw him. I think I know why you're reluctant to say anything that might get him into trouble, but I already know he finds homes for unwanted babies. I'm also told the babies go to homes where they are wanted and as a result can look forward to a much happier life than they would otherwise have had.'

'Who told you this?' she demanded.

'That doesn't matter, Zillah and it's nothing that either I or my superintendent are going to make our business. I am only mentioning it so you don't feel you need to hold anything back from me. If we are going to find your father I must know *everything* about his disappearance. I would also like you to give me a full description of him, remembering I have never met him.'

Hesitating for only a moment, Zillah said, 'I can do better than that. I can show you a photograph and also a drawing I made of him – which I think is more of a likeness than the photograph. Both were done about two years ago when we were still on Sharptor. A man came around with a camera taking pictures of the mines and miners living around the Minions workings and said he'd like to take pictures of Dado and me. He gave us two pictures of us together. I'll fetch them for you.'

Hurriedly climbing the six ladder-steps curving up to the gypsy wagon, Zillah emerged moments later carrying a silver frame which held a photograph of her smiling as she stood beside an expressionless man with a thick tangle of uncombed black hair.

'It is a very good photograph,' Tom said, although he was looking at the image of Zillah rather than her father. 'May I take it with me?'

'No but there's another behind it in the frame. You can have that as long as you take good care of it – and I want it back. Dado didn't like it very much because it has him scowling but, in all honesty, it's an expression that comes more naturally to him than a smile!'

Handing him a small sheet of paper, from a number held in a cardboard file, she added, 'Here's a drawing I did of him, you can take that too.'

It was a good pencil sketch and Tom was impressed by the skill it showed … as did the other sketches in the file, but he much preferred the photograph which included Zillah. He thought she looked radiant and was about to tell her so, but stopped himself in time. He was satisfied she had accepted he intended helping her to find her father, but realized she was still unsure about his motives.

'If you look after them you can take all the sketches, they'll be safer kept together in the file but remember, I want them back.'

With the photograph and sketches carefully sandwiched between two pieces of linen-covered pasteboard and secured with a length of ribbon, Tom placed it in the saddle-bag of the horse, commenting on the fact that the pasteboard file had once protected a book of poetry.

'Yes, it's my favourite reading,' Zillah said. 'I've read the book so often that the cover became worn – as you can see – and Dado rebound it with pigskin. He's very clever with things like that.'

'Isn't it unusual for a girl living a gypsy life to be reading poetry?'

Zillah shrugged, 'Perhaps, but one of the women in the camp at Sharptor had been teaching at a school before marrying a gypsy. She and my mother were friends and I was taught by her. It was she who gave me the poetry book, among others. I think she must have been a very good teacher because when we moved here I went to school at North Hill for a while, but found I knew more than the teacher, so I left!'

Tom was impressed, but he had other things on his mind. He was aware that he was very attracted to Zillah, but there was the nagging suspicion that the absence of Jed Smith was somehow tied in with the murder of Kerensa Morgan and the disappearance of baby Albert. He hoped it was not true for Zillah's sake, but there were a number of questions that needed to be asked before he left the gypsy girl and Slippery Hill.

Chapter 14

ON THE WAY from Slippery Hill Tom met up with the man who delivered letters to the area and learned that he had delivered letters to the Ring o' Bells landlord postmarked Laverstock, Wiltshire. It was a name he would pass on to Verity.

The nurse had spent less time than expected at the village school. Only two of the girl pupils came even remotely close to the standards expected of Florence Nightingale's nurses and neither was interested in taking up such a career. One was already unofficially engaged to the son of a farmer and the other's ambition was also directed towards an early marriage and a life of domesticity in the area where she had been brought up.

It was disappointing, but Verity was not particularly surprised. Florence Nightingale set extremely high standards and only girls with a burning ambition to nurse were likely to succeed in meeting them.

However, the day had not been a waste of time for the two policemen. Tom had found an address for Alfie Kittow's wife and Amos was delighted that his sergeant had also struck up an acquaintanceship with Jed Smith's daughter. He was deeply suspicious of the fact that the gypsy had not been seen since the night of Kerensa Morgan's murder and the mysterious disappearance of her baby.

'I agree it looks bad for him,' Tom said, 'but it sounds as though Jed Smith was asleep in his wagon at the time we believe Kerensa was murdered. Zillah said they were woken up in the early hours of the morning by someone who persuaded her father to go off with him. Unfortunately, she never saw the man and has no idea who he was.'

'Do you believe her story?'

'Yes, I do. She is basically an honest and straightforward girl.'

'She is also very talented … and extremely pretty!' This from Verity who had untied the ribbon around the photographs and sketches of Zillah and her father, handed over by Tom from his saddle-bag. 'Where did she learn to sketch like this?'

'I should imagine she taught herself. She is a bright girl – but very defensive about her background. Her mother was *not* a gypsy, but came from a remote farm in the heart of Bodmin Moor. She died some years ago, although Zillah's grandmother still lives there. That's where she was coming from when I met her, she had been to see whether her father had been there … and, yes, she is a very pretty young girl. For that reason alone I'm worried about her being on her own in that gypsy wagon; it's in a very remote place and there is a killer on the loose….'

Tom left the sentence unfinished but the others were aware of his meaning.

'Well, we'll do what little we can about finding her father,' Amos said, 'but we'll need to be careful what we disclose about it. Colonel Trethewy would have an apoplectic fit if he thought we were concerned about a missing gypsy – especially with a murder hunt going on. If he had his way they would *all* disappear … permanently. The best idea might be to circulate a notice that we are trying to locate the whereabouts of Jed Smith, without giving a reason. Should Colonel Trethewy hear about it we can always say we feel Smith might have some information that could help us with our enquiries.'

'What will you do about this gypsy girl in the meantime?' Verity asked. 'I agree with Tom that she is far too young and pretty to be left on her own.'

'She is,' Tom declared, 'but I've already suggested she should stay with her grandmother at her farmhouse on the moor, leaving a message in their wagon to tell her father where she is, but she wouldn't hear of it. She intends staying at Slippery Hill until his return. That's the way she feels at the moment, anyway.'

'*If* he returns,' Amos pointed out, grimly. 'Despite what the girl has said there is always the possibility Jed Smith *is* involved in the murder of Kerensa Morgan and the disappearance of her baby. If so he'll either not return at all, or end up on the scaffold if he does. Then his daughter will *have* to find somewhere else to live.'

'That's all sheer speculation,' Tom said, impatiently. 'Let's try to find him first. In the meantime I'd like your permission check on Zillah whenever I come this way.'

Tom did not see Verity's raised eyebrow, but Amos did. Nevertheless, he said, 'Of course, and if Jed Smith does return we'll need to have words with him. Now, I don't suppose you have had time to check on either George Kendall or Jowan Hodge, so if Verity will excuse us for a short while we will do that now.'

'Of course,' Verity said, 'While you are doing that I will have a look around the church, it looks most interesting.'

The first house the two policemen visited was the home of George Kendall, ex-Trelyn gamekeeper turned miner, the married man who was known to have had a tempestuous affair with Kerensa and who had made threats against her when she met Horace Morgan and brought an end to the affair.

Kendall's home was only a short distance from North Hill village and unlike the other cottages in the riverside hamlet his house had a garden that was unkempt and overgrown. When the two policemen reached the door it was opened to them by a thin, tired woman who looked as though she was weighed down by the cares of the world. She was also heavily pregnant.

In answer to their question about whether her husband was at home, Martha Kendall replied, 'No, I'm not expecting him until he's drunk his pay away and that could be a long time. He and his mates have had a couple of good weeks and yesterday was settling day. He'll be some landlord's best friend until the money runs out.'

'Do you have any idea where he might be drinking: I understand he's been barred from the Ring o'Bells in North Hill.'

'He's been barred from most of the inns around here but a landlord is quick to offer forgiveness when a miner comes in with money on settling day – even him at the Ring o' Bells. He'll get more of my husband's money than me and the kids will see, that's certain.'

'Do you think that's where he might be?'

Martha Kendall made a gesture of helplessness. 'Your guess is as good as mine – better, probably – but if you intend arresting him then do it before he's spent all his earnings. The kids are crying out because they're hungry and I've got nothing in the house to feed them.'

'Much as he might deserve it, I can't arrest him for that,' Amos said, regretfully. 'I just want to ask him one or two questions that's all, same as we're asking many of the North Hill men. In fact you might be able to answer for him. What he was doing on Tuesday night, for instance?'

'Tuesday night ... you mean the night Kerensa Morgan was murdered? He went out to work on night shift and as far as I know that's where he was. The other men on his pare would be able to tell you for certain, but if he hadn't turned up they'd have sent someone round here to fetch him. They'd found a rich lode and when miners do that they're like terriers with a rat; they wouldn't think of leaving it alone until it was worked out. He'd have been there with them, for certain. In fact *I* should be more of a suspect than him; no one could be happier than me at seeing that little whore dead. I believe George and me might have made things work for us if she hadn't taken a sudden fancy to him. It's not even that it meant anything to her ... not the way it did to me and the kids, and to George too. If I'm honest I could happily have killed her for it – and would have done given half a chance, but unlike Evangeline Hodge I have nothing to fight her with.'

Jowan Hodge was the last of their suspects and Tom said sharply, 'What do you mean by that, Martha? What does this Evangeline Hodge have that you don't?'

'Her looks, for a start. Five girls one after another, with the next one due at any time has done for mine ... and her husband loved her when they got wed. George married me because he'd got me pregnant and if the parish hadn't got him my pa would have, God rest his soul. I wish he was alive now, he wouldn't have stood for George treating me the way he does, he'd have murdered him long before this. But he was killed in an accident up at Wheal Notter soon after my eldest was born and by the time another three months had passed my mother had joined him....'

Almost angrily Martha Kendall brushed away the tears that had welled up in her eyes. Making a perceptible effort to pull herself together, she said briskly, 'But that's all in the past, I'm not a silly young girl any longer, I have a family to look after – and George is still my husband. I married him for better or worse, although I've seen little enough of the *better* side of him.'

'Have you *no* idea at all where he might be, Martha?'

'None … although, the last I heard, the Cheesewring Inn up at Minions was the only one he hadn't been banned from, so you might be lucky and find him there.'

Before leaving the cottage, Amos gave Martha Kendall a florin, 'to buy something for the children to eat'. When she protested that despite her situation she had not resorted to accepting charity, Amos said he would retrieve it from her husband – when they found him!

Once outside, Amos said to Tom, 'We know George Kendall is reputed to be violent when he's been drinking so we won't take any chances. I can think of a man who would be able to handle him. Ride back to Bodmin and find Harvey, then the two of you go in search of Kendall. Try the Cheesewring Inn first. If he turns violent when you question him – as he most certainly will – arrest him and take him to the lock-up at Trelyn. If he has any money left on him take it and give it to his wife. Sergeant Dreadon can release him once he's sober, but he's to warn him that if he tries to take his anger out on his wife he'll be arrested and taken before a magistrate to face three months in gaol.'

Harvey Halloran was the Cornwall constabulary's sergeant major. A long time friend of Amos, he had served with him in the Royal Marines during the Crimean War. Brought up in a London slum, he had been a bare-fist boxing champion in his younger days and was still a formidable fighter when a situation called for such skills. Amos was confident he had the ability to successfully deal with George Kendall, whether the violent miner was drunk or sober.

'Couldn't we charge Kendall anyway?' Tom asked, hopefully.

Amos shook his head, 'He'd only be given a fine and I'd rather Martha had his money than the court. When you've found Harvey take a horse from headquarters for him and get after Kendall before he's spent out. I'll go and collect Verity now. She can either remain in the church for a while longer, or come with me to find Jowan Hodge. I doubt whether he'll have very much to say about Kerensa Morgan or baby Albert so she'll be able to wait with the pony and trap while I interview him ... that's if he's back home yet.'

Chapter 15

HARVEY HALLORAN WAS drilling a group of new recruits to the Cornwall Constabulary when Tom found him and the force's sergeant major welcomed the interruption with some relief. The latest additions to the force were mainly farmhands and general labourers, most of whom seemed unaware of the difference between left and right and had no concept of co-ordinated movement with their fellow recruits. The thought of performing a task that promised some excitement appealed to him.

Minions was a village at the heart of the copper mining industry despite being only a short distance from the peace and tranquillity of Trelyn. On the way there Tom brought his companion up-to-date on details of the inquiry into the murder of Kerensa Morgan, the mystery of her missing baby and George Kendall's part in the affair. He also told Harvey what he knew of Kendall, including his propensity for violence and his reputation as a fighting man, especially when he had been drinking.

'Has he ever been a Royal Marine?' Harvey queried.

'Not as far as I know. He was a gamekeeper on Colonel Trethewy's estate before he went mining.'

'Then he'll be no match for two ex-marines,' Harvey said confidently, 'but if he becomes violent step back and leave me room to deal with him.'

Having seen Harvey in action on a couple of previous occasions when his particular 'skills' had been called upon, Tom was happy to agree. The Cornwall Constabulary's sergeant major was in a class of his own when it came to fighting. Tom would be ready to help in the unlikely event that his assistance was required, but until then he would be quite content to stand back and allow Harvey to dictate the action.

On the return journey from Bodmin, in company with Harvey Halloran, Tom met Amos and Verity returning from North Hill. Jowan Hodge had not been at home and a neighbour had told Amos that the wealthy miner and his wife were absent looking at houses. In view of his success the miner-turned-adventurer and his wife were expected to move out of the area in order to pursue a life more in keeping with their newly acquired affluence.

The neighbour also disclosed that Evangeline, Jowan's wife, was the daughter of a Bible Christian minister who had recently been given responsibility for a large district in North Devon and was destined for higher office within the ministry. She wanted to be closer to her family in order to enjoy the success that had come to all of them.

'Does that mean we are going to strike Hodge off our list of suspects?' Tom queried.

'Not until we have a positive lead in another direction, or Hodge can satisfy us he couldn't have been involved,' Amos replied. 'This is the most wide open case we have ever had to deal with, Tom, and I don't like it – but I mustn't keep you, it's something we can discuss at length later. If you don't get to Minions soon there are likely to be other miners drinking with Kendall and however much he might be disliked by some of them, they'll dislike policemen more. By the way, I have had a word with Sergeant Dreadon at Trelyn. I told him he can expect to have Kendall in his lock-up tonight. He pointed out that even if you find him right away it will be dark before you are ready to return to Bodmin – and it wouldn't be safe to cross the moor in darkness. He's going to double up his children in their beds and make room for both of you to stay at his house for the night. It's a good idea because we need to question Kendall and I doubt if you'll get any sense from him tonight. By morning he'll be sober enough to answer questions, but too befuddled by drink to lie convincingly.'

'That makes sense,' Tom said. 'I'll take any money in Kendall's possession to his wife tonight and after we've questioned him Harvey can return to Bodmin while I go back to Slippery Hill to see whether Zillah's father has returned….'

Aware of the reason for Amos's quizzical look, Tom changed the subject hurriedly. 'I'll make quite certain Kendall isn't released until he's been given a stern warning about being violent towards his wife and she's had time to spend some of his money on food for herself and the kids.'

'Fine!' Amos had not missed Tom's sudden change of subject after mentioning Zillah and he added, 'Be careful of your dealings with that gypsy girl, Tom. Sergeant Dreadon confirms what you have mentioned about her being attractive, but it seems she will not put up with any nonsense from men. He said that when one of the miners up at Sharptor took too close an interest in her she drew a knife on him. Apparently the miner only bled a little and was anxious to keep the incident quiet, so no action was taken by Dreadon, but she's not a girl to take liberties with.'

'I never thought for one minute she was,' Tom replied indignantly, at the same time more pleased than he should have been to hear Amos's testimonial to Zillah's character. 'But her father might be able to give us the first positive lead to our murderer. Knowing what we do about Jed Smith's activities he might have been contacted in the middle of the night by someone who wanted to get rid of a baby in a hurry. If that was the case the baby could have been Albert Morgan.'

'True. Do whatever you think is necessary, Tom – and the best of luck to both of you in your dealings with Kendall. I look forward to having a report from you in the morning, Harvey, but don't be too rough with him. Remember, he's the breadwinner for his family, albeit a reluctant one.'

Arresting George Kendall at the Cheesewring Inn proved a much simpler task than had been anticipated, even though the unpredictable miner had already been involved in a fracas which had resulted in a rapid evacuation of the miners' public house. Kendall remained in a belligerent mood and the publican, used as he was to dealing with drunken miners, did not try to evict him but continued to serve him with drinks in the hope he would eventually collapse in a drunken stupor and could be carried outside to sleep off his protracted binge among the fern and gorse of the surrounding moorland.

However, Kendall was a hardened drinker and seemed to have an unlimited capacity, showing no signs of succumbing to the undoubted potency of the inn's own brew. When Tom and Harvey entered the tap-room it was occupied only by Kendall and two elderly retired miners who had consumed enough to distance themselves from anything going on about them. When the two policemen entered the premises the landlord showed an unprecedented eagerness to assist the constabulary by pointing out their quarry.

In response to Tom's question as to his identity, George Kendall glared at him through bloodshot eyes and slurred, 'What's it got to do with you?' Then, recognizing the uniform of Harvey, he demanded, '... and what's *he* doing here?'

'We're here to ask you a couple of questions, that's all,' Tom replied in a placatory tone of voice. 'If you co-operate it shouldn't take more than a few minutes.'

'It'll take less than that to throw you out of here,' Kendall's jaw was thrust forward belligerently. 'I'm enjoying a quiet drink and have nothing to say to you ... or any other Peeler, so sod off.'

'I'll go when you've answered my questions,' Tom replied, more authoritatively now, adding, 'and your money would be better spent on your wife and children than in here.'

'Who are you to tell me how I should spend my money...?' Kendall rose to his feet menacingly, albeit unsteadily. 'I've had enough of people telling me what I should do today, and I'll deal with you the way I did with them—' Tom was suddenly pushed aside as Harvey confronted the drunken and belligerent miner.

'My colleague has asked you very politely for your co-operation, so I suggest you sit down again and think very carefully before you do anything you're likely to regret.'

'It's you who'll do the regretting,' Kendall growled. 'Out of my way while I deal with him ... then it'll be your turn.'

He moved to shove Harvey out of his way, but when his arm was pushed to one side he was suddenly galvanized into action with a speed which displayed why he was considered such a dangerous man, drunk or sober and lashed out at the large policeman.

Unfortunately for Kendall, Harvey Halloran had been involved in far too many brawls to be taken by surprise in such a manner and the punch was brushed off almost casually.

Letting out a bellow of rage, Kendall lunged at Harvey, but once again the policeman was too quick for him. Stepping back with a speed which belied his height and weight, he threw just one punch. It landed squarely on the other man's chin – and it was enough.

The drunken miner sank to his knees and then fell forward to land face down on the slate floor, unconscious.

'Well, that was so easy it was hardly worthwhile my coming all the way here,' Harvey said, regretfully. 'I reckon you could have dealt with him yourself, Tom.'

'I doubt that very much,' Tom replied, relieved he had not needed to tackle Kendall on his own, 'but when the landlord closes his mouth and looks intelligent once more, he can fetch a bucket of water to throw over Kendall to bring him round. The walk to the Trelyn lock-up should help sober him. He might feel more inclined to tell us what we want to know by the time we get there.'

Contrary to Tom's prediction, by the time the lock-up at Trelyn was reached George Kendall was out on his feet. Whether it was the drink he had consumed, sheer tiredness after his marathon binge, or a combination of the two, was impossible to tell, but it would be many hours before he was in a fit state to be questioned.

Before being settled in his temporary lodging, the drunken miner was relieved of the sum of seven pounds and fourteen shillings, which Tom said he would take to Martha Kendall right away, commenting that when the drunken miner woke in the morning he would probably not remember whether or not he had spent the money on drink – and Tom doubted whether his long-suffering wife would enlighten him.

Unfortunately the motive for arresting Kendall in the first

place suffered a serious set-back. During a meal cooked for the policemen by Sergeant Dreadon's wife, the Trelyn policeman said he had been speaking to two of the men who worked in the same *pare* – or 'team' – with the arrested man. They had confirmed he was working with them throughout the whole of the night of Kerensa's murder and the disappearance of the Morgan baby.

'Do you think they were telling the truth?' Tom asked.

'They had no reason to lie,' Dreadon replied. 'I wasn't even questioning them. It came out in general conversation that George Kendall was working all night at the time in question and it was their casual observation that had he not been with them he would have been a prime suspect in view of his association with Kerensa and the threats he has made against her in the past.'

'Thanks for the information,' Tom said, trying to hide his disappointment that the man *he* considered the most likely suspect had been given an alibi, 'but don't mention anything about the murder to Kendall before I have an opportunity to speak to him in the morning. I also intend reading the Riot Act to him about the way he treats his wife and kids and warn him that Harvey won't go so easy on him another time. Not only that, I will *personally* see to it he has nothing but a prison wall to vent his anger on for a very long time afterwards.'

'Are you upset that Kendall is not the man responsible for Kerensa Morgan's murder? I know you had a strong suspicion that he was the guilty man.'

Harvey put the question to Tom later that evening after the money taken from the drunken man had been given to his grateful wife and the two policemen were preparing for bed in the room usually occupied by two of Sergeant Dreadon's children.

'I'm disappointed we haven't found the murderer and, yes,

Kendall fitted the bill very nicely. Of course, there's always the possibility his friends are covering for him, knowing he would be top of our list of suspects. Miners would take on the world for one of their own. Still, looking on the bright side of things, if he is in the clear then we've ruled out one of our suspects, but it still leaves us with too many!'

'My money is on this gypsy,' Harvey said. 'I was talking to Sergeant Dreadon's wife while you were writing up the report about Kendall's arrest and she was telling me it's well known for miles around that he makes money from trafficking in unwanted babies.'

'I don't doubt it – but there has never been a shortage of such babies anywhere in the country. He has no need to kill to get hold of one, especially if it would involve the wife and son of an important man like Colonel Trethewy's estate steward. Besides, everyone I've spoken to agrees that Jed Smith's not a violent man.'

'I suppose it could depend on who the baby was for and how much someone was prepared to pay for it.' Giving Tom a quizzical look, Harvey added, 'It's not like you to rule out a possible suspect purely on hearsay, Tom. Don't tell me this daughter of his has got to you? I'll have to see if *I* can find some pretty young gypsy girl to give a ride to on my way back to Bodmin.'

Tom made no reply, but the expression on his face told Harvey far more than words could have done. Realizing there was more truth in his half-joking remark than he had thought, he did not pursue the matter.

Tom, too, was aware that Zillah was the reason he had defended a man he had never even met. He was relieved that Harvey said no more on the subject.

When George Kendall was released from custody he seemed

to have taken Tom's strongly worded warning about his future conduct towards his family seriously.

It was also evident he had been chastened by the ease with which Harvey had subdued him in the Minions public house and Tom felt almost sorry for him when the dejected figure left the Trelyn lock-up and headed off in the direction of Berriow Bridge, head down and suffering from a monumental hangover.

Kendall had confirmed the story told by his fellow miners on the night shift at the Notter mine and by the time Tom returned to Bodmin he had reluctantly accepted that Kendall had not been directly involved in the murder of Kerensa Morgan.

Chapter 16

AS THE DAYS and nights passed without any news of her father, Zillah's concern for him grew and, despite her assurance to Tom that she was perfectly safe in her wagon home, she was increasingly aware of her vulnerability.

It was brought home to her in a frightening way one afternoon when she was hanging out some washing on the rope line stretched between two trees close to the spring that sprang from the hillside only a short distance from where the wagon stood. Most of the clothing she had washed belonged to her father and was already clean but it made her feel somehow closer to him and was a comforting thing to be doing in his absence.

As she finished pegging the final shirt to the line she saw two men approaching from the direction of the lane that bisected the valley. It was the lane's winter steepness that was responsible for the name of the valley farm and the tiny nearby hamlet.

The two men wore clothing Zillah associated with mining and as the gypsy wagon was not parked close to any known route taken by miners going to and fro from their places of work she was immediately apprehensive. It was heightened when one of the miners looked in her direction, nudged his companion, and after laughing together, both men changed direction and headed towards her.

Without appearing to hurry, but wasting no time, Zillah made her way to the wagon and, climbing the steep wooden steps, went inside, closing the bottom half of the stable-type door behind her and slipping the bolt into place.

Once out of sight of the approaching men she hurried to a shelf situated behind the stove and took down a broad-bladed meat cleaver which hung from a hook by a short leather thong. Then, with the cleaver hidden from view behind her back she returned to stand in the shadows just inside the wagon door. Zillah hoped the men would pass by without incident but she was taking no chances.

Her caution was well founded. The miners showed no intention of passing by and made their intentions clear immediately they reached the wagon. Stopping at the bottom of the steps, one of them called out, 'Hello in there, girl. Word's going around that your pa's gone off and left you here on your own. We thought we'd come along to make sure you're all right and give you a little company.'

Without showing herself at the doorway, Zillah retorted, 'I'm perfectly all right, thank you – and I don't need any company.'

'Well, seeing as how we've walked all this way 'specially, you can at least show your face. Better still, come out here and have a proper chat, then if we find we get along with each other we've both got money to spend and with your pa away you wouldn't have anyone to share it with – and we'd never say anything about it.'

Stung by the implications of his words, Zillah said, 'I'm sure you wouldn't say anything to him. If he was here right now he'd ram your words right back down your throat and choke you with them.'

'Now I do like a girl with spirit – especially a gypsy girl.' This time it was the second miner who spoke and he added, 'Let's just come inside your wagon and have a little fun, eh?'

There was the sound of a heavy miners' boot clumping on the first step leading to the wagon door and, stepping forward quickly, Zillah showed herself – and the meat cleaver. Holding it menacingly in front of her she said, 'You put a hand on this door and you'll lose all your fingers – and that's a promise!'

The man on the step hesitated before saying, 'You wouldn't dare....'

He threw his head back suddenly, losing his footing on the steps and stumbled backwards to the ground. Had he not done so the cleaver would have gashed his face and left him permanently disfigured.

Visibly shaken, he cried, 'You bitch! You could have killed me!'

'Try me again and I won't miss.'

The other man took hold of his companion's arm, 'Don't do it, Jim, I remember her now. She's Jed Smith's girl, her as stabbed Charlie Crago and put him off work for nigh on a month when she and her pa were living up by Minions. If she'd done as she said and cut off your fingers you'd never have worked again – and I believe she'd do it too.'

The man who had just had a narrow escape hesitated and glared at Zillah, who was still standing behind the closed half-door grasping the meat cleaver.

'All right ... but there'll be another time, girl – and that's *my* promise.'

He backed away from the steps but Zillah didn't put down the meat cleaver until she had watched the two miners pass from view on their way to the lane. Then, suddenly shaking she sat down and came close to tears.

She told herself it had nothing to do with being frightened by what had happened, but because her *dado* was not there to comfort her.

Zillah was a light sleeper and that night she was wakened by the sound of a dog barking at the farmhouse, a short distance away across the field. The dog, a working collie, was kept shut in an outhouse at night and often barked when it was disturbed by a passing fox or badger – but tonight its barking was different. The sound carried an urgency that was reserved for the occasional prowling itinerant paying a nocturnal visit to the remote farm in the hope of finding something of value left lying around.

The two miners who had threatened Zillah earlier in the day had unsettled her and having been woken she could not immediately get back to sleep – which was why she heard a noise some minutes later that was much closer to the wagon. It sounded as though someone had slipped and stumbled on a patch of damp and muddy ground close to the spring.

Sitting up in her narrow bed she felt a thrill of excitement. Perhaps it was Dado returning home at last! But then there was another sound, this time from a different place as someone walked into the line where her washing had been hanging and she knew her *dado* would never have done that.

This sound was followed by hoarse whispering and she realized there was more than one man outside. She suspected it was probably the miners who had called on her earlier in the day. She suddenly remembered that the window on the far side of the small wagon was open!

Hurriedly throwing back the blanket that covered her, she reached the window just as one of the unseen men outside stood on a spoke of the wheel that was below and to one side of the open window and reached out to the window sill.

Releasing the window catch Zillow slammed it shut, trapping the man's fingers and causing him to lose his footing on the wheel.

Judging from the response to his cry of pain Zillah realized that there were at least two other men outside with him and she released the window momentarily, allowing the injured man to pull his fingers free before she closed and fastened the window once more.

'She's broken my fingers!'

The injured man's cry brought no sympathy from his companions, one of whom growled, 'You're lucky, she threatened to chop Jim's fingers off with a cleaver when we were up here earlier today.'

The comment confirmed to Zillah that the two miners had returned as they had promised, and had brought company with them. Groping her way across the dark interior of the wagon she located the meat cleaver and lifted it from its hook.

She felt safer with it in her hand and called out to the men, 'I've got the cleaver here and if any of you try to break in I'll use it and you'll lose more than your fingers.'

'Then we won't try to come in....' The voice was that of one of her earlier visitors. 'Instead, we'll let you come out to *us* – and you will. We'll use some of the wood you've got stacked out here to light a fire under your wagon. We'll have you one way or another, girl ... raw or roasted.'

One of his companions began to chuckle but the sound was cut off by a woman's voice. 'Oh no you won't! You'll get on your way – and you'll go running 'less you want your families to come here on my farm to take away what's left of you. I've got a two-barrelled scattergun that I've used to get rid of all the other vermin I've had around here.'

'There's no need for such talk, missus. We're just having a bit of fun with a gypsy girl, that's all.'

'Just fun, is it? Well, you move away from that door and I'll pass this gun up to her and let her choose how best she's going to join in this fun you're talking about.'

Zillah could see nothing of what was going on outside the wagon but she could hear the conversation and there was a three-quarter moon that was bright enough for the indomitable woman farmer to see the three miners. When the one who had been talking took a step towards her she pulled one of the two triggers of the scattergun.

The noise of the shot was almost matched by the shrieks of pain from the man who had precipitated the firing of the formidable weapon. It had been fired into the ground between the woman and the nearest miner but there was a large flat stone here, placed *in situ* by Jed Smith who used it on which to chop wood. Pellets from the gun had struck the stone and ricocheted into the miner's legs and lower body.

His shrieks were lost on his companions who were already fleeing from the scene when Mrs Hocking shouted to the remaining wounded miner, 'I have a second barrel here and you'll have the full benefit of it if you haven't caught up with the others by the time I pull the trigger....'

Forgetting his suffering the miner did not remain on the scene to argue with her. Hobbling painfully after the others he was soon lost.

Calling out in the darkness, Mrs Hocking called out, 'Are you all right, Zillah?'

'Yes, thanks to you.' Zillah opened the top half of the wagon door. 'How did you know they were here?'

'The dog woke me up with his barking and I knew there was

something wrong. He's a damned nuisance sometimes, but he lets me know if there's anyone around who shouldn't be. Now, the men who were here will be too busy licking their wounds to bother you again I've no doubt, but just in case one of 'em has more guts than the others, I don't think you should stay here. You'd best come to the farmhouse and spend the rest of the night there. We'll think what we're going to do about you, come morning.'

Chapter 17

THE POLICE WERE no closer to finding a more likely suspect or learning the whereabouts of baby Albert when Tom returned to North Hill, sent by Amos to find out whether Jowan Hodge had returned to the village.

There was still no sign of him and Tom decided to travel on to Slippery Hill to check whether Zillah had received any news from her father. When he reached the gypsy wagon he was taken aback to discover the site tidied up and the gypsy horse harnessed. It would appear Zillah was on the move.

An exchange of greetings between the two horses alerted Zillah to Tom's arrival and she came to the door of the wagon. Tom thought she looked tired and drawn, as though she had slept very little during the night.

'What's happening, Zillah, are you moving off somewhere? Have you heard something from your father?'

'No ... have *you* learned anything?'

'I'm afraid not. All police stations in Cornwall have been notified that he's missing, and to make certain the information isn't ignored we've added that it's Superintendent Hawke who wants news of him ... but where are you going, and why? I thought you wanted to stay here until he either returned or you had news of him?'

'That's what I intended, but news seems to have got around that I'm here on my own. A couple of miners came around yesterday suggesting I might like company. I sent them packing, but last night they returned – and they'd been drinking. Fortunately they made so much noise that Mrs Hocking, the owner of the farm we're on, heard them and came down here with a shot-gun. One barrel from that sent them all running, but she insisted I went back to the farmhouse with her for the night. By then it was so late anyway that I had very little sleep and came back here at dawn and got ready to move off.'

Aware that Mrs Hocking could get into trouble, Zillah said nothing about the shot that had been fired wounding the drunken miner, but Tom was far too concerned about Zillah to question whether the gun had been fired *at* anyone. 'It's what I was afraid could happen, Zillah. Do you have any idea who the men were?'

'No, only that they were miners.'

'But where are you going now, back to the camp where you and your father were before you moved here?'

'I wouldn't be welcome there. I'll go to my grandma's farm, up on the moor. When Dado comes back Mrs Hocking says she'll tell him what's happened and where I am. She's been very kind to me and I'm grateful to her for what she did last night. I've settled up here and she's said I needn't worry about leaving a bit of a mess. She has someone in to help her on the farm and says she's paying him too much for doing too little, so it will give him something to do to earn his wages.'

Zillah was making an attempt to be jocular but she appeared desperately tired and could almost have been crying. Tom guessed that as well as worrying about her missing father and the upsetting incident with the drunken miners, all her problems would have crowded in on her during the hours of darkness when she was alone and at her most vulnerable.

Anxious to do something – anything – in attempt to take her mind off her situation, Tom asked, 'Can I help in some way?'

Giving him a weary but quizzical look, Zillah said, 'I think everything's done, all I need to do now is hitch the horse to the wagon and get on my way.'

'Have you eaten this morning?' Tom had noticed smoke trickling from the chimney of the wagon's stove, but there was no smell of cooking.

'I've been too busy – and didn't feel like eating anyway.'

'I'll tell you what, I've had a hard ride from Bodmin, and an unsuccessful visit to North Hill. I see the stove inside the wagon is lit, if I hitch up and tie my own horse behind the wagon, we can get you moving while you make a pot of tea for us both.'

Once again she looked at him uncertainly, 'Why? Why should you want to be so helpful to me?'

'Because we both have something to gain from it. I fancy a cup of tea – and you look as though you have need of one.'

Tom held his breath, waiting for an angry response from her.

Instead, and quite unexpectedly, she said quietly, 'All right. The horse's name is Delengro, which means "kicker" and it wasn't given that name for nothing, so you've been warned.'

In truth, she was grateful to have someone around to help and make decisions for her.

The gypsy horse was aware it was about to be put to work and was an unwilling participant in their plans. However, by refusing to allow the animal to turn away from him and kick its way out of gainful employment, Tom eventually succeeded in backing it between the shafts of the wagon and hitching it up in readiness for the journey to the moorland farm of Zillah's grandmother.

Frustrating the aspirations of the fractious horse had taken a long while. By the time the task was completed Zillah had made and poured the tea. As they stood beside the wagon, drinking, she asked, 'Are you any closer to finding who killed Kerensa Morgan and took away the baby?'

'We are not as near as I would like to be just yet,' Tom replied, honestly, 'but we *are* coming closer. I can't say more than that right now because we're waiting for more information to come in, but neither Superintendent Hawke nor I will rest until we've found the person responsible and have some news of your father.'

Satisfied he had been able to dispel at least some of the deep unhappiness engendered by the lonely night hours, Tom tipped the grouts in his cup to the ground and nodded towards the horse which was stamping its hoofs and shaking the harness impatiently. 'Shall we get moving now before Delengro thinks up some form of mischief?'

Zillah had the reins for the first part of the journey, but passed them to Tom once they left Slippery Hill behind. Guided by her they took a different route to the one he usually used when crossing the moor. Zillah explained that although slightly longer it was easier travelling for the wagon. It also avoided villages, hamlets and, in particular, the mining communities where they would receive unwelcome attention.

The deviation suited Tom and once on the high moor, having travelled for some three hours he readily agreed to Zillah's suggestion that they should stop to rest the horse. She added that while it grazed she would cook something for them to eat as she was feeling hungry now.

Aware that it was a sign she was returning to something close to normality, Tom agreed and was impressed by the speed with which Zillah had an outside fire going. She soon produced a meal comprised of ham – which she said came from a pig bred by her grandmother – new, unpeeled boiled potatoes and green vegetables which Tom was unable to identify.

When he queried them, Zillah explained it was a mixture of wild plants, the only one she felt he would know being dandelion, adding, 'If you don't like them I'll take them off your plate....'

'No, I'm enjoying them, I didn't know what it is, that's all. The whole meal is delicious ... just right. You're a very good cook, Zillah.'

Trying not to show the pleasure she felt at his compliment, Zillah said, 'It's just an ordinary meal, but I've never before cooked for anyone but Dado and me.'

Her sudden change of expression told Tom that mention of her father had reminded her of the present circumstances and he said hurriedly, 'The rest of the world doesn't know what it's missing by not tasting your cooking, Zillah, I can't remember when I enjoyed a meal more.'

This was quite true. There was something magical about eating a meal prepared by Zillah over an open fire and surrounded by the empty beauty of the moor.

'I think your wife might be upset to hear you say that,' she said, unexpectedly. Shifting a blackened kettle of erupting, spitting water to one side of the greedy wood fire, she avoided looking at him while awaiting his response to her remark.

For a moment Tom was taken aback, but then he said, 'There is no wife to be upset, Zillah, I've never married.'

She looked at him now and, satisfied he was not lying, asked, 'Is there any particular reason why?'

It was the second occasion in recent weeks his marital status had been queried although the two women who had posed the question could hardly have been farther apart, either in breeding, or their mode of life.

'My work has always had a lot to do with it. I was a Royal Marine from the age of thirteen, serving around the world, and then I became a policeman in London before coming to Cornwall which means I've never been left with time to get to know anyone well enough to think of marriage.'

Even as he was speaking the thought of Flora, the ex-Laneglos housekeeper sprang to mind, but it somehow lacked the clarity and sense of loss such memories had once evoked.

'What about you, Zillah, I thought gypsy girls usually married when they were scarcely more than children?'

'Most do, but because my mother was a *gorgio* I'm not recognized as a true Romany. Not that it's ever troubled me as far as marriage is concerned because I've never met a Romany man I felt I wanted to marry. When a true Romany woman marries she's expected to devote her whole being to her husband and have no real life of her own. That's never appealed to me, there is far too much I enjoy doing on my own.'

From their first meeting Tom had been aware that Zillah was very much a free spirit and he said, 'Well, you're not likely to meet many men up here on the moor on your grandmother's farm, so you'll be able to devote as much time as you like to your drawing.'

'I intend to – and I'm certainly not looking for a man, especially while Dado is still missing.'

In spite of all Tom's efforts the conversation had once again returned to the disappearance of her father and he said, hurriedly, 'Of course. I'm sorry, Zillah, I should have thought before I spoke. You have enough to worry about right now.'

'You have no need to apologize to me … for anything. No one could have been kinder, although I still don't understand why. Constables are landowners' men … and landowners hate Romanies.'

'I don't know a great deal about landowners, Zillah, there weren't too many of them in the part of London where I worked – but there *were* gipsies and I found them no worse than anyone else who lived there. In fact, many of them settled and proved themselves good, law-abiding people.'

'That still doesn't explain why you've been particularly kind to me. Look what you're doing today, for instance. Why, Tom?'

He had told her his Christian name when he had introduced himself on their first meeting, but it was the first time she had used it and the fact gave him a moment of pleasure.

'I think I answered that question once before, Zillah. As I said then, I see it as part of what I'm being paid to do and, as I also said, it comes so much easier when it's being done for someone who is as attractive as you.'

'That's the second time you've said you're attracted to me, yet you've never tried to do anything about the way you feel. I think most men would.'

Coming from any other woman her words might have been construed as an invitation, but Tom believed Zillah to be guileless in such matters and he replied accordingly.

'I'm no different to any other man, Zillah, but I'm very aware you're concerned about your father and wouldn't try to take advantage of you because of that. Besides, if I *did* make advances towards you and you rebuffed me it would make things very difficult between us. I don't want that to happen.'

Giving him a straightforward look, Zillah said, 'Thank you for the first reason, Tom, it's what I've come to expect of you. As for the second…? Well, let's wait and see what happens, shall we? Now, I think we ought to be moving again. You still have to go on to Bodmin after we've reached the farm.'

Their conversation had brought about an indefinable change in their relationship and both were aware of it. It created an initial awkwardness between them, but they were easier in their talk together by the time Gassick Farm, the home of Zillah's grandmother was reached.

Tom left the farm, warmed by a kiss with which Zillah had brushed his cheek when he was about to depart, but then he put his horse into a lively trot in order to arrive at the Bodmin police headquarters before Amos finished work for the day.

Although the two men were close friends, in Amos's capacity as a senior officer of the Cornwall Constabulary, he might not approve of the manner in which one of his sergeants had spent the day.

Much to Tom's relief, Amos hardly listened to his explanation of how he had spent the day. Brushing it aside impatiently, he waved a letter at him, saying excitedly, 'Read this, Tom, it's a letter from Verity. She's kept her promise about helping us. Someone from her stepfather's force has been to Laverstock, the village in Wiltshire where Alfie Kittow's letters came from. His wife *is* there … and she has a baby with her! What's more, the constable who found her has made a few discreet enquiries and learned that when she first arrived in the village she was desperate to find a wet-nurse, claiming her own milk had suddenly dried up. It's far more likely, as old Bessie Harris claimed, that she was never pregnant in the first place and that the baby is not hers! This could be the break we've been waiting for, Tom.'

'So what do we do now, bring in Alfie Kittow?'

'Not yet. Check the file and make absolutely certain we have a full description of baby Albert, any birthmarks, whether he's bald, or has a mass of hair, that sort of thing. You'll be leaving by train for Salisbury first thing tomorrow morning and once there Laverstock is only a short distance away. I've discussed it with the chief constable and he's approved your journey. His clerk will have details of train times – I believe you'll need to change trains a couple of times along the way. He'll also provide you with money for the journey and a letter for the superintendent at Salisbury's divisional headquarters. Wiltshire Constabulary was formed some years ago and has an established detective branch, so I think you'll find them helpful, especially as you're friendly with their chief constable's stepdaughter! Now I think you ought to be getting home to have an early night. Your train leaves at seven-thirty.'

Chapter 18

THE RAILWAY STATION was situated at Bodmin Road, some distance from the town and Tom waited on a draughty platform until the Great Western broad gauge train, with its impressively tall smoke stack puffed fussily into the station. The only previous journey he had made by train had been when he came to Cornwall from London, a few years before and then he had travelled third class, in a carriage that was little more than an improvised cattle truck. Travelling second class today, at the expense of the Cornwall Constabulary was far more comfortable and almost enjoyable, for all that it lacked the luxurious 'armchair' comfort afforded those who travelled first class.

It took a little more than three hours to reach Exeter, where Tom was obliged to change trains and wait for another belonging to the London and South Western Railway which would take him to Salisbury, another four hours' journey.

It was three o'clock in the afternoon when Tom walked into the busy Salisbury police station and presented his letter of introduction from the Chief Constable of Cornwall. The superintendent in charge of the police station was aware of the inquiry going on in respect of Kerensa's murder and the disappearance of baby Albert and he sent for one of his detective sergeants and instructed him to give Tom all the assistance he needed.

Detective Sergeant George Farmer had been a founding member of the Wiltshire Constabulary when it was first formed in 1839. A quiet, self-assured man, he greeted Tom formally when they were introduced, but once outside the superintendent's office he relaxed and said, 'You must be tired out after travelling all that way by train. It was one of my men who made the enquiries at Laverstock about this woman and baby you wanted to know about so I was expecting a visit from someone about it. I've arranged for you to stay with me and my wife and family while you're here, but it's too late to begin our inquiries today. We'll go home for a meal and a glass of ale and visit Laverstock in the morning. On the way you can tell me something about the case, it sounds intriguing.'

Detective Sergeant Farmer lived in a police house with his homely wife, a daughter in her late-teens and a ten year-old son. They were obviously a close family and Tom, unused as he was to family life, was made to feel he was a welcome guest.

Although little was said about the case that had brought him to Salisbury, while they were eating the evening meal, Tom happened to mention that it was a meeting with Verity Pendleton that had subsequently provided information leading him to Laverstock. His words brought an immediate awed response from the daughter, Millie.

'You've actually spoken to Miss Pendleton?'

'Yes, we spent some time together when she was staying with my superintendent and his wife, in Cornwall.'

'You'll be able to do no wrong now,' declared Millie's mother to Tom. 'Miss Pendleton has been Millie's idol for years.'

'The Wiltshire newspapers have always covered Verity Pendleton's exploits in great detail,' George Farmer explained.

'Partly because she is a Wiltshire woman and the chief constable's stepdaughter, but also because she has lived a very adventurous life. Actually, I believe she is here in Salisbury at the moment, doing something at our hospital and staying with a friend of hers who was with her in the Crimea.'

'Oh, Dad, why didn't you tell me? I would love to just *see* her!' A distraught Millie looked across the table at her father.

'I'm sorry, love, I forgot.'

'If she is still in Salisbury I would like to speak to her and thank her for her help and let her know how the investigation is going,' Tom said. 'She spent some time in Cornwall and has taken a very keen interest in the murder of Kerensa Morgan and the disappearance of her baby.'

'I'll send someone along to the hospital in the morning to find out if she is still here,' George Farmer replied to Tom, at the same time doing his best to avoid his daughter's accusing gaze.

Later that evening, when the two men were seated on a bench in the garden, enjoying a smoke in the soft warmth of the summer evening, the detective sergeant said, 'I didn't *forget* to tell Millie Miss Pendleton was in Salisbury, it was deliberate. The newspapers used to be so full of what she was doing in the Crimea and then in India, that Millie got it into her head she, too, wanted to become a nurse. She would become very heated when I told her nursing wasn't the sort of work any decently brought up girl would do. During the Crimean War we had a military hospital here in Salisbury for returning soldiers. The so-called "nurses" who worked there spent more time in the public houses or police cells than in the hospital. I swear they were responsible for putting more men *into* hospital than ever came out healthy. I'd never let Millie become one of them.'

'I'd keep your views to yourself if you ever meet up with Verity Pendleton. She is working very closely with Florence Nightingale to change the image of nursing – and my superintendent and our force's sergeant major were both in Scutari Hospital during the Crimean War and will vouch for what *she* did there. Miss Pendleton is helping her choose a very select band of girls who will be trained properly and known as Nightingale nurses. She was down in Cornwall for that very purpose, staying with my superintendent, Amos Hawke and his wife for part of the time.'

'You sound as though you got to know her quite well … yet she was staying with your superintendent?'

'Amos and I were both in the Royal Marines and also both in the Metropolitan Police,' Tom explained. 'It was him who persuaded me to join him in Cornwall. He's the most senior superintendent in the force but we are still good friends and I work pretty closely with him in the Bodmin headquarters.'

'It's never a bad thing to have friends in high places,' George Farmer commented, with a hint of cynicism in his voice.

'True – but getting back to Verity Pendleton. Very few girls measure up to the high standards she is setting for those who are taken on as Nightingale nurses. Those who do can look forward to a very good and worthwhile career – and a respectable one. The nurses of the future are going to be very different to those you and me have seen in the past, George. It's something you should think seriously about. Millie seems to be a very bright girl. If she came under Verity Pendleton's wing you'd one day be very proud of her … and coming to the attention of the chief constable's stepdaughter wouldn't do your own career any harm, either!'

The following morning it took Tom and Detective Sergeant Farmer no more than twenty minutes to walk from the Farmers' police house to Laverstock village. A pretty village beside the River Bourne, it contained no more than eighty houses and they made their way to a thatched cottage in the heart of the village where the wife of the landlord of North Hill's Ring o' Bells public house was known to be living.

The door was opened to them by Florrie Kittow herself. She looked well and happy, but her expression changed to one of dismay when Tom introduced himself to her.

'Wh ... what do you want with me?' she asked, wide-eyed.

'I would like to ask you one or two questions, Mrs Kittow,' Tom replied.

'You've come all this way from Cornwall just to ask me questions? What about?'

Tom thought that if Florrie Kittow had nothing to hide, her natural reaction to having a Cornish policeman call on her would be to immediately assume that something had happened to her husband.

The cottage had very small diamond-paned windows and the inside was somewhat gloomy, but he could see another woman standing in the shadows behind Florrie and he said, 'Can we go somewhere more private to have a talk?'

The second woman moved out of the shadows towards them, saying, 'This is *my* home and I'm Florrie's elder sister. I'd like to hear anything you have to say to her.'

'I appreciate your concern for her, but I am here to ask your sister some questions about a murder that has occurred in Cornwall. It is possible she may be able to help me.'

'A murder?' This from Florrie. 'Who's been murdered – and why should it have anything to do with me?'

'Because the victim is someone you knew … Kerensa Morgan.'

'Kerensa…? Oh my God! It's nothing to do with Alfie, is it? He's not involved?'

'We are not absolutely certain *who* is involved at the moment, but why should you even think it could have anything to do with your husband?'

'I *don't* … of course I don't – but why else would you come all this way to speak to me if you didn't believe one or other of us has something to do with her murder?'

Choosing not to give an answer to her question, Tom said, 'Alfie told me you have a baby now. I'd like to see him – it *is* a boy?'

Tom thought he detected a brief flicker of alarm before she replied, 'Yes, it's a boy, Harry, but he's asleep now and I'd rather not wake him.'

In a sudden and unexpected contradiction of Florrie's statement there came the staccato sound of a baby's waking cry from upstairs and she said hurriedly, 'He's just waking up and will be hungry. The wet-nurse will be up there with him.'

'I'll go upstairs and make sure she *is* there,' said her sister. 'You know what she's like!'

Tom was convinced that talk of the wet-nurse had been an attempt to dissuade him from insisting upon seeing the baby, but he was not to be so easily deterred from his main purpose in travelling to Wiltshire.

When the sister could be heard hurrying up the stairs, Tom said, 'Shall we go into the garden where we are less likely to be overheard, Mrs Kittow? I feel you would rather your sister didn't hear some of the things I have to say.'

There was no mistaking Florrie's fear now as she stepped uncertainly from the house to follow Tom. George Farmer said,

'You go ahead, Tom. I'll stay here and make certain Mrs Kittow's sister doesn't come out and interrupt you.'

By the time Tom and Florrie reached the gate of the cottage garden she had gained sufficient control of herself to ask, 'Why *have* you come all this way to speak to me? I know nothing about Kerensa's murder, it must have happened after I left North Hill – and I'm equally certain Alfie had nothing to do with it. He was aware that Kerensa was trouble and was as relieved as me when she got married and left the Ring o' Bells. She wouldn't have stayed working for us as long as she did if he hadn't felt sorry for her having no close family.'

'I don't think that's the only reason, is it? From all I hear she was good for business and brought in the customers.'

'She also brought in more than her share of problems, but you still haven't explained why you're here to see *me*.'

'In all honesty it's not really *you* that's brought me all this way,' Tom said, 'and I haven't told you any of the details of Kerensa's murder yet. You see, she'd gone up to Hawk's Tor with her baby when she was murdered and although her body was found, the baby is missing. We've had police, villagers and even miners out scouring the moor and the adjacent countryside, but there's been no sign of him. Now, there's a very strong rumour going around North Hill that you weren't pregnant when you left North Hill, or, if you were, you certainly weren't close to giving birth, yet here you are only a couple of weeks away from home with a baby and looking fitter than any newly delivered mother I've ever met up with. Not only that, I find you're employing a wet-nurse because you're unable to feed it yourself.'

Florrie had been looking at him with increasing agitation while he was speaking and now she said, 'Are you saying you believe Harry is Kerensa's missing baby?'

'I'm not saying that yet, certainly not until I've seen him, but I *am* saying you are not baby Harry's natural mother.'

Florrie opened her mouth to speak, but Tom held up a hand to silence her, 'Before you say something that could give me a reason to arrest you, I want you to hear what I have to say. When I see the baby you have here I hope to be able to confirm whether or not it's baby Albert immediately. If it's not, then as far as I'm concerned that's the end of the matter, but I ought to tell you that I've learned about the activities of the gypsy Jed Smith and his skill in finding homes, albeit good homes, for unwanted babies. I would have spoken to him and saved myself a long journey and the Cornwall Constabulary unnecessary expense, had he been around, but he too disappeared on the night of Kerensa Morgan's murder. Now, I've said that if I'm satisfied the baby you have is *not* baby Albert I'll go away and you'll hear nothing more about it but, if I'm *not* satisfied I'll be taking you back to Cornwall with me and that could mean a lot of people, including your family here, in Wiltshire, becoming sceptical about baby Harry being yours.'

Twice Tom thought that Florrie was about to break her silence and interrupt him and on the third occasion, with an expression of anguish on her face she could contain herself no longer.

'Alfie and me will give Harry a happier life than he'd have otherwise had and I love him so much already....'

Tears sprang to her eyes as she choked on her words and Tom said gently, 'I don't doubt any of that, Florrie. If he's not the Morgan baby I'll go away content in the knowledge that he'll enjoy the sort of family life every baby should have. But I *must* know the truth. Did Jed Smith get the baby for you?'

Still finding it difficult to speak, Florrie Kittow could only nod miserably.

'When was this?'

Giving him a date that was a full week before the murder, she added, 'Jed gave Harry to Alfie and me outside the station at Liskeard, then I boarded the train with him and left Cornwall. I stayed at Templecombe, in Somerset, at a place Alfie and I knew of, before coming on here. I took on Lily, the wet-nurse, as soon as I arrived in Laverstock because I'd tried Harry with cow and goat's milk, but he wasn't doing very well.'

'Does your sister know anything at all of this?'

'No, she believes Harry is mine ... mine and Alfie's. Do you have to tell her?'

She was pleading now and Tom said, 'If the baby isn't Albert then I'll go back to North Hill and leave you in peace ... but how old was the baby when he was given to you?'

'A week.'

As Albert was two months old when he disappeared it meant that if Florrie was telling the truth there should be a considerable difference between the two babies and he would have had a wasted journey from Cornwall.

Florrie was aware of the difference between the ages of the two babies and she said, 'Harry is a small baby, too – and it wasn't helped that he wasn't fed properly before I found Lily. It was a great worry at the time, but Lily lost her own baby and although she's scatterbrained she fusses over Harry as though he was her own....'

Suddenly tearful once more, she pleaded, 'You *won't* take him away from me, will you? Jed told Alfie his real mother was a young unmarried girl and that she and her mother would probably have killed and buried him if he hadn't said he'd take him from her.'

'I've already given you the answer to that, Florrie, but do you have any idea where Jed might have gone … or who might have wanted to kill Kerensa and take *her* baby?'

'Jed never said a word to me. He gave the baby to Alfie, took the money he was given and went. As for Kerensa … I never really knew her that well. I had little to do with the running of the Ring o' Bells, I left that to Alfie, but from what I heard about her there was no need for any *man* to kill her because she'd give him whatever he wanted anyway. Her husband was the only man I can think of with reason to do her harm. Mind you, it would be a different story if you thought a woman was involved. Most of the wives in North Hill would be suspects, myself included … but, of course, I was here in Wiltshire when it happened,' she added hurriedly, remembering to whom she was speaking.

'In that case, let's go back to the house and you can show the baby to me.'

'I can't go in like this, Harriet will want to know what's wrong!'

Aware that Florrie was talking of her sister, Tom said, 'You can tell her you're upset about Kerensa's murder. After all, she did work at the Ring o' Bells. You can also say my reason for seeing the baby is so I can tell Alfie all about him when I return to Cornwall.'

Chapter 19

'IT'S BEEN A fruitless journey for you, Tom.' Detective Sergeant Farmer made the comment as the two policemen walked back to Salisbury after their interview with Florrie Kittow at Laverstock. Tom had seen the baby she had and it was so unlike the description he had of baby Albert that he was satisfied he was not the missing Morgan baby.

'It hasn't produced any positive results,' Tom admitted, 'but it's stopped us wasting any more time pursuing the theory that Florrie Kittow might have baby Albert.'

'Are there any other suspects?' George Farmer asked the question as he acknowledged the greeting of a passing wagoner, who raised a hand to his hat as he passed by on the road.

'Alfie Kittow, Florrie's husband, isn't off the hook yet. The murdered girl worked with him for a long time and it's generally believed in the village they were a whole lot closer than landlord and barmaid. Especially as Kerensa had the reputation of sharing her all with whoever was around, married or single. Her husband was new to the village when he married her and probably didn't know of her reputation. If he found out later then he too has to be a suspect. We know he was violent to her on occasions and there's some mystery about his background, much of which was spent in India with the East India Company. That's another reason why I want to speak to Verity Pendleton. She was in India – as you know – and was going to try to find out something about him for us.'

'It would seem our chief constable's stepdaughter has been very helpful to you,' George Farmer mused. 'What sort of a woman is she?'

Glancing quickly at his companion, Tom replied, 'She's a well-bred, well-educated and intelligent woman. She's also very attractive, but totally committed to her work. She takes a keen interest in police work too, which must please her stepfather. Why don't you come along with me and meet her?'

'I'd like to,' George said, uncertainly, 'but she's used to meeting with the most senior men in our force, I'm only a sergeant.'

'So am I, but there's nothing pretentious about Verity, she's seen far too much of life for that. You'll like her … I do.'

'Well, when we reach the station we'll see whether they've been able to arrange a meeting for you.'

Verity Pendleton's message for Tom was that she would be at the Salisbury Hospital until about four o'clock that afternoon when she was returning to London. She would be delighted to see him if he could find time to call on her there before she left.

He arrived at the hospital shortly after noon in company with Detective Sergeant Farmer and Verity Pendleton welcomed him with a warmth which took Tom's companion aback, but then she greeted the Wiltshire detective with such relaxed friendliness that it was not long before he had forgotten he was talking to his chief constable's stepdaughter.

When Tom told Verity of his interview with Florrie Kittow, she expressed her sympathy for the North Hill woman. 'She must have been terrified you were going to take the baby from her, poor woman, but are you completely satisfied it is not baby Albert?'

'There can be no doubt about it,' Tom assured her, 'The baby she has is obviously younger than Albert Morgan and its hair and eye colouring are wrong. That was something I really should have thought of having someone check before coming all this way.'

'Had someone made those inquiries and it *was* baby Albert it could well have frightened her away,' Verity said. 'You had no alternative but to come here and see for yourself – and it meant that we are able to meet again so I am delighted. How are Amos and Talwyn...?'

The next few minutes were spent talking of her visit to Cornwall, but then Tom asked if she had been able to make any progress in her enquiries into Horace Morgan's service with The East India Company.

'The friend I have in the company was able to tell me that Morgan is in receipt of a pension from them. Unfortunately, the clerk responsible for the department dealing with the affairs of employees and ex-employees has recently left because of alcoholism – no doubt a consequence of his years in India – and the files are chaotic. They are currently being reorganized and he has promised to make finding details of Morgan a priority. I will be calling on him tomorrow morning when I am back in London and will send any information I gain off to Amos immediately.'

Their talk then moved to include George Farmer and Tom felt that the Wiltshire detective sergeant was assessing Verity whenever she spoke of her work. He was not surprised that when they spoke of leaving the hospital he suddenly said to her, 'The plans you have for the nurses you are recruiting ... will it really make nursing a respectable career for a girl?'

'A *highly* respected career,' she affirmed, firmly. 'Miss Nightingale would accept nothing less – and neither would I. Why do you ask?'

Taking a deep breath and avoiding Tom's interested gaze, George Farmer said, 'My daughter Millie has followed your career with a passion that has sometimes alarmed me. She desperately wanted to be a nurse too, especially when the reports of what you were doing during the Indian mutiny were published in the newspapers, but I told her in no uncertain terms that nursing was not a career for any girl of mine.'

Showing embarrassment, he explained, 'I formed my opinion from the women in this very hospital where we are now and who were supposed to be nursing soldiers brought back from the Crimean War. They didn't impress anyone.'

'I can assure you there will be no more nurses of that type,' Verity declared fiercely. 'Such women have made the task of Miss Nightingale and myself so much harder than it should be – but we are winning. The nurses of the future will be highly trained and entirely above reproach. The slightest hint of a scandal involving any one of them will lead to instant dismissal. We are building a service of which Miss Nightingale will be proud – and she is not easily pleased.'

'Yes, Tom explained that to me,' George Farmer said, 'but I am happy to have it confirmed by you.'

'How old is your daughter,' Verity asked.

'Eighteen. She has been helping out Miss Pretty at the local school for some time.'

'She is a very bright girl,' Tom put in, 'and still just as keen to be a nurse. I stayed at Sergeant Farmer's home last night and

Millie showed me a book on nursing she had bought only a few weeks ago with money she earned at the school. It was about Miss Nightingale's notes on nursing, as I remember.'

Verity's interest quickened immediately, 'I have a copy myself; it was published only last year and sets out many of her ideas on nursing. Anyone reading it and taking in what it says is likely to make the sort of nurse we are looking for.'

Shifting her attention to Sergeant Farmer, she said, 'Are you still opposed to your daughter becoming a Nightingale nurse?'

'Not if it is to become a respectable career, but—'

Verity cut him short. '*Nightingale* nurses are already recognized as being "respectable" and all the girls we choose to become her nurses will undergo a year's training under strict supervision and when qualified will have international recognition as true professionals. In truth, with such training and after some experience of hospital work our girls will be eagerly sought after to take charge of nursing in any respectable hospital in the world.'

'Then I couldn't possibly have any objection to Millie taking up such work. In fact I would be very proud of her.'

Verity looked up at the clock on the wall of the office where they were talking. It showed 12.50. 'My train leaves for London at a quarter past four – is it possible for Millie to come here to see me before then?'

'She has been teaching until noon today but should be home by now. I could have her here in half an hour.'

'Splendid ... while you are fetching her Tom can tell me more about how his murder investigation is coming along – and whether he has seen any more of the pretty young gypsy girl whose father went missing at the same time.'

Tom managed to steer their conversation away from Zillah for much of the time he and Verity were chatting, but his reticence about talking of her intrigued Verity and she kept returning to the subject of the gypsy girl. He was relieved when George Farmer arrived at the hospital with a very excited Millie and Verity explained she would like to question her without the two men being present.

Outside the hospital where the two men went to enjoy a smoke while they waited, George Farmer said anxiously, 'I'm still not absolutely convinced I'm doing the right thing by letting Millie meet Miss Pendleton, Tom. If she's accepted she'll be going away from the family, and if she's turned down she'll be broken-hearted, so either way her mother and me lose out.'

'You'd be losing her before long anyway, George. She's a very attractive girl and I'm surprised she has stayed single for so long. If Verity Pendleton accepts her as a Nightingale nurse you'll know that she is very special and you and your whole family can be very, very proud of her.'

'And if she doesn't?'

'As you say, she's going to be very disappointed, although that will pass with time … but let's not imagine what *might* be. In a few minutes you'll know, one way or another.'

In fact, the 'few minutes' turned out to be more than half an hour – but the wait proved worthwhile. Verity was smiling when the two women returned to the hallway where Tom was waiting with the Wiltshire detective sergeant and Millie was positively radiant.

Verity was the first to speak. Addressing herself to George Farmer, she said, 'Millie and I have had a long talk together and Tom was not exaggerating when he said she is a very bright girl. She is also a most determined one and has the commitment that

Miss Nightingale looks for in every one of her nurses. I am most impressed with her.'

'Does that mean ... you want her to train to become one of your nurses?'

Tom was unable to decide whether the detective sergeant was proud of Verity Pendleton's approbation of his daughter, or apprehensive of what it would mean to have her leave the family home. He decided it was both.

'I do. She is still a little young to take on the responsibilities that go with being a fully qualified Nightingale nurse but until she reaches a suitable age, and with your permission, I would like Millie to become my personal assistant, with pay of course, to help me with my duties of selecting other girls for nurse training, and inspecting hospitals to ensure they meet the increasing demands of government. It is work that will undoubtedly prove invaluable for Millie's future and she will always be under my personal supervision.'

The silence that followed her words lasted so long that Verity felt obliged to prompt Millie's father. 'What do you think, Mr Farmer?'

George looked to where Millie was waiting for his reply, an expression of anguish on her face. 'I think her mother and I are going to miss her very much, Miss Pendleton, but we will be happy knowing she is working for such a responsible person and proud that she will be helping you and Miss Nightingale make nursing the caring and respectable profession it should be.'

Millie hurled herself at her father with a squeal of delight that would have gladdened any father's heart and as her father hugged her tight in return, Tom said to Verity, 'You and her father have just made her the happiest girl in Salisbury.'

'I think she has you to thank for making it possible by persuading her father that she is being offered an honourable future, Tom, but it would not have stopped her from pursuing a career as a nurse because she is a determined girl who knows what she wants from life. When she reached an age when she could decide her future for herself she would have taken the step anyway, but you made it possible for her to do it with the approval of her family and come to us with their blessing. That is most satisfactory for all of us … but there is a lesson in this that you, as a policeman, should never forget.'

When Verity stopped short of an explanation, Tom prompted, '… And the lesson is?'

'That you should never underestimate the determination and resolve of a woman if something matters enough to her. Because of the way our society is she may have to work twice as hard as a man and show a mental – and indeed a *physical* strength – far beyond the norm in order to achieve her aims, but some women are possessed with such strength, as Miss Nightingale has shown. I believe Millie is cast in a similar mould. I am happy for her that she has not found it necessary to prove it to anyone.'

Chapter 20

WHEN TOM RETURNED to Cornwall the following day and reported the results of his journey to Laverstock, Amos echoed the frustration felt by his friend.

'That's another line of inquiry that seems to have come to a dead-end, Tom and we are no closer to finding baby Albert – or Kerensa Morgan's murderer. I think we need to go through the details of all we have done once again and check what we have, what everyone has said to us, then see if we can come up with some new ideas. Unless Kerensa was murdered by someone who hasn't yet come to our notice, it's beginning to look as though Horace Morgan is our sole remaining suspect.'

'Let's hope Verity turns up something on him at the East India Company. She'll be there today.' Tom told Amos of his meeting in Salisbury with Verity, touching briefly on the part he had played in obtaining training for Detective Sergeant Farmer's daughter as a Nightingale nurse.

'Verity is showing a very keen interest in the case and I'm glad you were able to be of some help to her, Tom. You seem to have built up an excellent relationship with Wiltshire's detective branch too. That might stand us in good stead at some time in the future, so your trip hasn't been wasted. Spend a quiet day tomorrow writing a report about it and I'll show it to the chief constable. The day after is going to be a busy one for both of us. I need to set off early in the pony and trap to attend the funeral of Kerensa Morgan at North Hill. The coroner released her body after the inquest, while you were away. The jury returned a verdict of murder by person, or persons unknown. In view of the fact that Colonel Trethewy is involved, the chief constable feels we should be represented at the service.'

'Do you have anything special in mind for me while you're there?'

'Yes, Tom, I'd like you to pay a visit to the farm where this gypsy girl is staying and check whether her father has returned. If he hasn't, find out if she can tell us any more about his activities, or whether she knows of anyone else who might have been doing the same thing. Then you can go on to the Ring o' Bells to tell Alfie Kittow you've seen his wife and the baby. Frighten him a little and perhaps he can come up with something that might be useful to us. When you're done come on to Trelyn and meet me at Sergeant Dreadon's house. I've arranged to have something to eat there before returning to Bodmin. No doubt Dreadon's wife will be able to find enough for both of us.'

When Tom reached Gassick Farm he found Zillah in one of the stables grooming a moorland foal, one of three that would be put up for sale in the near future. She greeted him warmly, but was so despondent when she learned he had no news of her father he was unsure whether her initial warmth was at seeing him, or because she believed he had come with news of the missing man.

'I'm sorry, Zillah, but I'm on my way to North Hill and Trelyn now and while I'm there I'll be asking around to see whether anyone has any news of him. But how are things going, here at the farm?'

She shrugged, 'I'm keeping busy. There's plenty to do around the place, it's been neglected for far too long.'

'You haven't thought of anything else that might help us to find your father, or remembered something about that last night that might help identify whoever it was who called him out?'

'Nothing, but I'm about finished here now, would you like to come into the house for a cup of tea and meet my grandmother?'

Accepting her offer, Tom accompanied her into the farmhouse to meet the owner. Blanche Keach reminded Tom of Bessie Harris, the North Hill midwife. She was small and comfortably plump but, much to his relief, unlike the midwife's home, hers did not smell of cats. She was a busy, garrulous woman with a moorland Cornish accent which was so strong that initially he had some difficulty in understanding her. However, it soon became embarrassingly evident to him that she was sounding out his prospects as a possible future grandson-in-law.

Zillah was aware of it too and as soon as Tom had finished his tea she made the excuse that she had more work to do in the farmyard and ushered him out of the house. They left still pursued by the searching questions of the old woman.

'I am sorry for that,' Zillah apologized, when they were clear of the farmhouse. 'But Grandma doesn't meet many people up here on the moor and you're the first man I've ever brought into the house. It will probably be the last, I found it very embarrassing.'

'I'm sure she means well. She's probably concerned you'll end up as she has, looking after the farm on your own.'

'There are worse things to be doing – and when Dado comes back I'll suggest to him that we both stay here and work. We'd never be rich, but we'd never starve either.'

Riding away from the farm after spending about half an hour

in Zillah's company, Tom wondered what was likely to happen to her if Jed Smith *never* returned. Her grandmother would soon be too old to work about the farm and it would be a lonely and hardworking place for a young girl on her own. It was something that would be much on his mind in the days to come.

At North Hill the Ring o' Bells was quiet, the inn not yet open for the day's business although the cleaner had completed his work and a tired-looking Alfie Kittow was making everything ready for the customers he was expecting at noon.

Outside the church, which was only across the lane from the inn, a black carriage drawn by two plumed black horses stood outside the gate to the churchyard. Behind it was another carriage with the Trethewy coat-of-arms painted on the door and beyond that again Tom recognized Amos's pony and cart.

'You've arrived a little late for the funeral, although I see you're not dressed for it anyway. Can I offer you a drink?'

Declining the landlord's offer, Tom said, 'The village is very quiet, Alfie, is everyone in the church?'

'The only person from North Hill I've seen go in there is old Bessie Harris. Everyone else has stayed in behind closed doors. The mourners are all servants and workers from Trelyn Hall, attending the funeral on the orders of Colonel Trethewy. It wouldn't be good for his image if no one turned out for the funeral of his estate steward's wife, especially when no one in North Hill even bothered to come out to pay respects to the coffin as it passed by. I've never known such a thing before, not even when they buried an unknown Irish navvy who got drunk, wandered out on the moor and died in the snow when they were putting the railway in, down by Liskeard.'

'Did the villagers really hate Kerensa Morgan so much?'

'The men certainly didn't and that's the trouble. I can't think of one woman in the village who was ever friendly to her and there's not a man who'd dare come out and show respect for fear of what he'd suffer from the woman in his life!'

'Well, my superintendent is at the funeral to show that the Cornish Constabulary haven't forgotten her ... but talking of the women in our lives, I must congratulate you and your wife on your son. He's a bonny little chap. I must admit a family resemblance is not immediately obvious, but no doubt most people who see him will say he favours your wife's side of the family, just to please her. But, of course, you'll be aware of how he looks already, having been at Liskeard railway station when Jed Smith handed him over to her.'

The pewter mug being cleaned by the inn-keeper landed on its rim on the slate floor, severely distorting the drinking vessel. Leaving it lying where it had fallen, Alfie said, 'You've seen Florrie and the baby? But ... they're in Wiltshire!'

'That's right, Alfie, she and Harry are staying with her sister in Laverstock, at least, they were when I saw them. Florrie was very helpful, she told me all sorts of interesting things about baby Harry – and Jed Smith. Things you seem to have forgotten when Superintendent Hawke and I spoke to you. In fact I could be quite cross with you for not being truthful to us at the time.'

Alfie's first instinct was to plead innocence but he realized it would not only be futile but likely to antagonize Tom.

'I'm sorry, I didn't *want* to lie to you, but if word got around here about what we'd done, me and Florrie, there would always have been a stigma attached to the baby, and we wouldn't want that. We intend bringing the baby up as our own, him never knowing the truth and having no one else know, either.'

'You wouldn't get away with that, Alfie, at least, not if it's your intention to stay around here. Bessie Harris isn't the only one who's sceptical about Florrie's pregnancy and there would always be a chance the baby's real mother would hear the gossip, put two-and-two together and one day decide she wanted to see how he's growing up.'

'Me and Florrie have spoken about that and now she seems to be happy in Wiltshire with the baby I intend selling up here and taking a better class public house there, so Florrie can be closer to her family. But I suppose that depends on you, and what you decide to do now you've found out all about it.'

'Quite frankly it's likely to be out of my hands. You *could* still be of help to us, but having lied to us before I don't know whether my superintendent will believe anything you say to us in the future. Mind you, if you can possibly help us in any way then he and the chief constable might decide to forget anything else you've done. If they don't...?' Tom shrugged, 'The chief constable could object to you getting a licence to run a public house – and that would influence the magistrates in any other part of the country.'

'But that would take away my livelihood!' Alfie was genuinely dismayed.

'A licensee needs to be an honest pillar of the community, Alfie. Lying to the police doesn't exactly fit that bill, nor does keeping anything from them. You must learn a lot from the men who frequent this inn. Drink has a habit of loosening a man's tongue so I doubt if there's a rumour going around about anything in the community that you don't know about. The murder of Kerensa Morgan and the disappearance of baby Albert is one of the most shocking things ever to happen in this area and men will talk about it whenever and wherever they meet up. You must hear a lot of the talk and know what everyone is thinking.

I'd like to know about it, Alfie. Something someone says could well tie in with what we already know and so prove helpful in catching the murderer and getting baby Albert back.'

'I hear talk, of course I do, but don't take too much notice of it.'

'Well I suggest you do in future. Let me or Sergeant Dreadon know about any of the rumours that are going around and let *us* decide whether there's truth in any of them. It could make my chief constable change his mind about you.'

Alfie Kittow remained silent but, as Tom turned to leave, he said, 'Was Florrie upset by you going to Laverstock to see her?'

Turning back to the concerned inn-keeper, Tom said, 'I think she was afraid I was either going to take the baby away from her or tell her sister the truth, but once I'd reassured her she told me all about how she came by him. Had we known earlier it would have saved the Cornwall Constabulary the money that was spent going to check whether or not the baby was in fact Albert Morgan.'

'You thought he might have been Albert and you told her that? Oh, poor Florrie!'

'I told her about Kerensa's murder and that her baby had gone missing, but she was far more upset at the thought that Harry might be taken away from her. Had you told me the truth in the first place, and of Jed Smith's part in it, you could have saved Florrie all the distress she was caused. Talking of Jed Smith … when did you last see him? Was it after he gave the baby to you and your wife?'

'I had no reason to see him again once I'd paid him at Liskeard railway station.'

'So he never said anything to you about anyone else he might be getting a baby for?'

'No, but he wouldn't, would he? I mean, the most important

thing about what he does is to keep it quiet so that nobody ever knows where it's come from, or gone to. But if you think Jed might have had anything to do with Kerensa's murder you're absolutely wrong. He makes money by finding homes for unwanted babies – and might do one or two other things that aren't strictly honest by our standards, but he isn't a violent man. He'll go out of his way to avoid violence in any shape or form. Everyone who knows him will tell you the same.'

Tom thought Zillah would be touched to know what Alfie and others thought of her father, but he did not respond to Alfie's assessment of the gypsy's temperament and left the Ring o' Bells after reminding Alfie once more of the importance of listening to any gossip he heard in his public house and telling him to pass it on to Sergeant Dreadon at Trelyn.

Neither Tom nor Amos would pursue an investigation into the manner in which Alfie and Florrie had obtained baby Harry, nor would they suggest to their chief constable that he have the publican's licence revoked, but it would do Alfie no harm to think that either might happen. It meant he would be anxious to bring anything he learned about the case to their attention.

Chapter 21

THE FUNERAL SERVICE at the North Hill church had ended and Kerensa Morgan laid to rest in the tiny churchyard by the time Tom left the public house and was riding to Trelyn. He passed groups of Colonel Trethewy's servants and workers walking back to the estate.

Amos was talking to Sergeant Dreadon outside the entrance to the police house when Tom arrived there. Tying his horse on a loose rein to the post outside the garden gate, he joined them and told both men of his meeting with Alfie Kittow and the suggestion he had made to him.

'I'll make a point of visiting the Ring o' Bells more often on my beat,' Dreadon said. 'Just in case he's a bit shy of coming to visit me here. It's one of my duties anyway, but there's rarely any trouble there. Alfie Kittow runs a good inn and is quick to bar any troublemakers.'

'Well, let's hope he comes up with something of use to us,' Amos commented. 'We don't seem to be progressing very well at the moment with our own inquiries – but you were telling me what has been going on here, at Trelyn. It sounds as though things have been very quiet.'

'That's what I *was* saying,' Sergeant Dreadon agreed, 'but I think it's about to change!' He nodded to where a horse which possessed more skin and bone than flesh, was executing a shuffling trot along the lane towards them, a gnarled little old man dressed in farming garb jolting up and down on the animal's saddle-less back. 'It's Ebenezer Pender who farms up Slippery Hill way. He's always got problems with something or other and expects us to sort out everything from the weather to a poor harvest.'

When the horse was pulled to a halt in front of the police house the rider slid to the ground and scuttled along the path towards the waiting policemen as fast as legs shaped to the body of his pony, would allow.

'Well now, Ebenezer,' said the sergeant. 'That's the first time in all the years I've been stationed here at Trelyn that I've ever seen you in a hurry about anything, so I'm guessing you have something of importance to tell me.'

'It's important all right,' Farmer Ebenezer declared, 'and I daresay you'll think so too when I tell 'ee. I haven't been able to give my cows nothing to drink this morning because of it and they've got no water up there in the top field behind the old mine.'

'Well now, I know we've had no rain for nigh on four weeks and things are becoming critical, but it's the Lord's doing and there's nothing even a police sergeant can do about it.'

'I'm not talking about the weather,' the red-faced farmer declared, 'and it don't much matter whether there's rain or no. That well's never dried up in all my lifetime, no, nor my father's or grandfather's neither. 'Tis the *reason* why I can't get no water that I'm here to tell 'ee about – and though the Lord will no doubt be having plenty to say to the man involved about all the things he's done in his life, right now it's *you* who'll need to be sorting my water out.'

'I'm sorry, Ebenezer, you're not making any sense. What is it you think I can do about your well?'

'If you'd been listening to me there'd be no need for you to be asking damn silly questions. I want you to come to the well on my farm, up by the old mine explosive store and take away the body that's in there, stopping me from raising the bucket.'

'A body?' This time it was Tom who spoke. 'Do you have any idea who it is?'

The farmer gave Tom a disdainful look, 'It may not be a very deep well, but we don't have lanterns down wells here in Cornwall so I can't say as I recognized him, or even saw his face, but he seems to be lying on top of the bucket, which is why it wouldn't come up, and there's a red scarf caught on the stonework a little way down, the sort of scarf worn by a gypsy. The only gypsy I know of around these parts is that Jed Smith, who has his wagon on Harriet Hocking's land, beyond my place....'

The three policemen, aided by a couple of farm labourers finally succeeded in retrieving the body from the bottom of a well that was enclosed by a low wall, close to what had once been a small but sturdily built explosives store on an abandoned mine on Ebenezer's farmland, not far from Slippery Hill itself.

Sergeant Dreadon was able to identify the body immediately as being that of Jed Smith – but his was the *second* body recovered from the wall. Lying on top of the dead gypsy in the narrow well was another … that of a baby boy.

Hurriedly summoned to the scene Horace Morgan arrived accompanied by Colonel Trethewy, travelling in a light, four-wheeled open carriage. He immediately identified the second body as being that of his missing son, Albert.

Distraught and bewildered, he demanded, 'Why…? Why kill Albert as well as Kerensa? I know Kerensa made enemies during her lifetime, rightly or wrongly, but why Albert? He was just a baby who had never done a wrong deed to anyone. Why kill him too? He had so much to live for….'

'There's no sense trying to read the mind of a man like that,' This from Colonel Trethewy who had joined the men at the well. 'He could not possibly have had anything against either of them, it is just the way these gypsies are.'

From the moment the bodies had been discovered, the thought uppermost in Tom's mind had been how he was going to break the news of her father's death to Zillah, and the magistrate's words angered him, but before he could respond to the statement, Amos said, 'Sadly, it would seem that Jed Smith was a victim too.'

'Nonsense!' Colonel Trethewy spluttered, any grief he might have felt at the discovery of baby Albert outweighed by satisfaction that a gypsy had suffered a similar fate. 'You have the body of Morgan's son and there's a dead gypsy in the well with him. It's obvious he killed the baby after murdering its mother, then slipped and fell in the well himself after disposing of the baby's body.'

'It's a shallow well, Colonel, neither wide nor deep enough for anyone to go floating around and changing their position. The man who went down there on the rope found the baby's body lying *on top* of the gypsy. That means that baby Albert went into the well *after* Smith. Someone killed the gypsy and threw him into the well, then tossed the baby in after him.'

For almost half a minute Colonel Trethewy sought for a flaw in Tom's reasoning. Then, with a curt, 'Well, it's your case, you sort it out. I've told you what *I* think', he turned on his heel and stalked off, heading for his carriage.

Without turning his head towards Amos, Sergeant Dreadon watched the departing landlord and said, 'There have been many times when I would have liked to tell Colonel Trethewy that he was talking a load of nonsense but I've never had either the nerve or the courage of my convictions that I was right. You've just given me a moment to savour, sir. It's a memory I shall cherish.'

Tom was only half listening to his colleagues. He realized Amos's observations were correct, which meant that someone was responsible for the deaths of both Albert and Jed Smith and undoubtedly Kerensa Morgan too, but he knew Amos would ask him to ride to Gassick Farm and bring Zillah to the old explosive store to make a positive identification of her father.

It was not a task he relished.

When Tom arrived at the moorland farm, one look at his unhappy expression told Zillah even before he began apologizing for being the bearer of the worst possible news. She listened with increasing anguish as he told her of Ebenezer's grisly discovery and explained to her that although Sergeant Dreadon had said the body was that of her father, she needed to come with him to make a positive identification.

Not until they were almost halfway to the well, with Zillah riding bareback on a moorland pony beside him, did she ask, 'How did he die?'

There was no kind way of telling her and Tom replied, 'We think he was struck on the back of the head with an iron bar before being thrown down the well. We found what we believe to be the murder weapon at the scene.'

'So he was murdered … but why? He had more friends than enemies and I can think of no one who would want to kill him.'

'I can think of someone with a very good reason, Zillah. The man who called at your wagon the night Kerensa Morgan was murdered. If it is your father – and I am afraid there is little doubt about it – he and Kerensa were both killed by the same man. The fact that the body of her baby was also in the well, lying on top of your father is significant. It's possible your father was called out to take the baby and find a home for it but realized who it was. If that was the case he would know who the murderer of Kerensa was. He was probably the only one who did. Because of this the murderer had to get rid of him too. So, you see, it's more important than ever that you remember every single thing you can about the night that man came to your caravan, no matter how unimportant you believe it to be. The murderer has killed three times now and for all we know may well strike again.'

'To the best of my knowledge Dado never ever saw Kerensa's baby and we never knew she had been found murdered when he was called out.'

'So you told me, but the murderer wasn't to know that and once your father heard about it he would have realized he had been dealing with her murderer and that would have sealed his fate.'

'But why call Dado out at all if he was going to kill Kerensa's baby anyway?'

'That's one of a great many questions I can't answer just yet, Zillah. The whole thing is thoroughly baffling at this point.'

He did not voice a growing unease he had that the murderer might consider the possibility that Zillah could have seen him, or would recognize his voice if she heard it again. If it crossed the murderer's mind then she too would become a victim.

They travelled in silence for much of the remainder of the journey to the old mine and once there Zillah tearfully confirmed that the body found in the well was that of her father. She tried very hard to contain her grief but did not succeed and, taking her arm, Tom led her away as the others waited for a farm cart belonging to Ebenezer to arrive and carry the bodies away.

When they were some distance away from the others, Tom asked, 'What will you do now, Zillah? Would you like me to ride with you back to Gassick Farm?'

'What is going to happen to Dado now?'

'There will be an autopsy carried out on him to find out how he died and an inquest will be carried out by a coroner. When that's over the ... your father's body will be released to you.'

Struggling hard to remain in control, Zillah queried, 'How long will all that take?'

'I honestly don't know, Zillah. Much will depend on the findings of the surgeon carrying out the autopsy and then it's up to the coroner to decide. There will certainly need to be an inquest, but he could release the body before then. I wish I could be more specific but sometimes these things take time.'

Digesting this information, Zillah finally asked, 'When was he killed?'

'Again, I couldn't say for certain but I suspect it happened on the night he went off with the man who called at your wagon.'

This information resulted in another long silence. It was broken when Tom said, 'I'll keep you informed of all that's happening with our investigation into his murder. I'm really sorry about all that's happened, Zillah, but by the time you told me about your father being missing he had most probably already been killed, so there was nothing I could do to prevent it.'

'I know ...' Suddenly and unexpectedly the tears in her eyes spilled over and began running down her cheeks. Reaching out, she gripped his arm fiercely. 'I wish ... but, no, it doesn't matter *what* I wish. You'll find who did to this to my Dado and the others?'

Feeling deeply sorry for the bereft girl, Tom said, 'Yes, I'll find him, Zillah, and he'll pay with his life for what he's done.'

'Find who killed my father, have him punished and you'll learn what it is I wish ... but may I see the baby, please?'

'Are you quite certain you want to, Zillah, it's a very sad sight?'

'I'd like to see the face of someone who shared death with my father.'

'Very well, the baby's body is inside the explosives store. I'll take you there.'

Inside the stone-built building the sunshine streaming through the open door fell upon the tiny body and Zillah looked at it for a long while before saying, 'I expected to see it wrapped in the shawl I made for Kerensa Morgan shortly before it was born. Dado took it to her at Trelyn and said she was delighted with it.'

Tom had been over the evidence many times since Kerensa Morgan's murder and he remembered that in Jemima Rowe's statement to him and Amos when they had first met her, the retired Trelyn Hall housekeeper had specifically said that when she saw Kerensa pass by her cottage, carrying baby Albert, *he was wrapped in a shawl.*

Suddenly excited, he asked, 'This shawl, was there anything particularly distinctive about it? I mean, was it something your father might have recognized if he had seen it wrapped around the baby?'

'Of course. He admired it while I was making it and was so proud of it when it was finished he took it to Kerensa Morgan himself.'

'Then we might have found a motive for your father's murder.

If he was taken to the baby on the night he was called out from your wagon and recognized the shawl he would have known who the baby was and might have said something about it to the murderer, or perhaps refused to have anything to do with what was going on. The murderer couldn't have allowed him to go away because when your father heard about Kerensa's murder he might well have gone to the police. Is there anything particular about this shawl *I* might recognize if I saw it, Zillah?'

'Yes, Although you wouldn't see it immediately. I worked the initials "A" and "M" into the pattern because Kerensa said if it was a boy it was going to be called Albert after her father and if a girl, Agnes, after her husband's mother. If it's going to be helpful I could give you the drawing of the pattern I did before I started making the shawl....'

In spite of Tom's misgivings Zillah insisted on returning to the moorland farm alone and when she had gone to break the news to her grandmother that the body found in the well was that of her father, Tom took news of the identifiable shawl to Amos, explaining his theory that Jed Smith might have been murdered because he recognized it and realized who the baby was.

'The facts are there, Amos. Smith was called out from his gypsy wagon some time in the early hours of the morning, by which time Kerensa was already dead. It's hardly likely that whoever called at the wagon said, "I'd like you to get rid of this baby for me, I've just killed its mother"! I think we must assume that the object of calling upon Smith was to have him find a home for the baby, but I doubt very much whether he would have been told where the baby was from, or *why* there was such a sense of urgency about it.'

'It's a good theory, Tom, but after going to so much trouble why kill the baby as well as Smith?'

'I have no answer to that,' Tom admitted, adding. 'It's always possible Smith wasn't killed on the night of the murder but, in order to keep him quiet … but, I admit, that still doesn't explain why baby Albert was murdered.'

Despondently, he added, 'We have a great many possibilities, but very few *probabilities* and are no further forward in identifying a killer.'

'I have to agree with you,' Amos said. 'Although this shawl might eventually prove important if we ever find it, we'll say nothing to anyone about it at the moment and when we get the drawing we'll commit it to memory so that we'll recognize the shawl if we ever come across it. By the way, I can see why you are so taken with this gypsy girl, she's very attractive. Do you think she will go back to her father's people now?'

'No, she says they never forgave him for marrying a *gorgio* – a non-gypsy. She's going to remain with her grandmother on her moorland farm, but it's very remote and there are only the two women there. I'm concerned our murderer might get it into his mind that Zillah could recognize something about him, something she isn't even aware of knowing. If he does then she'll be an easy target for him.'

'Then we must keep an eye on her, we don't want anything happening to anyone else. Besides, there's always a chance she might remember something that will help us … but don't get too involved with her, Tom. Talking of help … with any luck we'll hear from Verity soon, giving us what information she's been able to glean about Horace Morgan. I'll leave you to tie things up here with Sergeant Dreadon, while I brief the surgeon from Launceston who'll be carrying out the autopsy. Then I need to produce a report by the morning for Chief Constable Gilbert on these latest two murders. He's not going to be happy! When the meeting with him is over I'll ride to Launceston to discuss the findings of the autopsies with the surgeon carrying them out. Oh, in case I miss you in the morning, ride to North Hill and check whether Jowan Hodge and his wife have returned home. If they haven't, make some inquiries among their friends and neighbours. His absence is beginning to look suspicious.'

Chapter 22

THE SURGEON WHO carried out the autopsies on Jed Smith and baby Albert was young and keen. He was actually hoping to pursue a career in forensic pathology and had recently returned from a visit to Bristol University in furtherance of this ambition. He told Amos he had completed the examination of both bodies but had not yet written up his reports on them.

'You can send the reports on to us at headquarters later,' Amos said. 'Just tell me what you found.'

The young pathologist leaned back in his chair and, displaying an enthusiasm for his subject that Amos found ghoulish, explained, 'The cause of the gypsy's death is perfectly straightforward, he had a number of cuts and abrasions caused by contact with the stonework of the lining of the well as he fell, but what killed him was a blow to the back of his head, delivered with such force that his skull was severely fractured. The weapon was undoubtedly the iron bar found nearby. Because it was rusty and had a rough surface I was able to find hair, blood and fragments of skin embedded in it ... The cause of the baby's death was far more difficult to ascertain and proved most interesting. However, I am confident I found sufficient evidence for my eventual findings to convince a coroner's jury of its accuracy.'

Pausing, the surgeon awaited a reaction from Amos. When

none was forthcoming, he continued, his enthusiasm undiminished, 'The baby's body had hardly a mark on it. The distance from the top of the well to the water was not great so there were no particularly noticeable marks caused by impact with the water and it does not seem to have touched the side on the way down.'

'So its death was due to drowning?'

'No,' said the surgeon, triumphantly. 'There was no water in the lungs. It means the baby must have been dead *before* it was thrown into the well.'

Amos was puzzled. 'But ... you said there were no marks on the baby's body, how did it die?'

'That is exactly what puzzled me – at first,' the surgeon said, adding with obvious pride. 'The baby had not been fed for some time before its death – but that had nothing to do with its death, either.'

Pausing once again for effect, he was satisfied with Amos's obvious bewilderment and continued, 'I found traces of wool, probably from a shawl, inside the baby's mouth and even a tiny fragment in its throat. I doubt that one in a hundred pathologist, no, not one in a *thousand*, would have been as thorough, Superintendent – but I was. As a result I am willing to swear on oath that the cause of the baby's death was asphyxiation as a result of being wrapped in a shawl which covered not only its body, but probably its face as well.'

'But there was no trace of a shawl around the baby, or in the well?'

'I certainly never saw one.'

Mulling over the surgeon's information, Tom asked, 'Would you say this was the result of a deliberate act, or an accident, Doctor?'

Leaning back in his chair and putting his fingertips together in front of his face, the surgeon said triumphantly, 'I have given you the cause of the baby's death, Superintendent Hawke, I suggest that exactly *how* it was caused is for *you* to ascertain!'

Riding across Bodmin Moor while Amos was on his way to Launceston, Tom was tempted to make a slight detour and see how Zillah was before riding on to North Hill to call at the home of Jowan Hodge. But he resisted the temptation, knowing he should be able to spend more time with her once his business was concluded at North Hill, especially if the wealthy miner was not at home.

Unexpectedly, he found the Hodges had returned home and the door was opened to him by Evangeline Hodge. A tall, stern-faced woman she looked him up and down disdainfully when he introduced himself and asked whether Jowan was at home. Then, in the stentorian tones of someone accustomed to addressing outdoor meetings of Bible Christians, she demanded to know what he wanted with her husband.

Patiently, Tom explained that he was investigating the murder of Kerensa Morgan and that purely as a matter of routine he needed to eliminate her husband from the list of those who might have had the opportunity to kill her.

'Well, you can eliminate Jowan from your inquiries here and now,' Evangeline declared. 'He was not even in Cornwall when the murder was committed. He was in North Devon, staying at the home of my parents. He had gone there the day before to look at a house we are thinking of buying and moving to. He liked the house and sent for me to join him in order that I might give my approval to the purchase, so there is no need for him to be troubled by you.'

'Thank you Mrs Hodge, I am grateful for your information, but I need Mr Hodge to tell me himself of his whereabouts on the night of the murder and I will need to have the names and address of your parents.'

'Are you doubting my word, Sergeant Churchyard?' Evangeline appeared to actually swell with indignation.

'No,' Tom replied evenly, 'and your corroboration will be duly noted, but I can't accept the evidence of a second person, I need Mr Hodge to tell me himself.'

Tom felt that the look she gave him should have reduced him to ashes on the spot, but with a snort that would have done credit to a medieval war-horse Evangeline Hodge turned away and called, 'Jowan, come here, there is someone who wishes to speak to you.'

Moments later a man appeared in the doorway of a room that appeared to be a kitchen, wiping his hands on a piece of towelling. Jowan Hodge was smaller that his wife and slightly built, but Tom felt that in order to have achieved the success he enjoyed as a miner he must be stronger than appearances suggested.

'This gentleman is a policeman who is looking into the murder of Kerensa Morgan. He wants to know where *you* were on the night she was killed. I have told him, but he won't accept my word for it and needs to hear it from you.'

Turning back to Tom, she said, 'I trust you have also spoken to those who might have had *reason* to kill her – and there are a great many. She was a whore and the wrath of the Lord should have fallen upon her long before it did.'

'And her baby and Gypsy Jed Smith … they deserved to be murdered too?'

Evangeline Hodge seemed taken aback by his question, but

only for a moment. 'The ways of the Lord are beyond our understanding, young man. Are you a Christian?'

'I am a policeman and I'm here to speak to your husband. Perhaps you will leave us, please?' Tired of her religious cant, Tom ignored her question and brought the subject back to the purpose of his visit.

'We have no secrets from each other and there is nothing that either of us has to say that can't be shared.' Then, aware from Tom's expression that he was losing patience, Evangeline Hodge added, frostily, 'But if that is *your* way of doing things...!'

Leaving her observation unfinished, the tight-lipped woman sniffed haughtily before turning and walking back inside the cottage.

Noticeably nervous, her husband said to Tom, 'What exactly is it you want with me? As Evangeline told you, I was staying with her parents in North Devon on the night poor Kerensa was murdered.'

'I'll need to take their address in order to confirm that, Mr Hodge, purely to eliminate you from our inquiry, you understand? At the moment a question mark hangs over the head of any man who ever knew her, and I gather from your reference to her as *poor* Kerensa that you don't entirely agree with your wife's opinion of her.'

Jowan appeared uneasy and when there was a sound from inside the cottage Tom realized that Evangeline Hodge was close enough to hear their conversation.

'Shall we walk in the garden while we are talking, Mr Hodge?'

After a hasty, nervous glance in the direction of the sound they had both heard, Jowan Hodge nodded his head in vigorous assent, without speaking.

When they were away from the house the miner-turned-entrepreneur relaxed, but only for a moment. His tension returned when Tom asked, 'You *do* know why I am questioning you, Mr Hodge?'

'Yes ... no! You said you are speaking to anyone who might have known Kerensa and I have told you I wasn't even in Cornwall when she was killed.'

'That doesn't necessarily mean that you weren't implicated in her death, Mr Hodge. I am only questioning those who knew Kerensa *particularly* well.'

'I knew the girl, I'm not denying that, but so did a great many men. After all, she was barmaid at the Ring o' Bells and it's a very popular public house, but I was only an occasional customer – Evangeline and my work saw to that. There are a great many men who spent far more time in there and knew her better than me.'

The two men were walking side by side along a garden path while they talked, but now Tom stopped so suddenly that Jowan Hodge was startled. However, looking questioningly at his companion, he stopped too.

'Mr Hodge, I am making inquiries into what has turned out to be three murders. It is an extremely serious matter and I am not playing games. I expect anyone I question to take it equally seriously and answer me truthfully. It's in their own interest to do so because if I learn someone is *not* being entirely truthful my assumption will be that they have something to hide and I will arrest them and take them to Bodmin police headquarters for further questioning. Now, having spoken to your wife I realize she has a very strong personality. Were I to arrest you she would undoubtedly want to know why and I'm quite certain my superintendent would feel obliged to tell her. I believe you knew Kerensa Morgan far better than you have intimated, especially when she was Kerensa Tonks, although I've been told your relationship did not end when she was married. You certainly knew her far better than most of the Ring o' Bells customers. Now, shall we begin again – or perhaps you would like the support of your wife while I am questioning you?'

Hodge glanced quickly towards the cottage to where his wife had appeared in the doorway – and he visibly paled. 'Can we walk down to the gate ... or, better still, along the lane a little way?'

By way of reply, Tom walked to the garden gate and held it open. After another nervous glance towards the house, Hodge scurried out to the lane.

They had not gone far before Jowan Hodge said, 'I'm sorry I haven't been as frank as I should with you. You're right, of course, I *did* know Kerensa better than I said. Better than I *should* have, being a happily married man, but there was never anything serious between us, it was just ... well, she was a pretty girl and I suppose I felt flattered – but I'd rather you didn't repeat my words to Evangeline. You won't tell her what I've said?'

'If you answer my questions truthfully and I'm satisfied you had nothing to do with her murder – or the murders of the others – there will be no need for me to say anything about your relationship with Kerensa to anyone, although it could still get back to your wife. More than one person I've spoken to has linked your name with hers. It's even been suggested it's you and not Horace Morgan who fathered her baby.'

'That's not true! It's just not true!' Desperate to be believed, Hodge added, 'I haven't been able to give Evangeline a baby and she was almost as desperate as Florrie Kittow at the Ring o' Bells to have one ... but, sadly, she's too old now.'

'Did Kerensa Morgan ever suggest to *you* that you were the father of her baby?'

'No.'

The brief reply was not entirely convincing and Tom said, 'Are you quite sure about that, Jowan? Why else would she seek you out after the baby was born? I would have thought she'd have wanted to settle down once she had a respectable husband and a baby son.'

It was a shot in the dark, but it paid off.

'Her husband might be looked upon as respectable but there was little love in the marriage and he was mean with his money, something that didn't go down at all well with Kerensa. She was free enough with her favours but she expected men to show their appreciation by giving her gifts, otherwise she certainly couldn't have afforded the clothes she wore on what she earned at the Ring o' Bells.'

'Did she expect you to be generous to her, Jowan? After all, you could afford it more than most.'

When no immediate reply was forthcoming, Tom prompted him. 'Remember what I said, Jowan, I need you to be absolutely honest with me.'

Reluctantly, Hodge replied, 'She asked me for money, yes.'

'And did you give it to her?'

Jowan Hodge nodded unhappily, 'She said she wanted it so she could leave her husband and take the baby with her. She even suggested we might go away together.'

This was a revelation indeed and Tom asked, 'What did you say to that?'

Evading a direct reply, Jowan Hodge said, 'She knew I would never leave Evangeline. I gave her money, yes, but only because she was very unhappy and didn't deserve a man like Morgan.'

'Was he ever violent towards her?'

'She said he was and showed me bruises to prove it. She once also had a nasty graze on her cheek that she said he'd caused.'

Somewhat sceptically, Tom asked, 'Do you have any idea why he should have had reason to be so violent towards her?'

After only a slight hesitation, Hodge replied, 'I don't know if Morgan had heard the rumours going about that the baby wasn't his, or had worked things out for himself, but she said that once, when he'd been drinking, he demanded to know whether he *was* the father of her baby and knocked her about a bit.'

Tom thought that if Horace Morgan really was in doubt about baby Albert's paternity it gave him a strong motive for murder – but he had one further question to put to Jowan Hodge.

'Where did you and Kerensa meet to discuss her problems – and to hand over the money you say you gave her?'

'Up on the moor, close to Hawk's Tor. There's an old mine not far from there that I spent some time inspecting. It was abandoned before it had a chance to come good and I thought of reworking it. I used to pass by the tor on my way home, but after giving Kerensa the money I took to coming home a different way and, like I said, on the night she was murdered I was many miles away, in North Devon. I'll give you the address so you can check I'm telling the truth....'

Riding back to Bodmin on his way from the home of Jowan Hodge, Tom thought over what the successful miner had said about the relationship between Kerensa and her husband. That they were not the happily married couple Horace Morgan would have the world believe was becoming increasingly evident. Had the Trelyn land agent seriously believed Albert was not his son it would have given him a powerful motive for killing both mother *and* baby. The reason for murdering Jed Smith was less clear, but that would no doubt be established in due course.

Equally certain was that if Jowan Hodge's alibi held up – and Tom had little doubt it would – it left only two known suspects and of the two Morgan was emerging as the more likely murderer.

However, Tom decided he would try to put Morgan out of his mind until he had been to Gassick Farm to speak to Zillah and collect the drawing she had made of baby Albert's missing shawl.

Zillah seemed pleased to see him and he felt she would have liked him to stay for a while, but it was not long before the murder of her father was mentioned and her grandmother, a normally cheerful woman, who had been extremely fond of her gypsy son-in-law broke down and this upset Zillah so much that Tom reluctantly decided it would be better if he left both women to comfort each other.

Although disappointed there had been no opportunity to talk to Zillah alone, he left Gassick with the drawing of the shawl Zillah had made for baby Albert safely placed in his saddle-bag.

Urging his horse to a lively trot, he hoped to reach the Bodmin police headquarters in time to compare notes with Amos on the progress, or lack of the same, in their respective inquiries.

Chapter 23

IN AMOS'S OFFICE a few days later he and Tom were discussing the murder case when the sergeant in charge of the front office entered the room. He carried an envelope in his hand and explained, 'The mail has just arrived, sir. This letter is addressed to you and marked "Urgent, Private and Confidential". I thought I should bring it up to you right away.'

'Thank you, Sergeant.' As the policeman left the room, Amos looked at the envelope and said, 'It's from London, Tom, it must be from Verity.' Hurriedly cutting the envelope open with a bone-handled paper-knife that had been a present from Talwyn, he took out a number of pages filled with small, neat handwriting.

'It *is* from her,' he said, excitedly and began reading.

Waiting for more information, Tom felt increasingly frustrated as he watched Amos's expression undergo a number of animated changes as he read.

Putting the first page to one side and moving on to the second, Amos added to Tom's frustration by saying, 'I think we may have him, Tom. Verity has unearthed a motive … a motive we could never have imagined in a million years!' Tantalizingly, Amos broke off what he was saying as he began to read the second page of the long letter.

When he reached the foot of the page and turned to the third, Tom could contain himself no longer. 'What does she say—?'

He stopped abruptly as, instead of replying, Amos held up his hand to silence any further questioning and Tom was obliged to curtail his growing impatience until Amos had read the entire contents of the letter.

Finally placing the last page face down on the others, Amos leaned back in his chair, his thoughts seemingly far away for a few moments. Then, coming back to the here and now and tapping a finger on the letter, he said, 'Verity has come up trumps once again, Tom. She has not only filled in much of Horace Morgan's Indian background for us but given us a much stronger motive for killing Kerensa and baby Albert than any we could possibly have discovered for ourselves, here in Cornwall.'

Biting back a question, Tom waited for Amos to explain … and the explanation was not long in coming now.

'It would seem that Colonel Trethewy's estate steward is reticent about his life in India for a number of very good reasons, not least of them being that he has a wife and children there!'

This was startling news indeed and Tom said, 'You mean he married Kerensa bigamously?'

'Most probably, although whether we could ever prove it in an English court is debatable. His wife there is an Indian woman named Shabnam and although the East India Company records have her recorded as his wife, Verity has been unable to ascertain whether they had a Hindu or a Christian church wedding. Whichever it was, Morgan and Shabnam have two children, a boy and a girl.'

'If Morgan had left them there and started a new life back here in Cornwall why should he want kill Kerensa and his baby son?'

'That's where his story becomes even more interesting, Tom.

The mutiny broke out in India, in 1857 and Morgan's family were living in Cawnpore when it was besieged by a very large army of mutineers. They, together with about four hundred other women and children took refuge in the hastily fortified army barracks, protected by some four or five hundred men, many being invalid soldiers and civilians. Despite this, and against great odds, they held out for three weeks. Desperately short of food and water their suffering must have been unimaginable until eventually they were driven to accepting terms of surrender from the mutineers who offered them safe passage from Cawnpore. But, instead of being led to safety, they were turned upon by their besiegers and all the men and many of the women and children were killed. The survivors were kept in appalling conditions until a British relief column was drawing near, when they too were cruelly murdered.'

'But if everyone was killed then Morgan didn't commit bigamy with Kerensa, he was a widower … but how did he escape?'

'Ah, this is where it all becomes very interesting, Tom! Morgan's story to the East India Company after the event was that when Cawnpore was sacked by mutineers he escaped and hid for days before making his way to Allahabad, further down the Ganges River, where he fell in with the British army column making its way to Cawnpore to rescue the women being held there. Unfortunately, the soldiers arrived too late to save any of them. His story was checked but there was such chaos in the country at the time that the East India Company had no alternative but to accept his story and because he was thought to have lost his family he was given a great deal of sympathy. When he expressed a wish to leave the company and return to England they repatriated him and awarded him a company pension.' Pausing and leaning back in his chair, he said, 'This isn't the story he told to Verity when they spoke at Trelyn, possibly because he didn't want to be questioned too closely about what *really* happened there.'

'You say he was only *thought* to have lost his family?'

'That's right. Apparently – and just how isn't known – his wife and the two children survived. Shabnam was Hindu anyway and both the children were dark-skinned, so with the help of one of the low-caste garden servants they made their way to the south, away from the area controlled by the mutineers, helped along the way by friends and family of the gardener. Shabnam eventually made her way to her parents' home. They are very wealthy and she and the family are now living with them.'

'But didn't she look for her husband when the mutiny ended?'

Searching through Verity's letter, Amos found the page he was looking for and replied, 'Shabnam explained that in view of the wholesale slaughter of Europeans in that part of the country she assumed he was one of the victims. The mutiny ended in 1858 and then the British Government stripped the East India Company of its powers and took over the running of the country. As you can imagine the affairs of the company were in turmoil, with so many of its employees dead, and property and documents destroyed, it was impossible to discover exactly what had happened to anyone. Morgan believed his family had been killed, and his family believed him to be dead. It was not until last year – two years after the end of the mutiny – that her father met up with someone who had known the Morgans in Cawnpore and was told that Horace Morgan had *not* been killed but had survived and returned to this country.'

'What did she do about it?'

The story related by Amos had brought Tom to the edge of his seat and he asked the question eagerly.

'She wrote to the East India Company, here in this country, telling her story and asking for information about her husband. She said that if the information about his survival were true and he was alive, her father was willing to pay for her and their two children to take passage to England to be together again and that they could either make their home here or return to India where Morgan could be assured of living a very comfortable life with her wealthy family.'

'When did Morgan receive the letter? It certainly gives him a very strong motive for doing away with Kerensa – and the baby too, especially if he had any doubts about being its father!'

'That's where there is considerable confusion, Tom. Because the clerk who received the letter was an alcoholic and had allowed his paperwork to get into an impossible mess, no one can say for certain whether the information about his wife being alive was ever passed on to Morgan, especially as the letter itself is still in the East India Company's office and there is no record of when it was received, or whether or not Morgan was informed about it.'

'But we do know Morgan received letters from the East India Company since coming to Cornwall,' Tom pointed out. 'The letter carrier has delivered letters to him with the company's seal on the envelope.'

'True, and the chances are that Morgan *did* know his wife and family had survived in India, but he could always say the letters he received were something to do with his pension. Until we get hold of the actual letter telling him they are still alive – or a certified copy of it – we can't actually confirm the motive, let alone prove he killed his wife and baby because of it. We need to build up a cast-iron case against him for killing not only them but Jed Smith too, and make certain he doesn't have a watertight alibi for his whereabouts on the night of the murder. We'll go over everything we've done so far and push some people a little harder, Tom. Jowan Hodge, for instance. Try to learn whether he really could have fathered baby Albert and, if so, was it possible Morgan somehow learned of it. Landlord Kittow might be able to help with that. Discover what his customers in the Ring o' Bells were saying about it and whether Morgan could possibly have heard the rumour there. I'll be happier when we have the letter sent by Morgan's Indian wife to the East India Company in our hands too, but our job isn't over, even when we have it in our possession. However strong the motive might be, we still have to prove the case against Morgan in court, Tom. We must gather every scrap of information that comes our way about Kerensa and Jed Smith ... whether it incriminates Morgan or not.'

Chapter 24

ALTHOUGH AMOS FELT there was as yet insufficient firm evidence on which to arrest Horace Morgan for the murder of his wife, baby Albert and Jed Smith, Colonel Gilbert, Cornwall's chief constable was not in agreement with him when the two men met later that day.

'I feel you have sufficient evidence to bring him to Bodmin for questioning, at least,' the police chief said.

'That was my first thought,' Amos explained, 'but Morgan is estate steward for Colonel Trethewy and in view of Trethewy's well-known opposition to us I felt it might be better if we left bringing him here until we had a watertight case against him.'

'If the information you have about Morgan's Indian family is correct – and in view of its source I am in no doubt about it – then he could run off to India at any time. This is an investigation into a number of very serious murders, Amos, and our duty is to bring the perpetrator to justice. At this moment Morgan is a suspect … a very strong suspect. I appreciate your concern about Colonel Trethewy, but leave me to deal with him. When the Cornwall Constabulary was formed, Trethewy and a few other die-hard "country gentlemen" made our work very difficult. Indeed, they posed a threat to our very existence. Fortunately, due in no small measure to the efforts of yourself and my other senior officers, the force has proved its value to the county and its people. Colonel Trethewy is now part of a fast dwindling minority who still show antipathy towards us. I will not allow him to hamper our investigation, whatever the outcome may be. Bring Morgan here to headquarters for questioning.'

Both men knew that Colonel Trethewy would be furious at the arrest of his land steward on suspicion of murder, but Amos realized Chief Constable Gilbert intended this to be a show-down between himself and the constabulary's most bitter and powerful opponent.

He would have preferred to be in possession of conclusive proof of Morgan's guilt before arresting him, but there *was* sufficient evidence to justify bringing him to Bodmin for questioning. Besides, Gilbert had always supported his policemen when criticism had been levelled against them during the early, difficult days of the force's existence, no matter how influential the complainant. He had earned the opportunity to hit back at one of his most virulent critics.

Horace Morgan would receive no special treatment because of the position he held at the Trelyn estate, but Amos realized *he* would need to be the one to make the arrest. He could not ask Tom to face the wrath of the Trelyn magistrate, although he would be accompanying him.

The two policemen left Bodmin for Trelyn early the next day to bring Morgan to Bodmin. Tom had expected they would be taking the light carriage kept at the headquarters station but Amos felt it would be quicker if they took riding horses. It would enable them to take a shorter route across the moor instead of needing to keep to the roads.

Morgan would have the use of an estate horse and be able to use it to return to Trelyn when their questioning came to an end. As Amos pointed out, unless Morgan actually confessed to carrying out the murders they would not be able to charge him.

They had been riding for a little more than an hour when Amos asked, 'Isn't the farm where your gypsy girl is staying somewhere near here?'

The question startled Tom because at that very moment he was thinking that he had not seen Zillah for a few days and wondered how she was coping on the remote moorland farm.

In spite of this, he said, 'If you mean Zillah Smith, yes, her grandmother's farm is only a mile or so south-east of here, across the moor.'

'Well, why don't we take a ride there and see how she's getting on? We're still early and the last time I saw her she was very upset at the death of her father. I'd like to see how she is.' Aware that Tom was smitten with the girl despite all his attempts to hide it, Amos added, mischievously, 'I've no doubt you would, too.'

In truth, just lately Tom had found himself thinking of Zillah with a frequency he found disturbing, but he had no intention of admitting this to Amos ... or to anyone else and, ignoring Amos's final remark, he said, 'I can't think of anyone bothering her right out here. Gassick Farm is as isolated a place as you'll find anywhere, but there's always the chance she will have remembered something of help to us, so as we're so close it won't hurt to call in to see her.'

Amos felt he had known Tom for long enough to know how he really felt about Zillah Smith, and he felt deeply sorry for him. Tom was a lonely man and she was a very attractive girl, but Amos believed it was a relationship that could have no happy ending. Romance between the two of them stood as much chance of success as, say, a romance between his sergeant and Verity Pendleton!

Much to Tom's disappointment Zillah was not at home when he and Amos reached the Gassick farmhouse, her grandmother, Blanche Keach, explaining that she had ridden off after completing the housework and feeding the livestock kept on the farm.

'Aren't you worried about her going off on her own knowing there's still a killer on the loose out there somewhere?'

Amos put the question to Blanche as he and Tom stood with her, watching their two horses drinking from a granite water trough in the farmyard.

'Of course I'm worried,' the elderly woman replied, 'but Zillah's a girl with a mind of her own. She doesn't take kindly to being told what she should or shouldn't be doing, for all that she's a good girl and does more than her share of the work about Gassick. But it's not what a young girl wants to be doing, especially one who's used to the gypsy way of life.'

Inclining her head in the direction of Tom who had walked away in order to lead both horses to a nearby hitching rail, she added, 'When she brought him to Gassick I had hopes she'd found someone she'd settle down with but I didn't know he was a policeman then. The good Lord should never have put gypsies and policemen in the same world, they're like oil and water, they don't belong together.'

Blanche had only put into words what Amos had thought, albeit for differing reasons, but he made no comment, saying instead, 'Do you have any idea in which direction Zillah went?'

'None. I wouldn't even have known she'd gone if I hadn't seen her riding off on that pony her father brought in off the moor a year or so back. He taught her how to break it in and so she did, although there's still no one but her as can ride it. I reckon the pair of them suit one another.'

'Well, thank you for allowing us to water our horses, Mrs Keach, we'll be on our way again now. I am sorry not to have seen your granddaughter, but please tell her we are doing everything in our power to catch the man who murdered her father.'

Riding away from Gassick Farm, Amos looked across at his companion and said, 'You look gloomy, Tom, are you disappointed at not finding your gypsy girl at home?'

'I enjoy talking to her,' Tom admitted, cautiously, 'but then I enjoy talking to a great many people.'

Remembering how Blanche Keach had spoken of her granddaughter, Amos said, 'You'd be wise to keep your relationship with her that way, Tom. I had a chat with her grandmother while you were tying up the horses and according to her Zillah is very much a free spirit.'

Tom stiffened perceptively, but Amos continued, 'She likened the girl to the pony she's riding. Zillah broke her in, but Blanche Keach says they are both more than a bit wild and not yet ready to conform ... but let's press on and get to Trelyn Hall, find Horace Morgan and do what needs to be done. Even if he's not guilty of murder it should be interesting to hear what he has to say about the double life he seems to have been leading.'

Riding out on the moor, enjoying the freedom she felt there, Zillah had seen the two riders earlier and would have given them a wide berth ... but then she recognized Tom. The recognition gave her a thrill of pleasure although had she troubled to analyse her feelings she would have told herself it was merely because she had spoken to no one but her ageing grandmother for many days.

Flushed and exhilarated as a result of the headlong gallop, she pulled her pony to a restless halt when she reached the two policemen. After merely glancing at Amos, it was Tom to whom she spoke. 'Hello, I didn't expect to meet up with you today. Have you come out here to see me … to tell me you've arrested someone for killing Dado?'

'Not yet, but we're getting closer. Superintendent Hawke and me are on our way to Trelyn and North Hill now to speak to someone and look into one or two things.' Hoping he had successfully hidden the pleasure he felt at seeing her again from Amos, he added, 'You really shouldn't be riding about the moor on your own like this until we've caught whoever is responsible.'

Working hard to control her pony which still had a great deal of energy left after the gallop and was uneasy in the presence of the two policemen and their horses, Zillah said provocatively, 'Well, you could always come along to keep me company!'

'I'm serious, Zillah, you could be in danger, I've told you that before.'

'I know and I *do* appreciate your concern, Tom, but much as I love Grandma Keach she's a bit of a fusser and I just have to get away from her sometimes or she'd drive me mad. I don't think I've spoken to anyone else since I last spoke to you!'

Amos had not missed Zillah's use of Tom's first name but, making no comment he said, 'Sergeant Churchyard is right, Zillah, you really shouldn't be riding about the moors on your own. It's not a good idea at the best of times and right now you really could be in danger.'

Aware that Amos's use of Tom's rank and surname instead of his Christian name was an indication of his disapproval, Zillah looked at him for a few moments before saying, 'Then I'd better not stay here wasting your time but let you get on with catching whoever it is I'm in danger from.'

With this she nodded at Tom, pulled her horse's head around sharply and, kicking her heels into its body, set off at a wild gallop once more.

Giving his companion a wry smile, Amos said, 'You've found a feisty one there, Tom, I should hate to cross her! But let's press on and get to Trelyn Hall, find Horace Morgan and see what he has to say for himself.'

Chapter 25

WHEN AMOS AND Tom reached Trelyn Hall they found a great many ponies tied up outside the great house, together with a few pony traps and a farm cart, not one of which was in anything approaching pristine condition. They were not surprised when a groom informed them they belonged to tenant farmers who were there to attend a meeting called by Horace Morgan in order to discuss a rent increase to which the farmers were bitterly opposed.

'It sounds as though this is not going to be one of Morgan's better days,' Amos commented, adding. 'Is Colonel Trethewy at the meeting?'

'No, he's got a few cases on over at Launceston magistrates court today,' the groom replied.

Amos felt relief that he would not need to face the wrath of the Trelyn magistrate, but he still had a duty to perform and he said to the groom, 'I'm afraid we need to speak to Mr Morgan. Will you ask him to come out here and meet us, please?'

'I don't know about that,' replied the groom, uncertainly. 'He won't like having to leave in the middle of the meeting.'

'He'll like it even less if we need to go into the meeting in order to speak to him,' Amos pointed out. 'Go and tell him we're here, please.'

Reluctantly, the groom did as Amos requested, pausing before entering the house to look back uncertainly as though he would ask a question. Thinking better of it he turned away and went inside Trelyn Hall through the servants' entrance.

It was some minutes before Morgan put in an appearance, accompanied by the groom and he was decidedly disgruntled. Before he had reached them he called, 'What is it you want ... have you arrested someone?'

'Not yet, Mr Morgan. We are still making inquiries and it's for that reason I would like you to come to police headquarters in Bodmin to discuss one or two points that have cropped up.'

'Come to Bodmin? I'm in the middle of a meeting, what is it that can't be sorted out here and now?'

'It's something that needs to be discussed at some length, Mr Morgan. I think you might find it less embarrassing if we do it there.'

'I am sorry, Superintendent, but I am in the middle of an important meeting – important to Colonel Trethewy and the Trelyn estate – I can't just tell all our tenant farmers the meeting is off and will have to be arranged for another day because the police wish me to go to Bodmin just to have a chat with them.'

'I realize it will be inconvenient to Colonel Trethewy, to the farmers and to you too, but it is important, probably *very* important. When do you anticipate your meeting will end?'

'Not until some time this afternoon.'

'Then, in order to inconvenience everyone as little as possible I am prepared to allow you to complete your business with the farmers if you agree to come to Bodmin police headquarters as soon as it is over.'

'Can't you tell me what it is about?'

'I could, but I would rather we all sat down together and had a chat – a long chat – in order to clear up a few matters that have arisen.'

'And if I decline to come to Bodmin?'

'Then I am afraid I will need to arrest you here and now and take you to Bodmin in order that you may help with our inquiries. I would rather not have to do that and I feel Colonel Trethewy would not be pleased with either of us should that prove necessary.'

Taken aback by Amos's positive reply, Morgan said, 'I am not happy with this, Superintendent, and I doubt very much whether Colonel Trethewy will be either.'

'You might wish to avoid involving your employer in this, Mr Morgan. If he keeps to his usual routine he will have dinner at the White Horse in Launceston after the court proceedings are over and remain there overnight, so it is possible he will not even know you have been absent from the Hall. Now, do I have your co-operation, or will I need to call upon the powers I possess and arrest you? The choice is yours.'

Aware that Amos was deadly serious, Horace Morgan said, albeit reluctantly, 'I'll come to Bodmin as soon as the meeting is over – but I want it known that it's under protest.'

'Whatever. I'll expect you there sometime late this afternoon, or early evening.'

Riding away from Trelyn Hall, Amos said doubtfully, 'Do you think it's a good idea to trust Morgan to come to Bodmin? What if he takes off?'

'We'll go and have a word with Sergeant Dreadon now and suggest he keeps an eye out for him. If he means to go off somewhere he'll take some of his belongings away with him. If Dreadon sees him leave the hall travelling light he'll be on his way to us. By giving him a choice he'll not think we have him down as a suspect – and what else can we do? Remember, all we have is a possible motive and nothing else to go on. Certainly nothing that would convince a court that he murdered his own wife and child. But now we're here we'll go and have a word with Alfie Kittow, perhaps he'll have come up with something for us.'

They had set off from Bodmin early that morning and when the two policemen arrived at the Ring o' Bells, it was still before noon. The public house had not yet opened for business but Alfie Kittow was up and busily packing.

In answer to Amos's question he said, 'I think I have a buyer for the Ring o' Bells. He's coming to see me this evening to confirm how busy trade is during the evening. I'm fairly certain he'll buy and when he does I'll be off to Wiltshire to join Florrie and the baby.'

'Do the villagers know you are leaving?'

'Not yet and I've been listening to their conversation like you asked me to. You'd have been particularly interested in the men I had in here a couple of nights ago. It was Jowan Hodge and the men he was working with when they struck it rich on the mine. It was an early farewell party because he's leaving soon.'

'Why was he having it early?' The question came from Tom.

'Because his wife was off at her parents, preaching at some meeting they were having there. She doesn't approve of him drinking here with his mates, in fact the truth is she doesn't approve of drink at all. He'd be teetotal if she had her way but it's one thing she hasn't yet managed to stop him enjoying. Mind you, she's not so fired up about him coming to the Ring o' Bells since Kerensa stopped working here.'

'Do you think his wife *knew* he was carrying on with Kerensa Morgan?'

'If she didn't she must have been the only one in North Hill who wasn't aware of what was happening – and there was very little that went on that Evangeline Hodge missed! There was certainly a lot of banter going on among Jowan's mates the night they were all in here together, he got quite heated with them.'

'What did they say that particularly upset him?'

'It was talk about Kerensa's baby in the main. They were saying the baby couldn't have looked more like Jowan if he'd been born with a pickaxe in his hands. Jowan got really cross with 'em in the end. When one of 'em said it was a good job Horace Morgan had never suspected anything, another chipped in to say he would have had to be more of a fool than anyone thought him to be not to realize it for himself – and Jowan walked out. Mind you, I think his mates were probably right. I've never really liked Horace Morgan, but he's nobody's fool.'

When the two policemen left the Ring o' Bells together, Tom said, 'I think I'm going to have another chat with Jowan Hodge, Amos.'

'If needs be we'll *both* have words with him, but we'll leave it to another day. Right now let's get back to Bodmin and wait for Horace Morgan. We'll see what he has to say before we do anything else.'

When Horace Morgan arrived at the Bodmin police headquarters he was not alone: Colonel Trethewy was with him – and the Trelyn landowner was in a foul temper. Court proceedings had been cut short because the defendant in a case that had been expected to last the whole afternoon had escaped from custody on his way to the courthouse from the prison where he was being held. It meant the colonel had no excuse for remaining in Launceston for the remainder of the day and spending the evening carousing with his friends. Then he arrived back at Trelyn Hall to find his estate steward preparing to ride off to Bodmin acting on the orders of the police…!

Storming into Amos's office ahead of Morgan he demanded, 'What do you mean by coming to Trelyn and ordering my estate steward to report to you here, Hawke? I can think of nothing he has to say to you here that could not have been said at Trelyn. Quite apart from the inconvenience caused to both of us, he has work to do there, work I am paying him good money to carry out. Can I expect to be recompensed by Chief Constable Gilbert?'

'I think you must put that question to the chief constable himself, Colonel Trethewy, but I rather doubt it. We are investigating the taking of three lives and the chief constable is following the case very closely. He and I discussed the latest evidence that has come to hand and we both feel Mr Morgan might be able to help us. I regret any inconvenience that may be caused, of course, but am quite certain that you of all people will appreciate that we *all* have a duty to perform to help bring the killer to justice.'

'I think you are wasting both time and money unnecessarily, Hawke. I said when you found the body of the baby and the gypsy in the well that you had your killer. The gypsy killed Morgan's wife, before going on to throw the baby into the well. Then, possibly in a moment of remorse, he killed himself as well … but I can see I'm just wasting my time talking to you. I'll go and speak to Chief Constable Gilbert and give him a piece of my mind. When I come back I will expect you to have finished with Morgan and allow him to return to Trelyn with me.'

'You will find the chief constable in his office, Colonel, but unless you intend remaining in Bodmin for the night I am afraid Mr Morgan will not be returning to Trelyn with you. I wish

Sergeant Churchyard to be with me when we question him and he has had to leave the office. As our questioning will take some time I intend to make a start early tomorrow morning. Mr Morgan will remain in Bodmin tonight.'

It seemed for a few moments that Colonel Trethewy would argue with Amos, but with a terse, 'We'll see about that!' he stalked out of Amos's office and set off to find the chief constable.

Horace Morgan had listened in silence to the conversation between his employer and Amos but now Colonel Trethewy had gone, he said, 'What is it you want with me? I've told you everything I can about the night of the murder. I can't think of anything else that might help. Certainly nothing that makes it necessary for me to stay here for the night.'

'I am afraid we have received some rather disturbing information that only you can clarify, Mr Morgan but, as you heard me tell your employer, I wish Sergeant Churchyard to be present when we speak about it and he won't be available until the morning. In the meantime we will house you in a cell until he returns – but you have had a long ride from Trelyn so I will have some refreshment brought to you there.'

'You are going to put me in a cell?' Horace Morgan looked at Amos in total disbelief.

'That's right, but Sergeant Churchyard and I will see you first thing in the morning – and I am given to understand you suffered far more serious privation during the final days you spent in India – and many of the questions we have to put to you concern your time there.'

Having given Horace Morgan food for thought, Amos summoned the station sergeant to his office to escort him to the cells.

*

It was a very disgruntled Colonel Trethewy who left the Bodmin police headquarters half an hour later. The meeting with Chief Constable Gilbert had been a stormy one, the voice of the Trelyn magistrate carrying to most offices in the building. However, the Cornwall chief constable was unmoved by the other man's threats and refused to be cowed by his bullying manner, pointing out that, unlike the days before the county had a police force, a magistrate no longer had the power to dictate *how* an investigation should be conducted and he, as chief constable, would not allow him to interfere with the work of his officers.

He further pointed out that Amos had kept him informed of the progress of his investigation since the beginning and he had given his approval for Morgan to be brought to Bodmin for questioning. He would be released if and when his replies satisfied the investigating officers – and, no, Colonel Trethewy would *not* be allowed to speak to his estate steward again until after he had been questioned.

Amos was delighted that Chief Constable Gilbert had supported him in such a positive way but it came as no surprise. The police chief was an ex-army man who had achieved a rank equal to that of Colonel Trethewy but, unlike the magistrate, he had seen considerably more action during service in Africa where he had earned a reputation for decisiveness when it was called for by the occasion. Amos felt he was more than a match for the irate landowner.

In the meantime Amos would return home where he would be joined by Tom, whose absence from the office had not been on a matter of any importance but, having mentioned to Morgan that his life in India was to be put under scrutiny, Amos intended he should spend the night thinking of the life he had led there and worrying about how much was known by them.

Chapter 26

I

LOCKED IN A darkened cell, Horace Morgan *did* think about India, even though he had spent some four years trying unsuccessfully to put that country, as he had known it, out of his mind. He wrestled with his unhappy thoughts in the darkness until the early hours of the morning, then, falling into an exhausted sleep, he began to dream of all he wished to forget … and the dream became a nightmare.

In common with most other European residents in the Indian city of Cawnpore, Horace Morgan was living in a state of nervous apprehension. It was May, 1857 and rumours were filtering through to the isolated garrison town of growing discontent among the sepoys of the Honourable East India Company's native regiments in various areas of India.

There were a number of reasons given for their restlessness, much of it due to a lack of understanding, or a disregard of Indian ways, on the part of those who ruled the company from England and many of those who carried out their orders in India. The latest and most serious blunder was the issue of a new type of cartridge for the rifles being brought into use for the army, which required the sepoy using it to bite the end off the cartridge to expose the gunpowder before ramming it down the barrel of his gun.

The cartridge was greased in order to make its passage down the barrel easier. Now there was a strong and justifiable suspicion that the grease contained animal fat, something which was abhorrent to both Hindu and Muslim sepoys.

Until now it had been taken for granted that the Indian population accepted its enforced status as being subservient to the European overlords – mainly the British – who ruled vast swathes of the great sub-continent and who lived in a style formerly known only to those who occupied the great houses of their homeland.

It was felt that the natives 'knew their place', despite being treated in a manner that ranged from patronizing to blatant brutality.

Cawnpore itself was a large and sprawling garrison city on the banks of the River Ganges with many thousands of residents, of whom the Europeans formed only a tiny minority.

In the garrison itself, too, Europeans were greatly outnumbered, 3,500 sepoys and *sowars* – native cavalrymen – being officered by less than a hundred Europeans. Although there were also some British troops in the garrison, they were outnumbered by fourteen-to-one by their Indian counterparts and at any one time a great number of them were suffering from some illness or another, brought about by the conditions of the country in which they were serving.

These figures began to take on a menacing aspect as rumours of unrest elsewhere continued to grow and Morgan and his fellow employees of the East India Company became aware that the sepoys and the company's employees were becoming increasingly sullen, and occasionally insolent.

All the signs of insurrection were in evidence but 67-year-old Major-General Sir Hugh Wheeler, officer in command of the garrison, dismissed any suggestion that the Indian sepoys – *his* soldiers – would ever contemplate mutiny against him.

If any officer should have understood the men he commanded, it was General Wheeler. He had served in India for fifty-four years, was married to an Anglo-Indian woman and they had a family here in Cawnpore, but Wheeler was to be proved tragically wrong, his faith in the sepoys who had served with him for so many years disastrously misplaced.

Tension mounted in Cawnpore when a telegraph was received at the Commissariat, where Horace Morgan had his office, that the sepoys at Meerut, 250 miles to the north-west had mutinied, mercilessly killing all the Europeans they could find, men, women and children, and setting fire to their homes.

This accomplished, the sepoys marched on Delhi, their numbers being swelled along the way by malcontents and criminal elements and carrying out an orgy of looting, arson and the murder of every European they encountered, regardless of age or gender.

When news of this latest outbreak of violence was conveyed to Wheeler, together with a rumour that the mutineers intended marching on Cawnpore when they had killed all the Europeans in Delhi, the general belatedly agreed to take measures to protect his countrymen in and around Cawnpore, while still insisting that it would prove to be unnecessary.

Because of this firmly held belief he went about the task in a half-hearted manner. It was assumed by those about him that he would fortify The Magazine, a spacious building within a high-walled compound built on the banks of the Ganges River about five miles to the north-west. Here were plentiful supplies of guns, ammunition and other items which would prove invaluable in a siege.

Instead, Wheeler ordered that an entrenchment be dug in the hard, parched ground around the army barracks which was situated on the very edge of Cawnpore. It was a decision which was strongly criticized by both his fellow officers and the civilians of the company, all of whom declared it to be virtually indefensible.

Horace Morgan was one of those who voiced this opinion, whilst at the same time hoping the general's optimism would prove to be well founded. Morgan was married to a Hindu woman, Shabnam, daughter of a wealthy family whose home was hundreds of miles to the north and they had two young children, a boy and a girl.

While the entrenchment was being dug with considerable difficulty in the rock-hard ground about the barracks, rumours abounded that the growing unrest was advancing down the River Ganges, moving ever closer to Cawnpore.

Then one day there was an inexplicable panic among the European community in the city, causing many of the families and their servants to flee from their homes to the dubious security of Wheeler's entrenchment.

The sheer panic of their hitherto arrogant and seemingly omnipotent overlords astounded those Indians who witnessed it ... and, suddenly, a *successful* uprising no longer seemed merely a pipe-dream. The realization brought about an undercurrent of excitement in the ranks of the sepoys that even the hitherto complacent General Wheeler could not ignore and when the telegraph wires linking Cawnpore to the outside world were cut, he too moved his family into the compound – and the die was cast.

Horace Morgan who occupied a fine bungalow bordering the river on the edge of town would have sent his family downriver to the perceived safety of Allahabad, another garrison town more than a hundred miles away but, unfortunately, the summer rains had not yet arrived and the River Ganges was as low as anyone had ever known it to be, the river's course interrupted for as far as could be seen by sandbanks which expanded with each passing day. The edge of the water which in other seasons lapped against the embankment at the end of the Morgans' bungalow was now little more than a trickle far away beyond litter-strewn mudflats.

Reluctantly, Horace Morgan decided it would be too risky for his family to attempt the long journey to safety via the river. A boat large enough to carry passengers in any degree of comfort would be forever grounding in the shallow water and, given the uncertain allegiances of those living along the banks of the great river and with bands of murderous mutineers roaming the countryside, he felt he had no alternative but to put his trust in General Wheeler. After all, he too had a family to protect and his knowledge of the sepoy temperament was superior to that of anyone else in Cawnpore … possibly in the whole of India!

So Horace Morgan moved his small family into the entrenchment, but it was not a happy move. Shabnam was dark-skinned, as were their two children and despite the present abnormal circumstances, the family found they were no more acceptable to the Europeans with whom they would be sharing the scant accommodation available in the barracks compound than they had been outside in more normal times.

Every room within the alarmingly overcrowded entrenchment was self-allocated according to rank. Officers and their families took over the permanent barrack accommodation; European wives and families of non-commissioned officers together with the families of Cawnpore merchants came next; Eurasian families followed and the few Indian wives and families were bottom of the social scale, taking whatever space they could, often in the open.

Horace Morgan was far from satisfied with the arrangement but there was nothing he could do about it, at least they had the protection of the few soldiers whose task it was to defend the entrenchment and this became increasingly important as days passed and stragglers late reaching Cawnpore spoke of hair-raising escapes from hitherto law-abiding villagers who were roaming the countryside in the company of dissident sepoys, killing and looting. It became increasingly apparent that it was only a matter of time before Cawnpore itself came under attack.

In spite of this threat Horace Morgan went to work each day in the Commissariat office in the heart of Cawnpore, even though only a small number of European staff was there to share the work of the East India Company agency and there was virtually no Indian staff to carry out menial work or operate the *punkahs* – primitive wood-framed canvas fans – each connected to a long cord which in normal times was operated by a native servant, hidden from view in a nearby cramped cubby-hole.

II

By the first week in June the situation in Cawnpore was exacerbated by even higher temperatures than was normal for the time of year and the Europeans in the heavily overcrowded entrenchment were tired and bad-tempered while many were in ill-health due to the unsanitary conditions.

One morning Horace Morgan went to work after a night

during which sleep had been made difficult by a great deal of unusual noise going on outside the makeshift fortification. Nevertheless, as the senior member of his particular department he felt it was his duty to be seen to be present in his office.

One reason was that he was compiling a long report to the East India Company's regional office in Calcutta, detailing what was happening in Cawnpore and the difficulties encountered by him and his staff in attempting to carry out their normal duties. When the report was completed he intended giving it to a particularly dark-skinned Eurasian member of his staff, disguising him as an Indian labourer and providing him with enough money to take it to Allahabad and forward it to the East India Company's Calcutta office.

Seated in his office and perspiring heavily, despite the early hour, he was suddenly disturbed by the most junior member of his staff, a young clerk who had arrived in India from England less than three months before.

Bursting into the office, the young man cried, 'We need to get out and go to the entrenchment right away, Mr Morgan!'

Alarmed, but trying to appear calm before the shaking clerk, Morgan said, 'Compose yourself, Robert. What are you talking about? Who says we have to go back to the entrenchment – and why?'

'One of the cleaners just came in to warn us! The sepoys have mutinied up at the barracks and killed many of their officers. General Wheeler has fired on them with cannon but they have run into town and with some of the townspeople are looting the bazaar. The cleaner said Nana Sahib and his army have joined them.'

Horace Morgan knew that if this information was true the situation was indeed extremely serious. Nana Sahib, the adopted son of the late deposed ruler of the area was a very influential man. He lived in great style and had always been regarded as a friend to the British despite their refusal to allow him to use the title 'Maharajah'. If he had now thrown his considerable influence and resources behind the mutineers then General Wheeler's own status would count for nothing…!

Just then another of the clerks called to Morgan from the doorway. 'Come quickly, the mutineers are setting fire to our bungalows. You can see the smoke from the windows.'

Looking out of the open office window Morgan could see in the distance above the rooftops of the nearby buildings, plumes of smoke rising into the air to join the dark pall of smoke already gathering above the enclave where he and other Europeans had their homes.

'Tell everyone to leave the building immediately and hurry to the entrenchment. They are to take anything of value with them – but don't waste time.'

The two clerks fled from the office and Morgan began stuffing papers from his desk into the office safe … then he became aware of a growing noise outside the building. It was the tumultuous sound of a frenzied mob interspersed with piercing screams of terror.

Running to a passageway window that overlooked the open square outside the Commissariat's front entrance, Horace Morgan looked out upon a scene that filled him with horror.

There was a huge crowd in the square, gathered like vultures around a number of circles of frenzied men wielding swords, bayonets, clubs and native knives, the weapons rising and falling frantically. As he watched, one of the groups erupted as a bloodied and severely wounded giant of a Scotsman, whom Morgan recognized as being one of the commissariat staff, momentarily rose to his feet before being overwhelmed once more beneath the mêlée of flailing blades.

Horace Morgan realized he was witnessing the murder of the men he had just sent from the building.

There would be no escape through the front entrance and hurrying back to his office, Morgan hurriedly removed a fully loaded Colt revolver from the safe and stuffed the various accoutrements for reloading it into his pockets. As an afterthought, he packed a number of bags of rupees into a satchel and with this over his shoulder and revolver in hand, he ran along the passageway to a set of stairs which led to the back door, putting the Commissariat between himself and the crazed mob.

At the doorway he collided with an Indian and was about to raise his gun to fire at him when the man said, 'Sahib Morgan … you must come with me quickly, there is a madness in the people and they are killing all who have fed and taken care of them.'

Morgan recognized the man as Jumna, an old East India Company servant who was in charge of the large force of commissariat gardeners. He was someone Morgan had always regarded as perfectly trustworthy … but now?

'Where do you want to take me?'

'You must come to my home, *sahib*.'

'I want to go to the barracks, where the other Europeans and my wife and children are.'

'There is no way you can get there now, Sahib Morgan. It is surrounded by sepoys and Nana Sahib's men … those who are not stealing everything from the bazaar. Your friends who were trying to reach the barracks were caught and are being killed. It is good for you that you came out through the back door. Come with me quickly, but say nothing in case you are heard. If we meet anyone you must try to hide, but we are not likely to meet many people along the way. The bad men are either stealing or killing and those who are not bad have shut themselves inside their houses.'

Horace Morgan was not happy at being dictated to by this low caste Indian, but he had no alternative but to trust him. The man proved himself loyal on three separate occasions on the way to his home. Twice when they met up with excited mutineers Morgan was forced to hide in deep doorways while Jumna distracted them and on a third occasion he hid in a hole in a broken wall while the aged gardener stood in front of it, hiding him with the folds of his robe.

Only Jumna's obvious advanced years and feigned infirmity prevented the rioters from insisting that he prove his allegiance to their cause by joining them. When they had gone out of sight Jumna led Morgan the remaining distance to the small home he shared with his equally aged wife.

The house was one of many built by the East India Company for its semi-senior employees many years before. It had fallen into disrepair but it had a small, low roof-space and it was here that Horace Morgan was hidden, safely out of sight.

III

Unable to sleep that night, or for many nights that followed, Horace Morgan lay awake in the roof space, listening to the constant sound of cannon and musket fire reaching him from the direction of the besieged barrack area, and agonizing over the possible fate of his family. He was aware that conditions inside the heavily overcrowded entrenchment must be unbearable.

His unlikely hosts were not immune from the attentions of the roving mob, who were eager to find more victims. It was known that Jumna was an East India Company employee and more than once he was visited by gangs of the rioters. Only his obvious poverty and the advanced years of himself and his wife deterred them from dragging him out and killing him.

However, their sudden and unannounced attentions meant that Morgan was unable to leave his cramped and dark hiding-place for even a few minutes. As a result his sanitary arrangements were of necessity primitive in the extreme and ablutions non-existent.

Fortunately, he was able to provide the elderly couple with more money than they had ever known before and using this they ate well and provided him with all the food he needed.

For two and a half long and uncomfortable weeks Horace Morgan hid in Jumna's home in the hope that either the siege of the entrenchment would come to an end or Cawnpore be relieved by a British army column which, so Jumna told him, was rumoured to be on its way.

By this time all three occupants of the tiny house were feeling the strain and Horace Morgan was beginning to have hallucinations, constantly fearful at any unexplained noise, birds that settled on the roof above him providing more than one alarm.

Then, one night, the sound of gunfire ceased. The unaccustomed silence that followed seemed somehow even more menacing than the constant noise of the bombardment and, deeply concerned, he called down to his hosts, asking what was happening at the entrenchment. Were the mutineers calling off their siege ... or had those within finally been subdued?

Jumna did not know but left the small house immediately to find out from the bazaar what interpretation was being put on the latest unexpected development.

When he returned, the old man carried news that filled Horace

Morgan with a hope that had been absent from his thinking for all the long hours of his unnatural confinement. The bazaar was buzzing with the news that Nana Sahib had sent one of the number of captive European women he was holding hostage to the entrenchment with a letter for General Wheeler. The missive offered terms for his surrender, promising safe passage for all those who had survived the weeks of constant bombardment and attack.

Jumna did not share Morgan's jubilation. Shaking his head, he said, 'There was a time when if Nana Sahib gave his word it was as though Krishna himself had spoken. That is no longer so. Today Nana Sahib speaks not with his own voice but with the voice of those who are guided by hatred and not honesty.'

'What do you mean…?' Horace Morgan ceased talking as a party of men could be heard passing by the door. When their sound had disappeared, he asked, hoarsely, 'Do you believe he is planning some treachery?'

'That is what is believed in the bazaar.'

'But … someone must warn General Wheeler.'

'Would you care to try, *sahib*?'

'I couldn't. I'd be taken by the mutineers long before I could even reach the entrenchment.'

'That is so, *sahib*, it is because you are a European. But if an Indian tried *he* would be killed by Wheeler's soldiers before he could reach them. We must hope General Wheeler is not deceived by what Nana Sahib is offering him.'

Morgan knew Jumna was right, but all that day he lay in the darkness of the roof space thinking of the situation without coming up with any solution, and late that evening he asked Jumna to go back to the bazaar to learn the latest rumours about what was happening.

When the Commissariat gardener returned he brought news that should have been reassuring, but Morgan was still concerned. General Wheeler had not accepted the original terms offered by Nana Sahib, but the two men had reached a compromise. Instead of laying down their arms as had been demanded in his first letter, those in the entrenchment would be allowed to leave carrying both arms and ammunition. Furthermore, transport was to be provided to convey the women to the river where boats stocked with sufficient supplies to carry the entrenchment's survivors downriver to safety would be waiting. The evacuation was to take place in thirty-six hours' time.

For all the day and most of the night before the evacuation was to take place Horace Morgan thought of ways he might possibly join up with those from the entrenchment, to be reunited with his wife and family, and escape downriver with them, but there seemed to be no way it might be achieved.

As Jumna pointed out, it would not be safe for Morgan to go out on his own to try to make his way to the entrenchment. It was still guarded by a tight cordon of sepoys who would kill him if he fell into their hands. The same fate would be suffered by Jumna if he tried to assist him by talking his way through the cordon.

The only solution, Jumna suggested, was to wait until the convoy of boats was on its way then, when night fell, he would guide Morgan, disguised as an Indian, out of Cawnpore to chase after the boats, either on foot, or using a small boat which Jumna would secure for him, using some of the money Morgan possessed. Either way, he should have no difficulty catching up with the convoy of boats. Heavily laden with passengers and provisions they would be unwieldy and slow-moving in the sluggish reduced flow of the river.

It was a scheme that *could* succeed, despite the obvious dangers and for the whole of the next day and night Horace Morgan's excitement grew as time for the evacuation of the entrenchment neared.

IV

Jumna left the house soon after dawn and was gone for more than two hours before he returned to say the evacuation had begun, but he was visibly shaken by what he had seen.

'Your people were approaching the river when I saw them, *sahib*, but many are hurt and all are as dirty as the poorest low caste beggar. There are not enough elephants or carts to carry all the women and children, many of whom have hardly any clothes to cover themselves. It looks as though their dresses and other garments have been torn up to make bandages for others. The people of Cawnpore left their homes to go and jeer them, but most were so shocked by what they saw that they fell silent as they passed by. Not so the sepoys who are escorting them. They are behaving as though they have won a great battle, beating those unable to keep up with the others, mostly the women, and shouting abuse at those who once commanded them … although not many of the officer *sahibs* remain.'

'Do you think you might have seen my wife, Jumna? She is a handsome high caste Hindu woman – with two children, a boy and a girl, both young.'

'I did not stay to watch them for long, *sahib*, my heart was too heavy for what I saw. The ways of your people are not always kind towards mine, but you are proud men and women and it hurt me to see them in such a state and I fear there are many who have not lived to see this day.'

Horace Morgan was silent for a long time before saying, 'Thank you for all you and your wife have done for me, Jumna. I will leave you half the money I have, which should make you a wealthy man. But no amount of money could ever repay you for all you have done. I will leave you tonight and by tomorrow I should have reached the others. God willing, I will find my wife and children with them.'

He had hardly finished talking when there came the sudden boom of cannon-fire. It was followed immediately by the sound of gunfire, sporadic at first but then continuous. There was also the shrill sound of the screaming of women and children and a roar such as might have been heard at a great outdoor event.

'What is it?' Horace Morgan demanded, although he knew there could be little doubt about what was happening.'

'Hide yourself and stay silent, I will go and find out what is happening.'

The sounds Morgan had heard came from the direction of the river and continued for almost an hour while he lay in the roof-space shivering in fright, his imagination running riot. Gradually the sounds died away, with only the occasional gunshot to be heard now. Then Jumna returned to the house and could be heard speaking to his wife.

Showing himself from the safety of the roof-space, Horace Morgan demanded to know what had happened.

When Jumna looked up at him, Horace Morgan was shocked to see tears streaming down his weathered cheeks. 'It was pitiful to see, Sahib Morgan. As I feared, there is no longer any worth in the promises of Nana Sahib. When the last of those to whom he promised safe passage had stepped from the shore to make their way to the boats a cannon opened fire, then many men he had hidden began shooting at them. When I hurried away from the river his men were among your poor people wielding swords to kill all the men and take the women as prisoners. I could watch it no longer.'

'Did any of them get away downriver? Any of the women and children?'

'I could not say. Perhaps … but I do not think so. I am sorry, *sahib* … there was nothing I could do to help them … nothing.'

Horace Morgan left Jumna's house two nights later dressed as an Indian mounted on a horse the Commissariat head gardener had managed to acquire for him, using some of the money taken from the East India Company's safe.

It was a good night on which to leave Cawnpore. Nana Sahib had organized a huge celebration for his soldiers and their many supporters and the town itself was quiet. Morgan intended travelling along the northern bank of the Ganges, but keeping far enough away from the river to avoid the many villages and small fishing communities scattered along its course.

Taking a tortuous route he would head for Allahabad, more than a hundred miles away, where there was a fort and a strong European military presence.

During his years in India and because his work had involved land ownership and management, he had come to know the area in which he worked better than most of his countrymen. This knowledge would stand him in good stead now. He was able to plan his journey through comparatively empty country, spending the nights away from human habitation, preferring to risk the danger posed by the carnivorous animals who lived in such places to that he would have faced in villages touched by the bloody hand of rebellion.

On the third night of his journey he lost his horse during a fierce monsoon storm that was accompanied by thunder and lightning. He had tied it to a tree using its rein, but the frightened horse broke it and galloped away, terrified by the noise of the tempest.

This posed a serious problem for him, but it was not a total disaster. He had been sheltering from the rain beneath an outcrop of rock in thick, jungle country, using his satchel for a pillow and inside the satchel he had the revolver, half the money taken from the commissariat and what remained of the food prepared for him by Jumna's wife.

When morning came he set off heading towards the river with the satchel slung over his shoulder and by noon had come within sight of a small riverside fishing village. There did not appear to be any untoward activity here, but Horace Morgan was taking no chances. Finding himself a hiding place well away from the village and its attendant canine population, he spent the remainder of the day studying the small riverside community.

That night there was more intermittent rain, but between the showers a crescent moon gave him sufficient light to make his way to the village, take one of the small boats left upside-down on the nearby river-bank just outside the village and drag it to the water. There had been a crudely shaped paddle beneath the primitive craft and, climbing on board, he propelled the boat clumsily away from the bank until he felt it taken by the current.

Progress was difficult at first, due mainly to clouds that kept scudding across the moon, preventing him from maintaining his course in the faster-flowing water to be found in the centre of the river and he grounded the boat on more than one occasion. Nevertheless, by the time dawn broke he was well on his way and out of sight of the village where the boat's owner lived.

There must have been a great deal of rain further up the river because before long the boat's speed increased and an almost constant rainfall meant that visibility was poor and the width of the river increased so much that for much of the time the boat would have been invisible from either bank and the few boats travelling the great waterway.

For all that day he continued his journey and at nightfall guided the boat into some rushes. Here, thoroughly exhausted, he slept for a couple of hours despite the rain that hardly ceased.

It was still night when he woke. The rain had mercifully stopped and the moonlight, peeping through wispy, speeding cloud was sufficient for him to see well enough to paddle the boat out of the rushes and back into the main stream of the river.

Morgan had no idea where he was now, but by morning felt he must be fairly close to Allahabad and he began to look for recognizable landmarks on the shore. It was difficult to see for any distance because for the moment the sky had cleared and the midsummer sun shining on rain-soaked ground resulted in a steamy mist that created a surreal effect on the landscape.

Morgan had manoeuvred his boat close to the shore when, suddenly, a party of armed horsemen emerged from the mist and, quickly raising their guns, a number of them fired at him. As bullets struck the boat and plopped into the water around it, Morgan dropped to the bottom of the boat, but before he disappeared from view he had observed that the riders were not *Sowars*, as he had first thought, but Europeans and he realized they were irregular British cavalryman.

'Don't shoot … don't shoot … I'm British!'

It was the first time Morgan had spoken for many days and his voice sounded strange, even to him but he called again … and again.

'Stand up and show yourself,' a voice called out in English and Morgan could sense the doubt in it.

'I'm standing up now … I'm Horace Morgan of the East India Company in Cawnpore – even though I'm wearing Indian clothing.'

Rising to his feet slowly Morgan held his hands aloft, expecting at any moment to receive a bullet from one of the many rifles pointing at him. Then one of the men said, 'Good God! It *is* Horace Morgan. I know him. He must have escaped from Cawnpore….'

V

The party of horsemen turned out to be members of an irregular cavalry troop formed from volunteers at Allahabad and sent ahead of the main body of British troops as scouts by Brigadier Henry Havelock, commanding officer of the relief column, preparing to march on Cawnpore.

The brigadier listened to Horace Morgan's account of the happenings at Cawnpore with dismay … and more than a little scepticism. General Wheeler was the most experienced army officer in India, he would never have allowed himself to be deceived in such a way, especially when he was responsible for the lives of so many women and children. Not until the same information was relayed to him the next day from two separate sources did he accept Morgan's news and send for him to tell him everything he knew about what had happened.

Havelock left Allahabad with his army determined to save the women and children, believed to now number at least 250, held hostage by Nana Sahib in Cawnpore, and he took Morgan with him.

His army marched on Cawnpore at a speed that left behind any man who could not maintain the merciless pace set by the brigadier – and it was a vengeful army. Sepoy deserters or possible mutineers met with along the route were arbitrarily executed and any village found harbouring them was burned to the ground and the men of the village hanged.

Halfway to Cawnpore, two regiments of Nana Sahib's army attacked the brigadier's advance guard, unaware of the size of his main force – and after a fierce battle they were soundly beaten. During the fighting Morgan, still not fully recovered from the ordeal of his escape from Cawnpore, stayed back with the baggage train, clear of the fighting.

There were two more fierce skirmishes along the way and by the time Havelock reached Cawnpore his men were close to exhaustion, but they suddenly encountered a native army almost three times the size of their own. Backed by a great many large calibre cannons they gave the British soldiers no time to rest before engaging them in battle.

It was a close fought and merciless engagement and Horace Morgan and the wounded, sick and non-combatants found themselves fighting off numbers of Nana Sahib's army, desperate to capture the baggage train.

Eventually the day was won by Havelock's army when his Highland Regiment made a wild but determined bayonet charge on Nana Sahib's soldiers urged on by the skirl of bagpipes. Soon, Nana Sahib's army was in full flight and the British Army sank down on the field of battle, totally exhausted.

They entered Cawnpore the next day and Horace Morgan went in with the vanguard, eagerly guiding them to the bungalow where he knew the women and children had been kept … but the sight that met his eyes was the crux of the nightmares that would bring him awake screaming for many years to come.

Not a woman or child of the 250 captives had been left alive. They had been slaughtered without mercy and their bodies thrown into a nearby well until it would take no more. The remaining bodies had been dragged away and hurled into the murky waters of the Ganges.

Evidence of the slaughter was everywhere and Horace was not the only man who was uncontrollably sick at the scene. Thinking of his wife and children who had been among those incarcerated in the house of death, Horace Morgan came close to insanity and the memory of that day would remain with him for ever.

.... This was the nightmare that returned to Horace Morgan during the night spent in the prison cell in the Bodmin police headquarters in Cornwall and, when he woke in the tiny enclosed and darkened space, his cries brought an unsympathetic gaoler to the cell with a warning that if he did not cease making such a noise he would be obliged to come into the cell and use his baton to silence him.

Chapter 27

When Amos reached police headquarters the next morning he was met by a concerned station sergeant who had been anxiously awaiting his arrival.

'That prisoner you and Sergeant Churchyard brought in yesterday evening, sir, I'm worried about him.'

'Horace Morgan? Why, what's he done?'

'I'm not altogether sure, but when I went to look at him when I came on duty this morning I found him sitting on the edge of his bunk, shaking like a leaf and sweating as though he'd just been in a prize-fight. I've kept an eye on him and when I last went down to the cells he looked so ill that I was about to send for a doctor when Sergeant Churchyard came in. He's down in the cell with him now.'

When Amos arrived at the basement cell where Morgan had spent the night he found Tom seated beside the Trelyn estate steward on the hard wooden ledge that served both as seat and bed.

Morgan had gained some control over himself now but as Amos entered the cell he began shaking uncontrollably and only ceased when Tom gripped his arm in a sympathetic gesture.

When the trembling had stopped, Amos asked, 'What's wrong with him?'

'He's had a nightmare about his time in India,' Tom replied, 'He says it's something that happens quite often, but the one he had last night was particularly bad, brought about by being shut up in the dark in a windowless cell. It seems it brought back memories of a similar situation he was in during the mutiny out there.'

Morgan had begun trembling once again while Tom was speaking and Amos said, 'Bring him up to my office, it's brighter up there. I'll have some tea brought up for him – although he looks as though he's in need of something stronger.'

Once in the office Morgan asked shakily if he might have the pipe and tobacco that had been taken from him when he was placed in the cell. Amos agreed and Tom went to fetch it.

After a few minutes spent puffing at his pipe and looking out of the office window at a rookery in the nearby trees, Morgan appeared to relax and gain control of himself once more, although he was still looking drawn and haggard when Amos said to him, 'Do you mind telling me what that was all about, Mr Morgan?' Amos and Tom had agreed the night before that Morgan should not be told that his wife and children were alive and well in India until they were satisfied he either had, or had not been informed of the fact.

The estate steward's thoughts had been far away but now, after breathing deeply a few times he gathered his wits together and said, 'For almost three weeks during the mutiny in India I was hiding in a dark roof space in a native's hut after seeing many of my colleagues murdered, all the while listening to the sound of mutineers' guns pounding the entrenchment where all the Europeans – men, women and children – were desperately striving to survive. Then ...' Here he choked on his words before gaining some control once more and continuing in a barely audible voice, '… Then they were all taken out and butchered.'

Morgan ceased talking abruptly and Amos said, 'We already know a great deal about your life in India, Mr Morgan, including the fact you were married and had two children there – something that you seem to have kept secret from everyone here. Suppose you tell Sergeant Churchyard and me something of your life there and *exactly* what this recurring nightmare is all about….'

Horace Morgan seemed about to dispute what Amos had said to him, but then his shoulders sagged and after a number of false starts and more than one break in the narrative when it appeared he might break down completely, Horace Morgan told his story. It went on for almost half an hour during which time both policemen listened in silent horror, occasionally exchanging sympathetic glances, and looking down at the floor when he was reduced to tears when talking about the massacre of the women and children at the bungalow, carried out on Nana Sahib's orders.

Both policemen felt deeply sorry for all that Morgan had suffered in India, but this was a murder inquiry and it had become evident that Horace Morgan was no stranger to violence and murder. There was also a very strong motive for killing Kerensa if he had been made aware that his Indian wife had *not* died in the massacre at Cawnpore. This remained the key factor in their questioning of him.

'Your last weeks in India must have been horrific, Mr Morgan.' The observation was made by Tom. 'It is little wonder you have nightmares about it even now.'

'They are *worse* than nightmares,' Morgan declared, fiercely. 'When they come I relive everything all over again. There are times – many times – when I have wished I died with my family out there.'

'But you had Kerensa and baby Albert,' Tom pointed out. 'Didn't they bring some happiness back into your life?'

Horace Morgan seemed to be struggling with his thoughts and feelings, then his shoulders sagged again and with resignation in his voice he said, 'Albert made me very happy, at least, at first he did. It's difficult not to be happy when there's a baby in your life.'

When he fell silent once more, Amos prompted him, 'You say he made you happy "at first", what happened to change it?'

Now Horace Morgan had told the two policemen about his experiences in India, it seemed he intended holding nothing back. 'I suppose when Kerensa said she would marry me I felt flattered. She is, or was, half my age but I let myself believe she loved me. I soon learned there was very little love for anyone in her make up. I knew nothing about the type of girl she was when I married her, but to be perfectly honest it wouldn't have mattered very much anyway if she hadn't thrown her past life up in my face whenever we had an argument – and our marriage was never short of those. It soon became clear she'd only married me to give herself some respectability, but she found respectability boring and began having affairs. This wouldn't have mattered too much either if she'd been discreet about it and been a good wife in other ways, but that was too much for her.'

Morgan paused again and when he felt the silence had lasted for too long, Amos asked, 'What did you do when you learned about these affairs?'

'I lost my temper one day when she bragged about them to me. It was the only time I did so, mind. To be perfectly honest I struck her. It made her cry and that hurt *me* so much I think I'd have forgiven her anything. I swore I wouldn't ever hit her again, and I never did.'

'When she was bragging about these affairs did she ever lead you to believe you might not have been Albert's father?'

The question took Morgan by surprise and he looked at Amos sharply, but when he replied it was with a curt, 'Yes.'

'That would have been enough to make most men feel they wanted to murder their wife!' Tom said sceptically 'Are you telling us you never felt that way?'

'To tell you the truth, I don't know how I felt. I didn't really believe her. When she became really angry she would say the first thing that came into her head, whether it was true or not.'

'Did she say anything about who the father of Albert could be if it wasn't you?'

With the shift of the questioning away from his past life in India Horace Morgan seemed to have regained control of himself and now he said, 'I think I've told you more than enough about my personal life with Kerensa. I never had anything to do with her death because I saw more violence in India than anyone should witness in a lifetime and I never expected it to follow me to England. No matter what Kerensa did I would never have done anything like that to her – and I would never ever have harmed baby Albert. That's the truth, I swear to it. All I'd like to do now is go back to Trelyn and try to pick up the pieces of my life as much as I can.'

'Are you still in touch with the East India Company, Mr Morgan?' Amos put the question.

'Not really, although I've had two letters from them since I came to Trelyn. Once to acknowledge the change of address I gave them and the second time three or four months ago asking me to confirm that I was still alive. That's because I have a pension paid by them into a London bank.'

'You've heard nothing else from anyone there?'

'No, why should I? I'm an *ex*-employee now and belong to a part of their history they'd rather forget about.'

'Had it not been for the massacre at Cawnpore would you have still returned to this country, or remained in India?'

'I would probably have stayed in India, but not with the Company. My wife's father was a very rich and important man in Northern India, a younger member of a maharajah's family. He owned a vast amount of land and always said he'd like me to manage it for him.'

'Have you never considered going back there and working for him anyway?'

Horace Morgan shook his head. 'There would be far too many memories. They were very happy ones until the end and there would be far too much to remind me of them every day of my life.'

'What if you were to learn now that your wife and family are still alive? What would you do?'

Horace Morgan's expression of pain could not have appeared more genuine had Amos struck him a physical blow and he said, 'That is a cruel thing to say at a time like this, Superintendent. I think I would like to return to Trelyn Hall now. Indeed, I can think of nothing you have said that is sufficient reason for bringing me here in the first place. Certainly nothing that couldn't have been said at Trelyn and saved me from suffering the torture I went through last night.'

Instead of replying, Amos took Verity Pendleton's letter from the file that was on the desk in front of him and handed it to Morgan.

'I think you should read this, Mr Morgan. It will give you a great deal to think about, as it did me, but for very different reasons. It should also satisfy you that I did have cause to bring you here to Bodmin for questioning.'

Horace Morgan was puzzled, but he took the letter and, after glancing at the address on the envelope, opened it. Verity's letter had been removed and only the copy of Shabnam Morgan's letter to the Honourable East India Company was enclosed. He was about to say something to Amos, but he was actually reading the first line when his mouth opened – and it remained wordlessly open as he continued reading.

Amos and Tom exchanged glances frequently while Morgan's face expressed a kaleidoscope of differing emotions as he read and both policemen arrived at the same conclusion without a word being spoken between them. They had considerable experience of interviewing criminals who had something to hide and if Horace Morgan had known the contents of the letter before today then he was a remarkable actor.

When he came to the end of the letter, Morgan returned to the beginning and, turning the pages, re-read some of the passages again. When he did look up there were tears in his eyes and a look of utter bewilderment on his face. 'When...? Where...? How did you come by this? Is it true? Is it *really* true? You're not just playing a cruel hoax on me?'

'It's true.'

'Then why haven't I seen it before? Who kept it from me ... and why?'

'It was turned up when I asked someone to make enquiries with the East India Company about your time in India. If you *really* knew nothing about the letter until today, it makes wonderful news for you and I can assure you nobody will be more delighted than Sergeant Churchyard and me. However, if we find the letter *was* sent to you then you are a very strong murder suspect indeed, especially as there is a rumour going around that you are not the true father of baby Albert. If it could be proved the rumours reached your ears there's not a jury in the land would find you "not guilty", however much they might sympathize with you.'

'But I've never seen the letter before! Had I done so do you think I would still be in this country ... or would ever have married Kerensa? Why *was* the letter never sent on to me?'

'I'm told it was addressed to the East India Company offices in London and that the clerk who dealt with correspondence was an alcoholic who failed to keep proper records. When he was dismissed, and someone was put in to clear up the mess he'd left behind, the letter was found, but it was assumed you'd been notified of the information it contained.'

'If only I'd known before I left India ... but after seeing the carnage around the bungalow where the women and children had been slaughtered ... and the well choked to the top with their bodies, I was told there had been no survivors. Oh God! How I've suffered all these years thinking they were dead and of the manner in which they died...!'

At this point Horace Morgan broke down in tears and, bowing his head and covering his face with his hands he wept noisily, much to the sympathetic embarrassment of the two policemen in the room with him.

It was a long time before he regained control of himself but every so often he sucked in a deep breath of air and his body shook with an uncontrollable sob.

'How long ago was the letter received?' he asked, eventually.

'I can't be certain, but from all I've learned it would be no more than six months and probably much less than that.'

'All those wasted years! I must let them know *I'm* alive … and get back to India as soon as I can.'

'I am confident you'll be allowed to go back there, Mr Morgan and that you knew nothing of the letter before today, but I can't allow you to leave the country right away. Do you have any idea where your family might be staying?'

'Shabnam will have taken the children to the family home near Simla, in Northern India. As I told you, she belongs to a royal family which rules one of the smaller states there.'

'If you write a letter informing your wife that you are alive and well and will be travelling to India as soon as is possible, I will send it off to London with a covering letter and ensure it's delivered to her through the Viceroy's office.'

Once again the news he had just received overwhelmed Horace Morgan. He was no longer the arrogant, overbearing man whom Amos and Tom had met at Trelyn when they had paid their first visit there and was almost timid in his manner when he asked, 'What happens to me now?'

'You are free to go, Mr Morgan. When you have written your letter to your wife give it to Sergeant Dreadon at Trelyn for urgent delivery to me and I'll see that it goes to India in a diplomatic bag from London. In the meantime remain at Trelyn until my murder investigation is completed – but there is no need to say anything to anyone about your interview here.'

'Thank you.'

Rising to his feet, Horace Morgan said, 'I owe you a debt I can never repay, Superintendent. Had it not been for you I might never have learned that my wife and family survived the massacre at Cawnpore.'

'I need no repayment, Mr Morgan, but if you think of anything that might help in my murder inquiry here, please let me know.'

Horace Morgan looked at Amos without speaking for a few minutes then, apparently making up his mind, he said, 'You asked me whether Kerensa had ever suggested to me that I might not be the father of baby Albert, but I never told you *exactly* what it was she said to me. In fact, during one of our arguments she *did* claim someone else was his father. She even told me where he was conceived: in the empty gamekeeper's house by the fish-ponds on the Trelyn Estate, she said.'

Both policemen were immediately interested and Amos asked, 'Who did she name ... one of the gamekeepers?'

'No. She said it was Colonel Trethewy.'

Chapter 28

'THERE IS NOTHING at all that can be done about it unless you can substantiate what Morgan told you, Amos.'

Amos was in the chief constable's office later that morning, having repeated to the police chief what Horace Morgan had told him.

'Even if it *is* true, Colonel Trethewy has broken no law … I assume there is no suggestion that Mrs Morgan was not a consenting party?'

'None at all, and even if there was the defence could call a whole army of men to give evidence of her promiscuity.'

'That is what I thought. We will keep the information to ourselves for the time being, but it does add Colonel Trethewy to your list of suspects.'

'It does, but although Morgan must remain on the list too, both Sergeant Churchyard and I are convinced he never received word that his Indian family survived the troubles they had there. If we are right it takes away the strongest motive he had for wanting to rid himself of his English wife.'

'Is there a chance we could charge him with bigamy?'

Amos shook his head, 'He genuinely believed he had lost his Indian wife and family and no jury listening to his story would ever convict him. Besides, it was in all probability a Hindu wedding and I am not at all certain that would be considered as binding in this country. Even if it was, we would have an impossible task obtaining the necessary documents to prove our case. Quite frankly I think he has already suffered far more than any man should, his is a harrowing story.'

'I will take your word for that, Amos – oh, by the way, will you pass on a "very well done" to Sergeant Churchyard for me? I have had a personal letter from the chief constable of Wiltshire asking me to thank Churchyard for the help given to his daughter when they met in Wiltshire. He says she is delighted with the girl Churchyard recommended to her. He also mentions in his letter that she is coming back this way to make some recommendations for a hospital to be built in Plymouth, so no doubt she will be visiting you and your wife.'

'I hope so, she is a very pleasant woman who has been a great help to us.'

Confirmation of Verity's proposed visit was not long in coming. There was a letter from her waiting for Amos when he arrived home that very evening. Addressed to both him and Talwyn, in it she confirmed what her stepfather had written to the Cornwall chief constable and said she would be in Plymouth for a full week. Apologizing for giving them such short notice, she asked if she might visit them for a day during the coming weekend, which was merely two days away. She explained she felt she could not possibly be so close to their home without visiting them, but that this was the only time she would have free during her stay in Plymouth.

Talwyn told Amos she had already replied, inviting Verity to stay with them for the whole weekend and she suggested to Amos that they invite Tom to have lunch with them on the Sunday.

Amos agreed, but he could not resist adding a wry comment about her all-too-obvious attempt at match-making having little chance of success.

Verity arrived by a morning train from Plymouth and was met by Tom at the Bodmin Road railway station. Despite his disparaging remarks about 'match-making', Amos had asked Tom to take a horse-drawn wagonette from the police headquarters to bring Verity to the Hawke home.

Verity was delighted to see him and, seated beside him, was smiling happily as they drove away from the station – and here they passed Colonel Trethewy, who was being driven to the station in a similar vehicle but had arrived late to meet a relative who had been on the same train as Verity.

The Trelyn landowner recognized Tom but did not return his polite nod of acknowledgement as the two vehicles passed each other. Tom did not look back at him but Verity did.

'Isn't that Colonel Trethewy from Trelyn?'

'Yes.'

'He is still watching us and has an expression as black as thunder! Have you or Amos done anything to upset him?'

Tom gave her a weak smile, 'I think Colonel Trethewy is permanently upset with us, but yes, we had Horace Morgan in the Bodmin police station overnight this week and the colonel was not at all happy about it. Actually, had Amos and I known the full story of all Morgan had been through in India we would never have subjected him to a night in a dark cell. He had a frightening nightmare and broke down completely when we showed him your letter.'

'Oh dear, poor man … but did you learn whether he knew his Indian wife and family are still alive?'

'I don't believe he did and Amos agrees. It came as a great shock to him. Even so, he was embarrassingly grateful to us – and to you – for giving him the news. He has written a letter to his wife there and Amos has had it sent to her through diplomatic channels. Morgan intends returning to India as soon as we find the killer of Kerensa and the others.'

'So he is no longer a suspect?'

'He has to remain a suspect until we have found evidence implicating someone else, but I really don't believe he is the murderer. Nevertheless, he has been able to help us in a way that we would never have considered had your letter not persuaded him to open up to us in the way he did.'

'I am pleased I was able to be of assistance to you, but how is the investigation progressing … and how is your young gypsy girl?'

Tom brought Verity up-to-date on where and what Zillah was doing but admitted he had not seen her for some days.

'That's a pity. I was hoping I might have an opportunity to meet her while I was here. I have been thinking of her rather a lot in recent weeks because I have a feeling she is a quite exceptional girl. It is probably because I think you have a good eye for someone out of the ordinary. You certainly recognized the potential in Millie Farmer. She is not only extremely intelligent and possessing more than her share of common sense, but she is also quick to learn.'

'I'm pleased. Her father will be too, he was very concerned in case he was committing his daughter to a life of sin by allowing her to go off and be a nurse.'

'He has nothing at all to worry about. Millie is a very moral girl and I really don't know how I could manage without her now. She has already lifted a great deal of work from my shoulders, whilst at the same time learning many of the nursing skills that have older women struggling. I am truly grateful to you for finding her for me, Tom.'

Chapter 29

VERITY'S WISH TO meet with Zillah was unexpectedly fulfilled the following day when the young gypsy girl paid an unprecedented visit to the Bodmin Police headquarters in search of Tom, riding from Gassick Farm in her usual manner, with no saddle and mounted on the pony she had broken in herself.

It was a Sunday and when she had convinced the sergeant in charge of the duty office that she was known to Tom and had some important information for him – and him alone – he directed her to the local church where one of the constables had reported seeing him attending the morning service with Superintendent and Mrs Hawke and their guest.

The service was over by the time she arrived, but the vicar was standing outside the church chatting to one of his churchwardens. Whilst not telling this rather wild gypsy where they actually lived, he was able to direct her to the road along which they would be travelling on their way to the Hawke home, adding in a disapproving manner that she would no doubt be able to catch up with them, riding as she was in such an unorthodox and unladylike manner.

Putting her mount into a brisk canter she soon sighted the party ahead of her, Tom driving with Amos beside him, while the two women were seated in the back of the wagonette.

It was Verity who first saw the rider rapidly catching up with them and called out to the men. 'We are being pursued by what appears to be a rather wild-looking girl on a horse. I suppose it couldn't be your gypsy girl, Tom?'

'I doubt—' Looking over his shoulder as he spoke, he broke off suddenly. 'It *is* her … it's Zillah!'

Hauling back on the reins he brought the horse and wagonette to a halt as Zillah reached them. 'Zillah, what are you doing off the moor, has something happened?'

After a quick glance at the two women in the vehicle who were looking at her with great interest, Zillah addressed Tom. 'I don't know if it's something you'd rather we spoke of in private. It's about the shawl I made for baby Albert.'

Both Amos and Tom were immediately interested and Amos said quickly, 'Everyone here knows about the case, Zillah.' Pointing to each of the women in the wagonette in turn, he said, 'This is Verity Pendleton who has been able to help us by gathering information from outside the county, and this is Talwyn, my wife … but, of course, if you have some *new* information for us it might be better if we discussed it in private.'

'Why don't you come home with us, Zillah?' Talwyn suggested. 'You can stay and have some lunch with us.'

Both women in the wagonette were dressed for church, while Zillah was her usual self, bareheaded and shoeless with the hem of her dress rising above her knees as a result of her unladylike riding position.

'I'm not dressed to go into anyone's house,' Zillah replied, making it a statement of fact and not an apology, 'and I need to return to Gassick for grandma.'

'What a pity,' Verity said, 'and you are the only one of us sensible enough to come out dressed for the weather. I can't wait to get back to Amos and Talwyn's home and take some of this off.'

'Verity is quite right,' Talwyn said, 'but at least come to the house, Zillah. I am so sorry about your father but I know how determined Amos and Tom are to catch whoever is responsible. They have both mentioned you so often I feel as though I know you myself and I've been longing to meet you.'

When Zillah looked uncertainly at Tom, he mouthed the word '*please*' soundlessly and, nodding her head in Talwyn's direction, she said, 'All right, you ride on and I'll follow … but I won't be able to stop for too long.'

'Splendid! Wouldn't you rather ride with us in the wagonette, Zillah, then we could chat as we go along?'

Shaking her head, Zillah said, 'The pony wouldn't let anyone else ride her and she'd play up and probably break free or hurt herself if she was tied behind a moving cart.'

Accepting her explanation, the party set off with Zillah either riding behind them or alongside, as the road allowed. When the Hawke home was reached and Zillah dismounted but hung back, Verity was particularly attentive to her, commenting on a scar that was barely visible on the gypsy girl's bare arm. Zillah explained that it had been caused by a fall from a moving caravan, when she was a small girl.

'Who treated it for you?' she asked.

'My Dado, he was very good at treating injuries of both animals and people.'

'He made an excellent job of it, Zillah, most people having a cut of that length and obvious depth would have been left with an ugly scar for life. Yours can hardly be seen. I wish I had been able to meet him and learn his secret.'

Praise of her late father made Zillah more at ease with them and when Verity went on to praise the sketches Zillah had given to Tom it opened up conversation between them even more,. However, when the gypsy girl entered the house and saw the comparative opulence of its furnishings compared with anything she had known she fell silent once more.

This time it was Tom who came to her rescue by bringing up the subject of the shawl.

'You said you had some information for us about the shawl, Zillah, is there something else you remember about it that might make it even easier for us to recognize?'

'It's more than that, Tom, I've seen it!'

There was a sharp intake of breath from everyone in the room; and, much to the frustration of Talwyn and Verity, Amos said, 'This could be very important news indeed, Zillah. I think we should go outside to the garden and you can tell Sergeant Churchyard and me all about it.'

Both Verity and Talwyn were familiar with police investigations and aware that if Zillah's information was of a sensitive nature it should not be discussed in the presence of anyone not actually involved in the case. Although deeply curious about what she had to tell, they curbed their curiosity, knowing Amos would tell them in due course, if at all possible.

When the men and Zillah had left the room, Verity said, 'What a very pretty girl ... and intelligent too. It is hardly surprising Tom is so smitten with her.'

Grimacing, Talwyn said, 'Unfortunately there can be no future in it for either of them. Tom is very well thought of in the Cornwall Constabulary but the chief constable would never allow one of his men to marry a gypsy, or even a half-gypsy, as Zillah is. She would be a pariah among her own people too if she became involved with a policeman.'

'What a sad world we live in, Talwyn. I thought that last night when Amos was telling us about that poor man whose wife was murdered. His Indian wife was quite obviously born into a rich and influential family, yet she would never have been accepted by any of the Europeans with whom her husband worked. I learned this lesson when *I* was working in India and had some extremely intelligent Indian girls nursing my patients there. I found it very frustrating at times ... but I must not bore you with my thoughts on such matters. When I last stayed with you I saw some sketches made by Zillah, does Amos still have them in his office, or have they been returned to her?'

'Neither, he brought them home because he doesn't want to risk having them mislaid at police headquarters.'

'Oh good! May I see them again, please? I was talking about them to an artist friend of mine in London ... a woman artist, no less, and one who is very well thought of in the London art world. She thought it fascinating that a gypsy girl should show such talent without having had any formal training. I would like to be assured I was not deluding myself by praising the sketches to her.'

'I don't think you were, I am very impressed with them too. I'll go and fetch them now and we'll look at them together while the men are outside talking to Zillah.'

Chapter 30

IN THE GARDEN the two policemen sat at the rustic table with Zillah, and Amos came straight to the point. 'I appreciate you coming here to tell us about the shawl, Zillah, tell us exactly where it is you've seen it.'

'Well, the people in the villages on our side of the moor have known for a year or two that I do crochet work and Dado sometimes sold my work to them. One of the ladies in North Hill had ordered a shawl for herself and I finished it this week, so took it to her yesterday. She was very pleased with it and after she had paid me and I was leaving her house we were talking at the garden gate when a woman came by with a number of small children with her and a baby in her arms. The baby was wrapped in a shawl that was much better than the scruffy clothes the rest of the children were wearing … and I thought I recognized it. I didn't know the woman and she wanted nothing to do with me at first, but I said I would like to see the baby and give it a Romany blessing and when she eventually let me hold the baby's hand I was able to have a close look at the shawl. There's no doubt about it at all … it's the one I made for Kerensa Morgan's baby!'

'Are you *absolutely* certain, Zillah?' Amos was excited by her news, but her information was so important he needed reassurance. 'Certain enough to stand up in a courtroom and swear to it?'

'Nobody said anything about a courtroom to me....'

'It shouldn't come to that,' Tom said quickly, 'You've positively identified the shawl and we should be able to take it from there, but did you learn the name of the baby's mother?'

'Yes, the woman I'd delivered the new shawl to told me. Her name is Martha Kendall. She's married to a miner and lives near North Hill, at Berriow Bridge and has a new baby boy.'

'Did she tell you how she came by the shawl? Was it given to her by her husband.' Amos asked the questions eagerly. George Kendall had been the number one suspect until his fellow miners had given him an alibi. This could prove they had lied and at the same time establish Kendall's guilt.

'I didn't ask, I thought you would want to put any questions to her. If I'd asked questions about it and she knew where it had come from she might have destroyed it, then you would have only had my word that it was the shawl I made for Kerensa Morgan's baby. The word of a gypsy girl wouldn't mean very much ... especially in a courtroom.'

'You did exactly the right thing,' Amos said, gratefully. 'It's a pity it's a bit late in the day to get to Berriow Bridge and back before nightfall, but there's nothing likely to happen to the evidence between now and tomorrow. We'll call on the Kendalls first thing in the morning. This is the most important piece of information we've had since we began this investigation. Now, thanks to you it could lead us straight to the killer of your father.'

Turning to Tom, Amos said, 'Although George Kendall was given an alibi by his workmates, you said at the time that miners are notorious for protecting their own, especially when police are involved.'

'I hope it *does* lead you to the killer,' Zillah said fiercely. 'If it does I'll feel I've done something right by the Romany code that Dado would have approved of. If someone does a wrong to you or your family it's necessary to avenge it. When Dado's murderer is hanged he'll be able to rest in peace. I'll go back to the farm now, but will you come and tell me when you've caught the man, Tom?

Amos had seen Tom's expression of disappointment when Zillah announced her intention of leaving and although he believed a romance between them could lead nowhere, he said quickly, 'Of course he will, Zillah, and I hope it will be soon, but don't leave us just yet, you've had a long ride. Come back inside the house and have something to drink at least, or, if you prefer you can stay out here talking to Tom while I fetch the others and have something brought out here for us all. I don't suppose there will be many more fine days left to us this summer, we might as well make the most of them while we can.'

When Zillah hesitated, Tom pleaded, 'Please stay, if only for a while.'

Giving Tom a look that made it clear it was *his* plea that had persuaded her, she said, 'All right, but I can only stay for a short while. My grandma isn't very well these days and I don't like leaving her on her own for too long.'

Leaving them together in the garden and going back inside the house, Amos could not help feeling perturbed by the obvious mutual attraction between Tom and Zillah. Their paths through life were so diverse he was convinced there could be no happy ending to their relationship. Nevertheless, when he entered the room where Talwyn and Verity were seated looking at the gypsy girl's sketches, he said, 'I've said we will all have something to drink together outside at the garden table. Zillah was reluctant to stay at all but Tom persuaded her. I felt she would feel more at ease out there. She and Tom are chatting together at the moment, we'll give them a few minutes to themselves before going out to join them.'

'You're a hopeless romantic, Amos, even though, like you, I don't believe anything can come of it.'

The scepticism came from Talwyn but Verity contradicted her immediately. 'Why not? Tom is honest and sensible enough to see the problems they are likely to face ... and after looking at her sketches I would say Zillah is no ordinary gypsy girl. She has a very real talent and it is something I would like to discuss with her ... but it can wait for a few minutes.'

In the garden there were a few moments of awkward silence between them before Tom asked, 'How are things up on the moor at Gassick Farm, Zillah?'

'Not too well at the moment and I can't see them getting any better. As you know, my grandma isn't too well and can't do very much about the farm. She's spent a lifetime up there on the moor and I think the dampness has got into her bones. Some days her rheumatics are so bad she can hardly stand. She keeps talking of giving up the farm and she'll need to do it one day soon.'

'What will happen if she does, where will you go?' Tom was genuinely concerned.

'She talks of going to live with a widowed sister who lives down on the south coast, somewhere near Penzance, it's warmer and drier down there. As for me ... who knows? Grandma says that when she sells the farm half the money she gets for it will be mine. It should keep me going until I decide what to do. I might take to the road again.'

Tom's dismay was evident, 'You can't do that, Zillah, a young girl travelling on her own in a wagon wouldn't be safe.'

'Well, I don't have to think about it immediately, although Grandma's already got someone interested in buying Gassick. He's a farmer who has a very large place on the edge of the moor and wants to buy somewhere on the moor to give him summer grazing. He has a son who wants to stay working with him but who has married and wants a place of his own. Gassick Farm would be ideal, not only does it have its own enclosed land but also has moorland grazing rights. Grandma would get a good price for it.'

'That's fine for your grandma but it leaves you unsettled – and I really don't think life on the road in a wagon is an answer.'

At that moment Amos and the two women emerged from the house, Amos and Talwyn carrying trays on which were tea and a jug of cordial, while Verity was holding the file containing Zillah's sketches – and putting these down on the table and seating herself, Verity was the first to speak.

'You're looking worried, Tom, is something troubling you?'

'Yes, Zillah has just said her grandmother is becoming too old for life on a moorland farm and is thinking of selling up and moving off the moor to live with her sister on the coast near Penzance. If that happens Zillah says she might go on the road with her wagon ... by herself. I've said I don't think it's a very good idea.'

'I agree,' Amos said, vehemently. 'A young girl travelling on her own in such circumstances would be a target for any predatory man – or men – and I'm afraid there's no shortage of them about.'

It seemed Zillah was inclined to argue, but she was forestalled by Verity. 'Can I say something that might – but I say only *might* – provide a solution?' Without waiting for a reply she said, 'Is there anything you particularly enjoy doing, Zillah, I mean *really* enjoy? Something that if you were told you could spend the whole of your day doing it would be your idea of heaven?'

'You have the answer right there before you on the table. I'm never happier than when I'm drawing or painting something, but I don't get much time for it at Gassick.'

'I thought … indeed, I *hoped* you might say something like that. When I look at your sketches I see something produced by an artist who not only has a very rare and real talent, but who truly loves the work she puts into it. I have an artist friend, a woman artist, who first had her work exhibited in the Royal Academy in London when she was only seventeen. She is still only a little more than thirty but has already attracted the attention of Queen Victoria and her work is rapidly being acknowledged in the capitals of the civilized world. She recently paid a visit to artist friends here in West Cornwall and was so impressed by what she saw that she has taken a studio close to them and intends moving in to it in the very near future. I would like to take some of your work back to London to show her, Zillah. If she sees the talent *I* believe you possess I am confident she would take you on as a pupil. It would not be far from your grandmother and you would still be in Cornwall. Of course, I can make no promises, but is it something you might consider?'

The suggestion left Zillah speechless and Verity added, 'You don't have to give me a reply right away, Zillah, think about it and let Tom know. He will be able to contact me through Talwyn … but *may* I take some sketches with me? I will ensure they are returned to you in due course.'

'Of *course* … and if your friend thinks I am good enough to become a real artist I have no need to think about it. It's something I've dreamed about for as long as I can remember, but that's all I ever thought it would be … a dream!'

Then, struck by a sudden thought, she said, 'But would the money I get from my grandma when she sells the farm be enough to keep me … and pay your friend for teaching me?'

Verity smiled. 'There will be no need for you to worry yourself about that, Zillah. If my friend thinks as I do, that you have talent, I will become your patron. In exchange for the occasional piece of your work I will support you until you are able to earn a living from it.'

Her expression one of disbelief, Zillah looked from Verity to Tom and back again before saying, 'But we have only just met for the first time, why should you want to do this for me?'

'It may be the first time we have spoken, Zillah, but I saw your sketches when I was last in Cornwall and believe you will one day become a very well-known artist indeed. When you do I will not only have the very real satisfaction of knowing I helped you along the way, but will probably have enough of your work to more than cover my expenditure if ever I decide to sell them. So, you see, not only will I be doing something to bring pleasure to myself and others, but I will have made a sound business investment.'

'Thank you very, very much…!' Turning to Tom, she added, 'And thank you too, Tom … Thank you all.'

Suddenly the tears Tom had witnessed on another occasion appeared in her eyes and she said, 'Dado would have been so very proud….'

Talwyn, used to dealing with upset and emotional pupils put an arm about Zillah's shoulders and said, 'Let's you, me and Verity go into the house for a while. We'll take the sketches with us and you can explain them to us while the men discuss the information you've given to them.'

Chapter 31

WHILE THE DIVERSE dramatic events were taking place at the Hawkes' house, not very far away a more acrimonious meeting was taking place at the home of Chief Constable Gilbert, adjoining the Cornwall police headquarters in Bodmin.

The chief constable had attended the same church service as Amos, Talwyn, Verity and Tom, where they all met and had a brief conversation, before parting and going their separate ways and, when they reached home the Gilberts found Colonel Trethewy waiting for them. The Trelyn landowner wasted no time on social niceties. Ignoring Mrs Gilbert, he launched straight into a verbal tirade directed at the chief constable.

'I want a word with you on a very serious matter, Gilbert ... or, to be more precise on *two* serious matters.'

'If this is police business perhaps you can call on me at my office tomorrow morning. I have a busy day but I will find time to discuss whatever it is that's troubling you.'

'It is very much police business – but also a matter of considerable public concern – and as your officers have called at Trelyn Hall unannounced and disrupted my routine I see no reason why your home should be considered sacrosanct.'

Chief Constable Gilbert could see that Colonel Trethewy had worked himself up into a state of barely contained fury. Turning to his wife, he said, 'You carry on into the house and see that cook has everything prepared for lunch, dear. I will be with you as soon as I have dealt with Colonel Trethewy.'

Glancing unhappily from her husband to the irate landowner, she asked hesitantly, as etiquette demanded, 'Will the colonel be with us for lunch?'

'No,' Gilbert said firmly, 'he will not be staying for lunch and he and I will have our discussion out here. I doubt whether it will take long.'

When she had gone into the house, still troubled, Chief Constable Gilbert said stonily, 'We will walk in the garden to discuss your grievances and, in view of the manner in which you have chosen to air them, I hope they are not of a trivial or imagined nature.'

Pointing along a broad gravel pathway that led between flowering rose bushes, he said, 'We'll go this way, out of hearing from the house.' With this he set off along the path without waiting for his companion.

Catching up with him, Colonel Trethewy said, 'My first complaint is something we have disagreed about before ... the treatment meted out by Superintendent Hawke to Morgan, my estate steward, after Hawke came to my house without prior warning and told Morgan he was to report to him at your headquarters, here in Bodmin. *Told* him, not *requested*, behaving as though he were a commissioned officer addressing a subordinate. As I told you at the time, my advice to Morgan was to ignore the summons but he felt it his duty to come here and learn what Hawke's nonsense was all about and I came with him. Hawke never informed him – or me – what it was all about at the time, instead, they arrested him and threw him into a cell, as though he was a common criminal. It was a disgraceful way to treat a perfectly respectable man and I dread to think what they did to him overnight, he refuses to tell me, but he returned to Trelyn a changed man, quite oblivious to everything going on around him. If he does not improve I will need to dismiss him and Hawke will have cost me a first class land steward.'

When Chief Constable Gilbert made no reply, Colonel Trethewy spluttered angrily, 'Well? Do you have nothing to say in explanation? I can assure you the police committee will be more forthcoming when I lay my complaint before *them* tomorrow.'

'You said you had a second "serious" complaint,' the chief constable said, laconically.

The reply angered Colonel Trethewy even more and he said, 'I intend to complain to the police committee about the waste of the tax-payers' money and the misuse of police property by Hawke's sergeant clerk, Churchyard. I had to go to Bodmin Road railway station yesterday and could hardly believe my eyes when I saw him driving away in the headquarters carriage with a young woman on the seat beside him. He had the impudence to nod a greeting to me as though I was one of his no doubt dubious acquaintances.'

'Sergeant Churchyard would have recognized you, Colonel, he is a very observant policeman … and a good one, probably the best in my force. In fact I had a letter only a couple of days ago from the Chief Constable of the Wiltshire Constabulary, asking me to thank Churchyard for something he had done while he was there on our current murder investigation.'

'Is that all you have to say? Am I to tell the police committee you actually *condone* the unauthorized use of police vehicles?'

'You may tell the committee whatever you wish, Colonel.'

The two men had reached the end of the long garden path now

and were faced by a solid studded gate set into a wall which had guarded an ancient priory that had once existed on the site where the chief constable's house now stood.

Stopping and turning to face his companion, Chief Constable Gilbert said, 'When you saw Sergeant Churchyard he was carrying out my instructions. The young woman with him is the stepdaughter of Wiltshire's Chief Constable, and someone who has provided us with information of great value in our murder investigation. Incidentally, you met her yourself, when she came to Trelyn and spoke to the girls at North Hill school. I detailed Churchyard to take the headquarters wagonette and bring Miss Pendleton from the railway station when I knew she was coming to Bodmin.'

Remembering somewhat uncomfortably that Verity Pendleton was close to the royal court in London, Colonel realized it might be better if he forgot the matter as far as reporting this particular incident to the police committee was concerned, but he had not finished with Chief Constable Gilbert.

'That doesn't explain the state of my estate steward after he was unlawfully detained in a cell overnight.'

'Horace Morgan was helping us with our inquiries into certain aspects of the murder of his wife and child and it was convenient for everyone to lodge him in a cell overnight rather than question him far into the night then send him home. As it happened Morgan proved most helpful ... and I have received no complaint from *him*.'

'All these unnecessary inquiries are a complete waste of police time and tax payers' money, Gilbert. I told Superintendent Hawke at the time the bodies of the gypsy and Morgan's baby were found in the well, that the gypsy was obviously the murderer of both the baby and Morgan's wife. The gypsy threw the baby into the well and accidentally fell in after it. Had all this happened in the days before Parliament forced a constabulary on us I would have explained this to the coroner and that would have closed the book on the matter, leaving the parish constables free to do something useful by stopping gypsies and vagrants coming into Cornwall and causing mayhem.'

'And leaving the actual murderer at large to no doubt kill again,' Chief Constable Gilbert retorted. 'I think the flaw in your conclusion was pointed out to you at the time by Superintendent Hawke and later confirmed by the pathologist. Jed Smith – the gypsy – was murdered, as was Mrs Morgan. The killer was also responsible for the death of the baby, although the circumstances of his death are less clear.'

'All fanciful hogwash!'

'Perhaps I should come along to this meeting and say my piece,' Gilbert said, amiably. 'As we get closer to the murderer our investigations have uncovered a great many unexpected but most interesting facts the committee would undoubtedly find of great interest, implicating as they do one or two men who hold high office in the county, all of whom must be breathing sighs of relief at the death of the unfortunate Mrs Morgan. Even though they might have had nothing to do with her actual death their behaviour, whilst not criminal in the accepted sense, can at best only be described as despicable and dishonourable. Were their names to become known they would find themselves ostracized by their peers and most probably removed from the prestigious offices some hold.'

Colonel Trethewy looked at the chief constable uncertainly. 'What are you talking about? Whose names have been mentioned … and why?'

'Sadly, it is a matter concerning the honour, and morals, of

Horace Morgan's wife and is not something I wish to disclose unless it becomes absolutely necessary and I feel it in the public interest to do so. Tomorrow's meeting of the police committee would perhaps be an appropriate occasion. I could put my information before its members and seek their opinion on how I should deal with it. I have no doubt their discretion could be relied upon to keep my information to themselves, in view of its extremely sensitive nature ... but notes will have to be made by clerks, of course, and they might find it more difficult not to repeat what they have heard. But tell me Colonel, is tomorrow's meeting scheduled, or is it one you are calling simply to air your grievances...?'

Watching from the doorway of his home as Colonel Trethewy rode away a few minutes later, Chief Constable Gilbert felt it was highly unlikely the police committee would be called upon to meet on the following day. He also doubted whether the Trelyn magistrate would be quite so virulent in his denigration of the Cornwall Constabulary in the future.

There was also the possibility that Amos's inquiries might yet reveal that Colonel Trethewy had more to hide than the cuckoldry of his estate steward.

Chief Constable Gilbert entered his house feeling the intrusion into his private life on this Sunday might well mark the beginning of a new and less acrimonious relationship between Colonel Trethewy and the Cornwall Constabulary.

Chapter 32

'IT WAS VERY kind of you to offer Zillah an opportunity to study with your artist friend.' Talwyn made the comment as they stood together at the window of her home. Outside, Zillah stood at the garden gate holding the reins of her horse as she talked to Amos and Tom.

'I would not have made such an offer had I not been convinced of her talent,' Verity replied. 'She has much to learn before she can become a professional artist, but I am very impressed with her and feel my friend will be too. Besides, they will provide support for each other along the way. The world of painters is much more relaxed about having women among their number than possibly any other vocation, but such an attitude is not fully shared by all members of the august academy in London which has the power to make or break an artist, but Zillah impresses me very much.'

'She also impresses Tom,' Talwyn said, as Amos turned away from the other two and made his way back to the house while Tom began to walk along the lane with Zillah, the gypsy girl leading her pony.

Fully aware that senior police officers laid down strict rules about the company kept by their men, even to the extent of giving, or withholding permission for them to marry, approval not being given until full enquiries had been made into the suitability of the future bride, Verity said, 'They make an interesting couple and I rather fancy the chief constable would look more favourably upon one of his officers courting an up-and-coming artist than a gypsy girl.'

Walking along the lane with Zillah, Tom thought she was happier than he had ever known her to be but, of course, the first time they had met she had been concerned for her missing father and until today little had happened to cheer her.

'Do you think Miss Pendleton really will speak to her friend about me and my drawings?'

Despite first names being used by Talwyn when introducing them, Zillah had been slightly in awe of the Hawkes' fashionably dressed and obviously well-bred guest.

'If Verity says she will do something you can rely on it being done. She has been a great help to Amos and me on a couple of occasions.'

'She is a beautiful woman, I am surprised she isn't married.'

'Verity is totally dedicated to her work. She and Miss Nightingale are determined to change the image of nursing … and they seem to be succeeding.'

'Have you known her for very long?'

Tom realized with a thrill that Zillah was surreptitiously trying to sound out whether there was a romantic link between himself and Verity. 'I first met her only a short time ago, when she came to Cornwall in a bid to recruit suitable girls to train as Nightingale nurses. She was staying with Amos and Talwyn then. I agree with you that she's not the type of woman you meet very often, but then I don't move in the same social circles as Verity Pendleton. She has even met Queen Victoria on a couple of occasions I believe. It came about because of the excellent work she did nursing with Miss Nightingale during the Crimean War.'

Zillah knew nothing of either Florence Nightingale or the Crimean War, but she knew about Queen Victoria and was suitably impressed. She was also satisfied that the huge social gulf separating Verity and Tom precluded any romantic link between them.

'Dado would have been proud to know someone else likes my drawings. He always encouraged me to do more of them, saying that one day we would make a lot of money selling them.'

'I'm quite sure you will. I'd be happy to buy one of them from you right now and I don't doubt Amos and Talwyn would too.'

'*You'll* never have to give me money for any of my drawings, Tom, however well I do with them. Even if I become famous one day you'll only have to say you liked one of them and I'll give it to you. If it wasn't for you, Miss Pendleton would never have seen any of my work and I would never have met her.'

'I'm pleased she recognized your talents, Zillah, just as I did the very first time I saw your sketches, when they were with the photographs that were taken at Minions. You ought to paint a self-portrait, most artists do at some time or another. If you did that I would love to have it to keep.'

They walked for a while without speaking before Tom said, 'With Verity as your patron I'm sure you are going to become a very successful artist, Zillah, but I'm glad her artist friend is coming to live in Cornwall. It means you're still going to be here … for a while, anyway. It means I should be able to see you sometimes … if you're not too busy with your new life, of course.'

He added the last sentence hurriedly as she turned her head sharply to look at him but he was delighted when she said, 'I'll never be too busy to see you, no matter where I am, or what I'm doing. You've been kind to me at a time when I desperately needed someone, yet you've never given me a reason – an *honest* reason – why.'

Encouraged by her gratitude, Tom said, 'All the reasons I've given you *have* been honest ones, even if they haven't said everything about the way I feel. If you really want to know, I find myself thinking about you on many occasions when I should be thinking about something else. If I leave the Bodmin police headquarters knowing I am going to meet you I'm as excited as a young boy setting out on a special treat but if I haven't seen you for any length of time I'm thoroughly miserable.'

Zillah was still looking at him and now she said, 'You've never before said anything about the way you really *feel* towards me, only the way you should *behave* towards me because you're a policeman. Why?'

'Because you might have been offended and said you didn't want to see me again. I just didn't want to risk that happening.'

Speaking quietly and seriously, Zillah said, 'I wouldn't have done either of those things, Tom, and I still wouldn't.'

They were out of view from the Hawkes' house now and when he kissed her she responded with a passion that excited and aroused him in a manner he had never before known. It might have continued had the pony she was still holding on a rein not pulled her away in its bid to reach grass on the verge at the side of the lane.

Regretting that the embrace had not lasted longer, Tom said shakily, 'Will I see you again, Zillah … soon?'

'I hope so, Tom. You know where I am living and I never go very far from the farm.'

'I'll make it as soon as I can … and hopefully bring you news on what we will have learned about the shawl.'

Reminding Zillah of her dead father effectively dampened the passion that had been aroused in her and the moment had gone, leaving them both with a feeling of confused embarrassment.

'I'd better be getting back to Gassick now but come and see me there … soon.'

His promise followed her as she rode away and before she passed from his view she turned and waved.

It was a somewhat bemused but light-hearted man who slowly returned along the lane to the Hawkes' home.

With the others, Verity watched him as he ambled towards them, deep in thought and she said, 'Whether or not either of them realize it, those two are very much in love … Zillah for the very first time I should think. I am not at all certain I am doing the right thing by taking her away.'

'You are doing *exactly* the right thing,' Amos replied, 'There can be no future for them the way things are. The chief constable would never agree to allow Tom to marry a gypsy girl. You've given her an opportunity that seldom comes the way of a girl in her situation. When she succeeds, as I believe she will, and becomes a fully recognized artist instead of an orphaned gypsy, the chief constable will think differently. If their love proves strong enough to survive the parting and the change in Zillah's circumstances they could have a very happy future together.'

Chapter 33

AMOS AND TOM set off on horseback from the Bodmin police headquarters soon after dawn the following morning, excited at the thought that this could be the day when they arrested the murderer of Karensa Morgan, baby Albert and Jed Smith.

There had been little opportunity to discuss the full significance of Zillah's information the previous day because after lunch, during which, by mutual consent, the murder case was not discussed, Verity needed to catch a train in order to return to Plymouth. Amos had suggested that Tom should deliver her to the Bodmin Road railway station in the wagonette and after returning the vehicle, take the opportunity to have an early night in order that they might set off together at first light and cross the moor to the Berriow Bridge home of George and Martha Kendall. They would be able to discuss their tactics along the way.

Once clear of the county town the two men were riding side by side when Amos said, 'Zillah is a very observant young girl; if this business of the shawl leads us to the killer I think she should receive some recognition for her part in it.'

'I'm not at all certain she would want that,' Tom replied.

'Helping the police won't make her very popular with the gypsies and if it turns out that George Kendall is our man it means he must have been given a false alibi by the miners he was working with. Any action we decide to take against them for aiding and abetting him would certainly result in a backlash against her by the mining community. The knowledge she has helped bring her father's killer to justice will be enough for her … much as I believe she deserves something more.'

After thinking about what he said, Amos agreed. 'You're probably right and you know her better than I do.' Giving Tom a searching look, he added, 'How well *do* you know her, Tom?'

'Not nearly as well as I would like to, although time could rectify that if I can get to see her occasionally when she has moved down west with this artist friend of Verity, but of course that will only happen if things work out and the friend offers tuition to her.'

'Do you think things could become really serious between the two of you … even as far as marriage?'

'It has crossed my mind but I haven't said anything to her yet, why do you ask?'

'Because if you and Zillah do reach that stage once she's taken up painting seriously, I could arrange for you to be promoted and sent down that way so you would be able to see more of each other.'

'That's a very generous offer, Amos, and I appreciate it, but first let's see what comes of Verity's recommendation to her friend. Right now I suppose we need to work out what we're going to do when we reach Berrow Bridge. Do you think George Kendall will turn out to be our killer?'

'It seems highly likely, Tom. Zillah is absolutely certain the Kendall baby is being wrapped in the shawl she made for baby

Albert, so unless Kendall has a very good story about how he came by it, he's not long for this world.'

George Kendall *did* have a good story and it was to be a frustrating day for the two policemen.

Kendall was in the house with his family when they reached Berriow Bridge and at first he showed deep resentment at their intrusion into his home. However, resentment turned to dismay when told by Amos there was reason to believe he *was* involved in the murder of Kerensa Morgan and the others.'

'We've already been through all this,' he protested, 'and I've proved I was working a thousand feet below grass when she was murdered. The men I was working with told you so.'

'They did,' Amos agreed, 'and if they lied for you they too will be in serious trouble.'

'They *didn't* lie,' Martha Kendall broke into the conversation. 'The wives of two of 'em will confirm that. They were working as bal maidens when their men came up to surface in the morning; they told me George was with them.'

'I believe you've just had a baby boy,' Tom said. 'Where is he now?'

'Out the back, in his cradle.'

'Can I see him?'

'Why?' Martha wanted to know.

'I'll tell you that after we've seen him. Will you go and fetch him, please?'

Suddenly fearful, she said, 'You're not going to take him away? George is behaving much better since the baby was born, he's always wanted a son....'

'We'd just like to see him,' Amos declared, sympathetically. 'There's no question of anyone taking him from you and if you prefer you needn't bring him here, Sergeant Churchyard will go with you to look at him.'

While Tom was out of the room with Martha, George Kendall demanded, 'What's this all about. What has the baby got to do with anything?'

'You'll find out soon enough. Ah! Here they are now, that didn't take very long.'

As he was speaking Tom re-entered the room with Martha. She was carrying a very sleepy baby … and Tom was holding a shawl.

Nodding at Amos, Tom said, 'It's definitely the one, see…?' He held it up to the light from the window but it took Amos a few moments to make out the initials 'AM' cleverly worked into the crocheted pattern of the shawl.

'It certainly is.' Addressing Martha, Amos asked, 'Where did you get the shawl, Mrs Kendall?'

Puzzled, she replied, 'George brought it home the day after the baby was born. Why do you want to know, it's not stolen or anything, is it? Whatever else George might have done I know he'd never steal anything, not from anyone.'

Instead of replying, Amos turned to her husband. 'Is that right, you brought this shawl home for the baby.'

'Yes, but what's this all about? Like Martha told you, I never pinched it, or anything.'

Holding the shawl up to show him, Amos said, 'This is the shawl that was wrapped around Albert Morgan when his mother was murdered and he went missing. In fact, if you look at it closely there seem to be a couple of stains on it that might well have been bloodstains until someone did their best to wash them off.'

His mouth dropping open in astonishment, George Kendall looked at the two policemen in disbelief. 'But that can't be. It just can't!'

Amos's response was to say, 'George Kendall, I am arresting you on suspicion of the murder of Kerensa Morgan, Albert Morgan and of Jed Smith … handcuff him, Tom.'

'I know nothing about their murders … I swear it!' George Kendall protested. 'If you're arresting me because of the shawl, I'll tell you where I got it. It was given to me by Alfie Kittow, landlord of the Ring o' Bells!'

Accompanied by a still-handcuffed George Kendall, Amos and Tom walked their horses uphill from Berriow Bridge to North Hill village, little more than a half-mile away, the shawl which had prompted the arrest of Kendall tucked safely in Tom's saddle-bag.

As they approached the village, Kendall held his handcuff-linked wrists out and said, 'Do you have to take me into the Ring o' Bells like this? I've only been allowed back in there since the baby's been born, anyone who sees me is going to think I've gone back to my old ways again.'

'If you're telling us the truth you'll be able to put them right,' Amos replied, 'but the Ring o' Bells might not have a landlord after we've heard what he has to say about the shawl.'

'You'd better hope he doesn't deny all knowledge of it,' Tom commented grimly. 'If he does, the chances are that you'll have had your last drink in this world.'

The thought of such an eventuality proved sufficient to keep Kendall silent for the remainder of the walk to the public house and, as it happened, the premises were not yet open for business.

Alfie Kittow had not been out of his bed for very long and he was in the tap-room, where a strong smell of beer and stale tobacco lingered from the previous evening's activities. The slate floor had been newly cleaned and dried and the landlord was spreading fresh sawdust about the room.

He looked up from his task with an expression of annoyance on his face which changed to a forced smile of welcome when he saw Amos. It turned to astonishment when George Kendall followed, his handcuffed hands held out before him.

'What's going on ... what's Kendall been up to now, and why bring him in here?'

'We've just been to Kendall's home, Alfie, to locate a shawl we'd been told his baby was being wrapped in ... That's it Sergeant Churchyard is holding.' He indicated Tom who had been the third man through the tap-room doorway, 'Have you ever seen it before?'

'Not that I can recall,' came the reply.

It caused Amos to look sharply at Kendall who appeared stunned by the landlord's denial. After a couple of failed attempts at speech, the miner cried, 'You *must* remember, Alfie. You gave me the shawl along with other baby clothes when Martha had our baby boy ... You *have* to remember!'

'Oh, was it among them? I remember giving you a bundle of baby clothes but I honestly don't remember what was in it.'

'What do you mean, you don't remember?' This from Amos. 'I think you'd better remember, and quickly if you don't want to share Kendall's handcuffs and join him in a cell in Bodmin police station.'

'Why? All I did was give him a bundle of baby clothes because I thought him and Martha could do with them, having another baby in the family, I didn't know what was there. But what's so special with the shawl anyway, was it stolen from someone important?'

'You admit to giving him a bundle of baby clothes, yet expect us to believe you had no idea what was in it?' Amos was sceptical.

'It's the sort of thing we do here in the village. If you have something you don't want and there's someone in need of it, you give it to them. But what's so special about this shawl?'

As the two policemen exchanged glances, George Kendall blurted out, 'For God's sake tell them, Alfie! It's the shawl Kerensa's baby was wrapped up in when she was murdered and he went missing.'

The blood drained from Kittow's unshaven face and he felt for the table behind him for support. 'I swear I didn't know that! How could I? I was given the bundle of clothes for Florrie's baby – our baby – but I knew she wouldn't want second-hand clothes for him so I took them with good grace and when George and Martha's baby was born I thought they would do for them.'

Amos felt inclined to believe the inn-keeper, but he asked, 'So where did the clothes come from? Who gave them to you?'

'They came from old Bessie Harris, the midwife. She's always being given baby clothes and passes them on to them who she feels is most in need of them. Me and Florrie have never been in need of anyone's charity, but Bessie thought she was doing us a good turn and it would have been churlish to refuse them, so I took them and passed them on to George and Martha ...' Breathlessly, he added, 'Thank the Lord I've agreed a sale for the Ring o' Bells, the sooner I leave this place the happier I'll be!'

Chapter 34

OUTSIDE THE RING o' Bells, Amos and Tom talked as they led their horses through North Hill village, heading towards the home of Bessie Harris. George Kendall had been released and, still badly shaken, was having a relieved drink with Alfie Kittow before returning home.

'This case has never been a straightforward one,' Tom commented, 'and it's certainly not getting any easier! Even finding baby Albert's shawl seems to be taking us round in circles and bringing all our original suspects back into the picture. With the sort of luck we're having we'll probably get to Bessie Harris's and find the shawl was left on her doorstep, or something! We'll soon run out of suspects – unless our murderer turns out to be Bessie herself!'

'I don't think she has either the build or the agility to kill *anyone*, especially a man like Jed Smith who was a man in his prime … but unless I'm mistaken this is Bessie Harris coming towards us now.' He nodded to where the midwife was walking along the village street towards them.

'That's a relief, at least,' Tom said. 'I was dreading having to go inside that house again, it reeks of those cats of hers.'

'It looks as though she's carrying some baby clothes with her now,' Amos observed. 'We'll wait here for her.'

When the local midwife reached the two policemen she would have passed on with no more than a nod of her head as greeting but Amos said, 'We're lucky to have met with you, Bessie, we were on our way to speak to you … but are you on your way to help someone give birth?'

'No, I brought a baby son into the world yesterday for a young girl who got married only a fortnight since. She was so excited about getting wed she's lucky the baby wasn't born in the church during the wedding … but having the baby's taken some of the shine off it all for her. She had a hard time during her labour and things aren't likely to get any better either. Her husband's a ne'er-do-well who's not much older than she is and they've not got two pennies to rub together between 'em.'

Indicating the bundle she was carrying, she added, 'I've got a few baby things here that'll no doubt come in handy for her.'

'Where do you get the baby clothes from, Bessie?' The question came from Tom.

Bessie shrugged, 'From anyone who has them to spare. Sometimes a baby will have outgrown them, other times a baby won't have survived. That's where the best clothes come from, a mother doesn't want to keep a reminder of whatever's happened to her baby.'

'Was that what happened with the clothes you gave Alfie Kittow? Did they come from someone who had lost a baby?'

For a moment Bessie frowned, then her expression cleared and, addressing Tom, she said, 'Of course, you were in Wiltshire recently and word went around that you'd seen Florrie's baby. It took me by surprise, I can tell you. I was as sure as anyone can be that she was never expecting in the first place! It just goes to show, some women think they're pregnant when they're not, while others don't know they're expecting right up to the time the baby's born! You can't take anything for granted when it comes to having a baby ... but how do you know I gave Alfie some clothes for Florrie's baby? You can't have seen 'em when you saw her in Wiltshire because I didn't give 'em to Alfie until a week ago, or it might even have been less than that?'

Choosing to ignore her question, Amos asked, 'Can you recall giving him a shawl, Bessie, a very nice crocheted shawl that looked as though it might have been quality?'

'Yes, I can, it was a beautiful shawl ... but why are *you* interested in it, it's not stolen, surely?'

'No, nothing like that, it's just that the shawl has come to our attention during the course of an investigation and it needs to be looked into. Can you remember where it came from?'

'I remember very well because I've seen one or two like it before. They're made by the gypsy girl who's the daughter of poor Jed Smith. They *are* quality, so much so she could make a good living selling them to gentry and they'd be passed down through their families, no doubt about it.'

'This particular shawl we're talking about, Bessie, can you remember where you got it from?' Amos drew her back to the question he wanted answered.

'Yes, I remember very well, it came from Jowan Hodge ... though what he was doing with it I don't know. He and that Gospel-spouting wife of his have never had children and are not likely to have any now in spite of all the money he's made lately. Mind you, it's probably just as well, Evangeline Hodge would have religioned any baby to death long before it ever grew up! But I mustn't speak ill of her, she and Jowan will have left us soon. I saw him setting off in a cart full of their belongings and he told me there was only one more load to go. She's already over there, although she'll be back with him come

Sunday because she's taking a meeting for the last time at the new Bible Christian chapel, down at Middlewood, along the road a way from Berriow bridge, then they'll both be off for good.'

'What do we do now?' Tom asked Amos as Bessie walked away from them, leaving them standing in the middle of the village's only road. 'Do we get a warrant and go to Exmoor to arrest Jowan Hodge?'

'I'm getting a bit frustrated with arresting people then having to let them go again, Tom, and Jowan Hodge has the strongest alibi of all our suspects for the time of the murder. He also has enough money to pay some clever lawyer to find any holes in our case against him. We'd need to make this absolutely water-tight before taking out a warrant to arrest a man outside the county … if indeed Jowan Hodge is our man. If we were forced to release him again we'd be a laughing stock, something I don't doubt Colonel Trethewy would be delighted with. Nevertheless, we *do* have to speak to Hodge about the shawl and arrest him if we're satisfied he's our man. We know where he and his wife will be on Sunday so we'll let her take the service at Middlewood Chapel, then tackle him when the service is over. In the mean-time, we'll try to tie up any loose ends, and I thought of one when we were questioning Alfie Kittow today. Zillah has ver-bally identified the shawl to *our* satisfaction, but if Hodge gets a lawyer to challenge our case when we take him before a magis-trate to commit him for trial, we'll need to produce a written statement from her. I'll get back to Bodmin now and tell the chief constable what's happening, but you go to Trelyn, collect some writing paper from Sergeant Dreadon, then go to Gassick Farm and get a written statement from Zillah before coming back to

Bodmin. I don't suppose that will prove to be a hardship for you.'

Tom's happy smile was sufficient answer to his question.

Zillah's delight at seeing Tom dispelled all the doubts that had been building up as he approached Gassick Farm. He had almost convinced himself that having had time to think about it her feelings towards him might have cooled. Her warm kiss of greeting dispelled his doubts and she grasped his arm happily as she led him inside the farmhouse.

Some of the effervescence faded when he told her why he was there but when he told her that he and Amos felt the written statement was needed in order to have a suspect committed for trial, she said, 'I'll do anything you ask if it helps to catch whoever killed Dado, but are you really that close to making an arrest?'

'Yes, I honestly believe we are. In fact, it should be only a matter of days now.'

'You'll let me know as soon as he's arrested?'

'Of course.'

The silence that followed was broken by Tom who changed the subject, 'Have you mentioned the possibility of you taking up art with Verity's friend to your grandma … where is she, by the way?'

'She's not feeling too good today and went upstairs to rest for a while, it's something she's doing more often now. I'll feel much happier when she moves in with her sister but, yes, I've told her and she's pleased about it. She says she can sell up here and move to her sister's home without worrying about me now and I should be close enough to Penzance to see her quite often … that's if Verity's friend agrees to taking me on as a pupil, of course.'

'I don't think there's any doubt about that. Verity wouldn't have built up your hopes in the way she has if she wasn't certain about it.'

'I hope so, Tom, I really do … but I don't suppose I'll be able to see you as often as I'd like to and that upsets me far more than I thought it would.'

Her words gave Tom the opening he had been struggling to find in order to speak his mind. 'Does the thought of not seeing me really trouble you, Zillah, even though you'll be starting a whole new life? What I mean is, can you see there being a future for us … together?'

Zillah studied his face seriously for a long time before saying, 'Why do you ask a question like that, Tom?'

'I'll tell you that when you give me an answer … an honest answer, Zillah, not one you think I *want* to hear. Please, it's important.'

Once again, Tom needed to wait for her reply, but when it came she spoke seriously and thoughtfully. 'I think I know where this is leading, Tom, and I'm sure of how *I* feel, but you need to remember you're a policeman … and I'm a gypsy.'

'It wouldn't make any difference to the way I feel about you if you were a mermaid, Zillah. Besides, you're going to be an artist soon … and I suspect you'll be a very successful one. When that happens it won't matter to anyone where you've come from, or what you've been, but I realize you're probably being offered the chance of a lifetime and I would never forgive myself – and you might never forgive *me* – if I was to stand in the way of the future that's out there waiting for you.'

'Need it stand in the way of anything we do, Tom? Amos and Talwyn both do what they want to do, couldn't we do the same?'

'Is that what you want, Zillah … *really* want?'

'Yes ... though it might not be easy for either of us, especially as we'll be at opposite ends of Cornwall.'

'It needn't be that way, Zillah, that's why I wanted to know how you really feel about me because Amos is fully aware of my feelings for you and he's said he'll have me promoted and transferred to command a division in the Penzance district if it was what we both want.'

'I know it's what *I* want, Tom, it would be a new beginning for both of us ... a new life together! I just ... I can't believe this is all happening, there's so much ... I feel I might burst.'

'In that case I think I had better do something about holding you together...!'

Chapter 35

THE EAGERLY AWAITED letter from Verity to Talwyn confirming that her artist friend would accept Zillah as a pupil arrived two days before Amos and Tom were planning to question Jowan Hodge and was promptly posted on to the gypsy girl at Gassick Farm. Tom would have liked to take it there himself on their way to the chapel where Evangeline Hodge was to preach, but Amos had decided they would take the headquarter's wagonette because it was likely to be useful if they arrested Hodge and brought him back to Bodmin.

Taking the vehicle meant they would need to travel on the roads which, although often of an indifferent nature were more suitable for a wheeled vehicle than the rough moorland tracks.

It took the two policemen longer than anticipated to reach the chapel at Middlewood and Amos was beginning to fear they might not arrive before the service ended, but he need not have worried. It was to be the last service Evangeline would conduct in the tiny chapel and she was making the most of the occasion.

By the time they arrived the service had been going on for one and a half hours and, according to a miner who left the chapel soon after they arrived, it was 'likely to go on for another hour and a half because she's only damned about half of those who live around here. I doubt if she'll finish until she's doomed the other half to purgatory in the hereafter.'

'Are you speaking of Evangeline Hodge?' asked an amused Amos. 'What is she particularly upset about?'

'Just about everything,' the miner replied. 'When she exhausted the subject of the Ten Commandments she made up a few of her own, including drink, tobacco and anything else that makes a miner's life half bearable. When I walked out she was likening this area to Sodom and Gomorrah … Ah! Here's someone else leaving and we're not the first. By the time she's finished ranting in there she'll be preaching to no one but her husband.'

'So Jowan is in there with her?'

'At the moment, but he's looking as uncomfortable as everyone else.'

The disgruntled miner went on his way and as the family who had left after him passed the wagonette, they were expressing similar sentiments about Evangeline Hodge's sermon, with the added complaint that her words were 'Not fit for the ears of children'.

'It sounds as though Evengeline Hodge is getting a few things off her chest before she moves to Exmoor,' Tom commented when the family passed beyond hearing.

'It certainly does,' Amos agreed. 'I wonder how much of it has been prompted by her husband's association with Kerensa Morgan?'

'We might soon find out,' Tom said, as another couple of miners emerged from the chapel. 'If she keeps on at this rate the first miner's prediction will come to pass and there'll be no one for her to preach to.'

But it seemed that some of the chapel's congregation were

more forbearing than others. Although some seven or eight men and women left the chapel prematurely, when the service came to an end half an hour later there were still more than twenty people who filed out having survived the promise of brimstone and fire with which they had been threatened.

When it was apparent there were no more of the congregation remaining, Amos said, 'That seems to be all of them, let's go in and have words with Jowan Hodge.'

When Amos and Tom entered the chapel many of the candles had been extinguished but those nearest the door were still burning and the light from another was visible inside a room to which the door was open, at the far end of the white-washed and starkly simplistic interior.

Jowan Hodge was extinguishing the candles and, startled by their unexpected appearance, he declared, 'You're the last people I expected to meet on our last night in Cornwall. Did you just happen to be passing, or are you here to bid us farewell?'

'Neither,' Amos replied. 'We're here because we have one or two questions to ask you in connection with the murders of Kerensa Morgan, Albert Morgan and Jed Smith.'

'I've already told you where I was on the night of Kerensa's murder, so I had nothing to do with it and know nothing at all that could possibly help you.'

'Then how do you explain this?' Tom had entered the chapel carrying baby Albert's folded shawl and now he shook it out to show to Hodge.

Frowning, Jowan Hodge said, 'What am I supposed to say about it, I don't think I've ever laid eyes on it before.'

It was not the reply that had been anticipated and for a moment both policemen were nonplussed but while the conversation had been taking place they had not observed Evangeline emerge from the room at the far end of the darkened chapel.

The first they knew of her presence was when she hurried towards them crying, 'What are you doing with that? It's mine.'

Reaching them, she would have seized the shawl from Tom but, stepping back he lifted it above his head and of her reach. Stepping between the agitated woman and Tom, Amos said, 'Just a minute, Mrs Hodge. The shawl was given to Bessie Harris by your husband, are you saying it was yours?'

Rounding on her husband, Evangeline said, 'You gave it away? What were you thinking of? It was among the clothes I've been saving for years, you had no right...!'

Confused and upset, Jowan Hodge said, 'It must have been among the baby clothes you'd collected. There was no sense hanging on to them now so I gave them all to Bessie to pass on to someone in need.'

'You gave them all away? What were you thinking of...? What if the Lord had decided to give us a baby now?'

Before her husband could reply, Amos said to Evangeline, 'Are you admitting that the shawl belonged to you? Where did you get it?'

'What's so important about a shawl?' Jowan demanded angrily. 'Can't you see you've upset her?'

'The shawl belonged to Kerensa Morgan,' Amos said, curtly. 'It was wrapped about her baby when she was murdered, but when baby Albert was found dead in a well the shawl was missing.'

Breaking into the conversation, Evangeline said fiercely, 'Her death was the Lord's will, she had to die for her sins.'

'Mrs Hodge, are you saying you carried out the Lord's will by killing Kerensa Morgan—?'

Interrupting Amos, Jowan said, 'I protest—!'

'Shut up!' The miner's words were cut short by Tom.

'She was a Jezebel,' Evangeline declared. 'While she was alive no woman's husband was safe from her evil.'

'What about baby Albert, did he deserve to be killed too?' Amos prompted.

'He wasn't killed.' Frowning, Evangeline said, more hesitantly, 'He must have suffocated while I was carrying him to the old explosive store over by Slippery Hill. I wrapped the shawl about him to keep him quiet when he began to cry. I thought he had gone to sleep, but the Lord giveth, and the Lord takes away. Who are we to question his actions?'

'What were you going to do with the baby?'

It seemed that an agonized Jowan was about to speak again in answer to Amos's question, but a stern look from Tom silenced him once more and Evangeline said, 'I was going to have someone take care of him until we moved to Exmoor, then I would have had him back and loved him because he was as much mine as hers. Jowan was his true father, not that foreigner who came up to Trelyn.'

'That isn't true, Evangeline, I told you it wasn't true.' This time Tom was unable to prevent Jowan from crying out.

'It *is* true. I saw you with her once, with the baby. I saw how you looked at him. It was a father looking at his son. I knew then he should have been mine.'

Moving so that he was between Evangeline and her husband, Amos asked, 'But what about Jed Smith, the gypsy? Why did you have to kill him?'

'I went to his wagon to ask him to find someone to look after the baby until we moved to Exmoor, but when we got to the explosives store we found it dead. The gypsy was frightened and said he wanted nothing to do with a dead baby but I knew that when word got around about the baby's mother he'd tell someone, so when he started to walk away I hit him with an iron bar that was in the store. Then I dragged him to the well and threw him in and threw the poor baby in after him … but not the shawl. It was beautiful and I kept it because it would always remind me of the baby that should have been mine.'

Looking past Amos to where her husband stood in a state of anguished shock, she said, 'You should never have given the baby things away, Jowan, especially not the shawl. It was all we had to remind us of the baby the Lord had intended should be ours. But because it had been born of Kerensa Morgan, he must have seen too much of the Devil in him.'

That night Evangeline Hodge was lodged in Sergeant Dreadon's police cell in Trelyn and Amos and Tom spent the night in the sergeant's house. There was little sleep for anyone because their prisoner spent the whole night alternating between hymn singing and loud demands that she be freed and not shut up for carrying out the wishes of the Lord.

The next day, accompanied by her husband she was conveyed to Bodmin and lodged in a police cell to await an appearance before a magistrate in order to be committed to the Assizes, to face trial for a triple murder.

When the committal proceedings were completed early that afternoon, Tom set out immediately to inform Zillah that the killer of her father had been caught and sent for trial.

Meanwhile, Amos returned home to tell Talwyn of the arrest.

'What will happen to her now?' Talwyn asked the question as she struggled with her feelings which shifted uncomfortably between relief that the investigation had been concluded and reluctant sympathy for Evangeline Hodge.

'She'll stand trial but will undoubtedly be considered insane and spend the rest of her life in an asylum. It's a dreadful experience for any woman although her husband's money should ensure she'll be treated reasonably. But I'm glad we have finally solved the case … thanks to Zillah.'

'Yes,' Talwyn agreed. 'It has been a dreadful time for so many people, yet, in spite of that, a surprising amount of good has come out of it. It means Horace Morgan can now return to his family in India; George Kendall has turned over a new leaf … and not only has Zillah's talent has been recognized but she and Tom have found each other and have the chance of a happy future together.'

'That's true,' agreed Amos. 'All things of which, in her saner moments, Evangeline Hodge might have approved. But the horrors of the past few weeks are over now. North Hill and Trelyn can go back to being the peaceful and caring communities they have always been.'